RAIN

LEIGH K CUNNINGHAM

RAIN

Vivante Publishing

Vivante Publishing
Singapore
inquiries@vivante-publishing.com

Cover design by Elizabeth Boté
www.coroflot.com/minium

ISBN-13: 978-981-08-8280-8

Printed in the United States of America

To my husband, Steve, my love, my life, my reason. Because of you, I have become me.

In memory of my brothers, John and Paul.

PART I

July 1965 – December 1974

One

July 1965

MAINE was a town with immunity from outbreaks of new ways of thinking. Bohemians had never penetrated its outer limits, nor had the beatniks, and the Hippies would go the same way—around the perimeter. The Aquarian age that blew through elsewhere releasing seeds that would sprout rebellion and enlightenment, passed over Maine at a great altitude.

Helena Wallin had no desire to leave her hometown, especially not for Sydney given the unfortunate family connection with the place. For Helena, Maine was a diamond in a black velvet bag—there was no need to display it, enticing outsiders who would bring with them the ways of a lesser world. The insularity was comforting, not at all claustrophobic, and a stagnant population of thirty thousand agreed. To leave would be to settle for a lesser gem, and Sydney, after all, was a mere emerald city.

Life was near perfect, but for a solitary discontent that vested in her heart and its potential receiver. Two decades earlier, the X-chromosome had not only prevailed in Maine, it had conquered, guaranteeing a battle to the aisle unless

1

reinforcements came from elsewhere, and at twenty-two, Helena was beyond her use-by date. At twenty-one, Grace was similarly disadvantaged, but to a lesser degree: she was a living commercial for an expensive shampoo while Helena was the Homy Ped: sensible and comfortable.

Helena's readiness to inherit the mill, passed father to daughter that generation, not to son, not to Robert, countered the absence of a husband and children. The mill would be hers, and she chose not to dwell on the circumstances that made it so. But there was atonement, and Helena added the cause to a childhood preoccupation with parental appeasement, which is how she came to date Greg Allerby albeit just the once.

Greg Allerby ranked one with parents who measured eligibility in terms of upbringing, education, and job prospects. His more widely accepted profile however, was that of veterinarian with the exuberance of a dead fish, startling resemblance to Groucho Marx, and member of The Lodge, which was in itself a reason to defer. Helena, and most definitely Grace, utilized other rankings based on looks, charm, and prowess, preferably of a sporting nature.

Michael Baden's appeal lay in his preeminence on one set of rankings and complete absence from the other given his known past and predicted future. Helena did not understand her interest in him, but figured she was merely following popular opinion unable to think clearly on the issue of men for herself. Whether or not Michael Baden could ever summon an interest in her did not matter while other obstacles stood in the way. First, there was Grace, who was free to choose whomever she wanted. Then there was the mill rule that prohibited employee fraternization, and her father's Wallin Guidelines, which recommended against consorting with sportspeople in general and footballers in particular. And the defining impediment—in male company, other than her father, Helena was a blubbering idiot.

While the latter obstacles were problematic, Grace Convention guaranteed that Michael Baden had just three months until he was cast adrift like his predecessors when the yellow patina of old varnish displaced his porcelain veneer. There was time for Helena to buoy her flagging confidence by shifting the resilient mass on her hips and thighs. She would start a new diet the following day when the bouquet of Millie's freshly baked apple crumble had dissipated.

December 1965

For three months, Helena plowed her way through sticks of celery, grapefruit doused in Sucaryl, boiled eggs, tomatoes, and not much else. It was worth the misery as a conspicuous loss of bulk revealed itself just in time for the regulation three-month Grace break-up and emancipation of Michael Baden. Motivation waned in the fourth month due to the momentum of summer, and Grace's failure to observe tradition with Michael Baden still in tow. Early morning walks became isolated events, then non-events when it became clear the incentive for the program had been a figment of a foolish imagination. By the end of the fifth month, Helena had regained the weight lost plus interest—the spinning pin, having rested at an alarming number, sparked a gastronomical bender.

If Grace had known the source of her sister's compulsion to eat everything in sight, she could have eased it, for Michael Baden was soon to be ex-ed arising from a deal she had struck with her father: funding for a salon and apartment in Sydney.

Grace had never surrendered her dream, and contrary to popular opinion, did in fact possess a mild sensitivity to other issues that crossed the grain of her self-absorbed marrow: her parents had lost their only son, and everything life might have been if not for that tragedy twelve cloistered years before, was mere speculation.

Unlike Helena, Grace did not care for the multi-generational Wallin sawmill nor crave the daily joy of working side by side with her father nor hold qualms for disappointing him as he had her. She was not Robert, the first-born, a son, or the natural heir to the mill, yet she had been educated beyond what was normal for a young woman in the day. Her life, because of her father, because of Robert, had been stifled and orchestrated, and Maine meant nothing but social deprivation and life in a cesspool of virtue where minds had been set in concrete. It was a place without soul, and Grace craved what Sydney offered.

But while she had protested through five years of high school and three more in business school, Grace had been mindful all along of the virtues of being one's own master not answerable to anyone—that was her desiderata. The mill however, was not part of the plan for she was born to coif. Before the ink on her graduate certificate had dried, Grace had applied for an apprenticeship at a local hair salon, started work, and informed her father by presenting him with a small yellow pay packet and a smile.

The terms and conditions of the Sydney deal raised the arch of a tailored brow, and had the scent of bribery. Her father stooped lower implicating her mother, Millie, in the decision making process, which was akin to labeling Mahatma Ghandi a violent anarchist. Grace wanted to raise an objection, but suspicion had not incapacitated good sense, and progress to this milestone had been a lifetime in coming.

The first condition had some legitimacy: self-sustainment within a year, which did not seem at all onerous for a woman with her potential and education. The second condition though, the dismissal of Michael Baden, was spurious. Irrespective, she chose freedom, no contest. There would be other Michael Badens.

Grace had taken up with him primarily due to his good looks, but also because it was sure to irk her father. Everyone knew the mill rule—no dating the Wallin girls, and so Grace assumed Michael's interest rose similarly from the challenge. There was no sign of a deeper caring, and she did not expect any grief from the imminent dissolution. The timing was also

4

right, as one always had a sense of life's possibilities when bathed in the summer's warmth.

The handsome duo ambled down Waterloo Street after the Friday night dance at the town hall, stopping under a lamppost to gather the fallen flowers of a Honeysuckle tree. Grace stroked the dark leathery leaves, and admired the silvery down on the underside. She lit a cigarette, Ingrid Bergman in style, and inhaled the nicotine with the midsummer scented with honey. As usual, she was purse-less, a wealth creation strategy that worked well for her.

"I have some news," she said.

"Good news?" he asked positioning a yellow floret behind her left ear.

"Great news," she said. "I'm moving to Sydney."

He probed her face and waited as she blew smoke into the moth-ridden light. "I'll come with you," he said when she failed to insist.

"You can't."

"I can."

"My father wouldn't like it."

"Your father? How come you're suddenly concerned with what he wants you to do?"

"I'm sorry, Michael."

"You're sorry?"

The question had no immediate answer, and Grace watched as reality set in causing deep lines to form on his forehead and around his mouth.

"You're breaking up with me?" he asked.

"You know this is what I want."

"It's not what *you* want, it's what your *father* wants, isn't it? Isn't it?" he yelled.

"Calm down, Michael."

"Calm down! Why is he against me?"

"This has nothing to do with you. You're over-reacting."

They walked together in silence, hands rigid by their sides. Grace lamented the demise of the flawless night, the Southern

5

Cross now fittingly masked by heavy clouds that subdued the constellation's domination of the night sky.

"He wouldn't have to know," Michael said after a while.

"He's not stupid. If you resigned from the mill, and suddenly left Maine at the same time, he would know."

"Explain to me again why it would matter if he knew?"

"Why are you making this so hard on me?" she asked resorting to a faithful tactic. She paused in search of kind words. Nothing came to mind. "The truth is, Michael, I don't want you to come. This is *my* dream, and I want to do it on my own."

Time was dormant. There was no way to know how long their feet occupied that land, his hurt evident. He kissed her with feather-like lips that rested on hers for the longest while. She stared into his eyes then stepped back before walking away. It was not a time for sentiment. "Because I love you," she heard him whisper. She stopped for a moment then continued alone into the soulless dark that came to life briefly under each lamppost.

Two

December 1965

THE Royal Hotel beckoned. Michael would stay until the pain mollified and he was no longer solvent or sober, whichever came first. Grace had lied—her kiss said so. The move to Sydney was not her idea, but a cowardly guise instigated by James Wallin who hid his prejudice behind a skirt. Michael was not worthy—on that point, there could be no argument—but he at least deserved the truth without prevarication.

Michael had always planned to marry-up given that there was no way to marry below his life's station: a ladder only had so many rungs. He hoped to like his future wife, even a mild liking would suffice, and then there was Grace. Loving her was unexpected, and she came with the Wallin affluence: moderate with distinction. He had long observed the wealthier classes from his objective ground zero, and recognized the dichotomy that was prosperity and respectability—moderate wealth with distinction always outweighed wealth that was obscene in dimension and nature.

At the base of Michael's suitor triangle, a Milky Way from the tip was a dense listing of acceptable, low to mid-tier non-

7

socialites from suburbs with slightly more respectability than Park Lane. A considerable number had already showered him with interest, but matrimony was not the objective—the institution of marriage relegated in favor of the institution of finance, and only one who had stood for a second in Park Lane footwear could possibly understand.

The whites of his pockets languished over dark trousers when he finally vacated his preferred stool at The Royal. As he tried to stand and scull the last few mouthfuls of beer, he found himself spread-eagled on the butt-layered tiled floor. A couple of patrons in a similar state helped him to his feet. One tied Michael's shoelace, hinting that it may have been the cause.

Michael staggered toward the west side of town, resting at each landmark along the way. With half the distance traveled, he reclined against a supportive tree trunk, one of many that lined the avenue-like entrance to the Wallin Oval. Even with his vision blurred, he could see shapes of words on a bronze plaque, and knew what they had to say—honor to James Wallin, his father, and father's father. Veins ruptured inside his head, pushing him from the arbores column. An agile leap, incredibly, catapulted him over the turnstile, and a forwarding momentum introduced a fist to the wall of the canteen. He jabbed with both knuckles in tandem until bloodied and exhausted he collapsed to the concrete and fell into a wasted sleep.

Sergeant David Mackelroth arrived at the Wallin Oval in response to a 000 call, without the siren or flashing lights. In Maine, residents dialed 000 for any unexpected occurrence whether an incident required immediate urgent action or not.

From the turnstile, his torch light converged with a holey wall and below it, a human mass in a curved position, almost fetal. Sergeant Mackelroth moved in for a closer inspection of the fibrolite panel, and its perpetrator, or victim.

"Come on, Michael," he said, bending to lift the lifeless weight to sit against the punctured wall. He huffed a few times to expand his energy reserves then yanked Michael up onto his uniformed back, tying flailing arms around his neck as an anchor. The sergeant heaved as his body took the weight. "I'm going to need your help here," he said as they approached the turnstile. "Stand up, mate…just for a second." After a brief stint on his feet that swung him through the revolving gate, Michael grounded again face first into the dirt. Sergeant Mackelroth hauled him to the patrol car with his hands gripped under odorous armpits as paralytic legs generated a light dust storm behind them.

Michael slept while Sergeant Mackelroth tapped words into his police incident report. He came to a halt after 'Baden', the word evoking memories of a schoolyard confrontation involving his guest for the night. He had tried for years to extinguish the retrospection—of an acerbic pack circling the youngest Baden on the playground—but the memory possessed its own disquieting longevity. In turn, they had run in from the perimeter to punch the eight-year-old while he fended off attacks from another direction. Occasionally, instead of a pummeling, his pants, handmade from a potato sack, found his knees. All seven of the Baden boys wore that particular beige textile, gathered around the waist with a piece of frayed cord. Their clothing was the primary source of their misery, and it served as an involuntary barrier to the outside world. Not surprisingly, they all left school by thirteen with their spirits squeezed sour like sugar-less lemonade.

David Mackelroth, twelve then, was not a participant in the persecution that day, but a bystander, and equal in guilt for being so. He joined the police force at the end of his final year of school compelled by that single incident to help the victimized in future instead of observing their torture.

Sergeant Mackelroth ripped the report from the typewriter's vice, crumpled it into a ball, and pitched it across the room at the injustices of the world. He turned his attention to other work to distract his mind. The image of that child—tugging at his pants clutched in one hand and flailing at assailants with the other—would never leave him. He shook his head several times in an attempt to dislodge it.

The night aged quickly and caught the sergeant off guard. He wanted Michael back in Park Lane in advance of the lightened sky when early risers would witness the delivery, and tongues would wag with enthusiasm for days, weeks, forever.

"Come on, Michael," he said, tugging at a lifeless arm. "It's time for you to go home."

Michael took a few moments to adjust to sitting before attempting a stand.

"What hurts more—your hands or your head?" asked Sergeant Mackelroth, guiding Michael toward the back door of the country station.

"My heart," he replied, and waited for the giddiness to pass before following Sergeant Mackelroth, unaccompanied, to the patrol car.

They drove a while in silence, Michael's head still not in sync with a morning. "How long before it ends up in court?" Michael asked as the patrol car crossed the railway tracks to the wrong side of town.

"What?" asked Sergeant Mackelroth.

"The shed…incident."

"Oh, you mean the damage to the canteen. Well, Michael, the problem I have is this—no witnesses. Happens that way sometimes. Comes with the job."

"Thanks, David," Michael whispered.

"Just keep those fists in neutral for a while. The Rotary has a working-bee coming up at the oval. We can fix the wall while we're at it. You might like to come along and lend a hand, pardon the pun, assuming your knuckles have regained some movement by then. They're going to be sore by the look."

Michael glanced down at the red-spotted white bandages expertly wrapped around his knuckles. "I'll be there, David, and thanks again."

The patrol car eased to a stop behind the water tower, away from neighborly inferences. Sergeant Mackelroth waited at the wheel, observing while Michael plodded the rest of the way like any man without hope. He stepped on to the footpath out front of a house that had seen a better day a long time ago.

Mrs. Baden scuffled out to meet him, panicky at the sight of her son with bandaged hands. She was a tiny, elderly woman, and kindly, having raised eight children in unenviable circumstances, and she showed all signs of battle weariness. Gossipers alleged she was not Michael's mother, but Sergeant Mackelroth had never subscribed to a mill that merely sought to push those who had no further to fall.

Michael glanced up at the distant patrol car and raised the palm of his bandaged hand. A new day had dawned, one without Grace, and one that had begun with an act of human kindness, something he had thought, until then, was an oxymoron.

Three

February 1966

JAMES Wallin had seen one future for his daughters: successful businesswomen, independent of any man. Young mothers, never, and education was the key. It was not *his* dream, but his dream *for them*. Ultimately, this enabled his decision to let Grace go, the epiphany striking one morning during an innocuous daily occurrence: the polishing of his shiny head. Grace had chosen a path that paralleled his vision, but he had not seen it until his scalp shone that day, his arresting fears finally quieted. A salon in Sydney was not the mill, and it was not Maine, but it was the dream as conceived, and if James had allowed the truth to surface at any time earlier, he may well have let her go then, or not. His daughters were safest when kept closest, and he merely 'oversaw' rather than 'controlled' for his actions were borne of the heart, and fear also since his only son was lost to them.

Grace had never cared about the family connection with the past, and had never loved the mill as he did, and Helena. The sawdust, she claimed, affected her breathing, and the truth was not so remote—she could not stand the smell of the place.

And if anything, her presence there during school holidays had always been a source of disruption with a sudden surge in insignificant administrative issues rising from the mill workers below, like ants marching to their queen.

James was ready to step aside, and Michael Baden would do likewise, his willingness not a prerequisite. Questions of prejudice and dislike did not factor into the equation—James had employed the lad at the mill when he was barely fourteen, uneducated, and with no other prospect, but benevolence had limits, especially when it came to his two daughters. The Badens did however have a particular lineage that any father would repel.

Faithful as always to a promise, James bankrolled Grace's move to the city, underwriting her business for twelve months at which time the salon had to be self-sufficient or showing a sign of future reward. If not, a one-way, economy bus ticket to Maine would return her to a monastic existence, the protectionist policies of her teens seemingly bohemian in retrospect. She would repay the accumulated debt of her failure with services to the mill, and if necessary, particulate masks would be provided to ensure grumblings about sawdust and milling scents did not devastate the otherwise amenable mood at the office.

Helena's office at the mill held expansive views over Maine's sapphire-colored lake while the larger, but similarly unpretentious office of James Wallin bore downwards, offering an unobstructed view of the timber chain. The first link, an indiscriminate pile of logs waited for sorting into species, size, and end use. A debarking process followed, and then the pièce de resistance: debarked logs entered the main building, the sawing mill, to be trimmed, dried, smoothed, and transformed into lumber that would one day support the weightiest roof.

One hundred and twenty-two timber steps separated the working class from management on the hill: hierarchically and in terms of comfort—one swathed in noise, diesel, and dust and the other in tranquil homeliness. The steps also enforced the employee fraternization rule introduced for Grace's benefit when her childish charms honed into a magnetic teenage spell. A gentle finger tap on her office window disturbed Helena. She peered over the rim of her cat eye frames to enjoy a view equal to the expanse of water that usually filled the pane. Michael's smile betrayed his eyes: one was bright while the others revealed a sense of abandonment. He leaned on her sill, more James Dean than the original, but without the leather, and mill grime had grayed his white t-shirt. Helena enjoyed the vista before sliding the glass across.

He wanted to hear about Grace, and Helena was happy to oblige, and there was no need to be clever with exaggeration or embellishment for any story involving Grace was remarkable enough to stand on its own merits.

Their conversations became ritual, expanding from ad hoc drop-ins to daily exchanges over lunch under the pergola—an area designated off limits to mill workers who had their own lakeside gazebo. As time passed, their conversations strayed on to non-Grace topics marginalizing Grace like a discussion on the weather.

Helena had no problem with fluency in Michael's presence, and did not babble as was usual, owing to a single, decisive factor—she now viewed Michael Baden as an acquaintance and nothing more. Months earlier when she imagined him as the father of her children, a demonstration of her wit and unexplored sense of humor would have been impossible. Then clarity came to her one day while watching a documentary on The Beatles. Inexplicable emotion engulfed girls of all ages causing them to laugh one minute then sob without control through declarations of undying love for any one or all four. As Helena lounged in a floral armchair at Waterloo Street, the irrationality of it all dawned on her, and she saw it reflected in her own quiet obsession with the uninterested Michael Baden. No one could love a stranger so completely and utterly without knowing them, unless one was under some kind of spell or the influence of alcohol, or still a child with love that was yet to learn its bounds. Helena realized then that she was no different to the besotted girls who loved the Beatles. She did not know Michael Baden, and only knew of the Badens generally like everyone else in Maine. It had been a foolish preoccupation, but now that she did know Michael Baden, she liked him, as a friend and confidante, and that was all.

"When did you learn Italian?" Michael asked during another rule-breaking sojourn under the office workers' pergola.

"School."

"Some school. We were lucky if we learnt English at the one I went to."

"Maybe you weren't there long enough," she replied.

"Touché. That's French, I think."

"Très bien, monsieur."

Michael shook his head. "I'd like to learn Italian, so I can talk to Vincenzo in his own lingo. Do you think you could teach me?"

"Sure."

"I never heard Grace speak Italian," he said, "the way you do with the mill workers."

"She can," Helena replied. "She chooses not to."

Michael nodded. "I'll help you with something in return."

"*You*, help *me*? With what?" she asked.

"Open your lunch box," he said with a smirk.

"What's so amusing?"

"I just haven't seen one of these since I was in pre-school. I used to wish I had one." Michael sifted through the contents. "Let's see...one carrot with leaves, a block of cheese, and a Caramello Koala."

"What's your point?"

"If you did some exercise you'd be able to eat like a normal person."

"This isn't normal?" she asked.

"So here's what I'm thinking...in exchange for a few Italian lessons, I'll get you fit, or fitter I should say—we are starting from a low base."

"What an amazing offer," she replied, shutting the lid on her lunch box. "I'll give it some thought."

"What about the Italian lessons?"

"That, I can do—more chance of you learning Italian than me trying to run."

"How about Sunday? We can have a picnic by the lake."

"Sounds great. I'll bring the books and the food."

"Thanks, but I've seen your lunch. I'll bring the food," he said with a laugh.

Helena was early for the lakeside rendezvous as was customary for her. Grace would not approve she thought, as she unfolded a tartan picnic blanket. Punctuality, according to Grace Wallin, was a flaw indicative of a staid personality. This, not-so-subtle observation had once swayed Helena into a deportment program by Grace designed specifically for Helena's particular level of social ineptitude. It introduced Helena to a seemingly useless art form, and included a lesson on sociable lateness, which was not to be confused with rude late—the latter apparently not acceptable according to Grace, although Helena had years of experience to the contrary. A number of other meaningless exercises caused unrivalled levels of anxiety and frustration for both, the source, to a considerable extent, being Helena's lack of conviction and unwillingness to embrace the learnings as essential life skills. The program was abandoned by mutual agreement. Helena laughed remembering how Grace had ended the agony, declaring the cause hopeless beyond anyone's capabilities, even hers.

Helena settled on the blanket taking time to decide on a posture to portray the requisite casual professionalism. Legs were crossed and uncrossed, hands rested behind her back, in her lap, then on her knees. She tilted her body to each side, and backwards then did likewise with her head. She assumed the preferred position, and waited with patience.

After the first hour closed with no sign of her student, patience waned. The stiffened pose had caused calf cramps forcing Helena to resort to an inelegant sprawl not approved of in deportment school. She had better things to do than lay around all afternoon under the willows in anticipation of Michael Baden, and of greater importance, for her lunch. The nature of 'better things' was not known, but doing nothing was not an activity she did well, and biding time with patience was mutually exclusive. Helena rolled on to her side, no longer concerned for prudent, correct form.

"Very lady-like," he said, staring down into Helena's exposed inner thighs.

"Lo and behold," she said, and attempted to free the blanket's corner from under the size nines.

"I'm a little late...sorry."

"Really?" she said, noting how he swayed in the faint breeze.

"I brought lunch!" He pulled a package from his underarm. "Fish and chips are served, madam!" The newspaper unraveled, showering Helena with its contents.

"Get them off me!" she yelled, as opportunistic seagulls converged.

He picked hot chips from a salted cowlick to throw them an enticing distance away.

"I can see you're in no state to learn anything today," she said, extracting greasy fish fragments from her Crimpolene skirt, "to make matters worse."

"Worse than what?"

"Worse than *what*? You're late, I'm starving to death, and wild birds just attacked me! It doesn't get any worse than that!"

"I'm sorry, Helena...but you look so...cute with your hair like...like a bird's nest!" He laughed and fell to his knees.

"You're not funny." She patted her hair into its usual faultless state, and re-adjusted her clothing. The resumption of order thawed her temperament, as did his words. He said she was cute—a word not applied to her in ordinary circumstances, and only once previously from memory when she wore a sailor's suit at a school recital at the age of five.

An uneasy silence followed, and as if time controlled

physical momentum, he slowly veered into her personal space, falling into her face to search like a blind man for her lips. It was all over before she recognized the rarity of the occurrence.

"I'm sorry," he whispered, backing away. "That wasn't right."

More silence followed. "Well, this is awkward," said Helena, patting at her skirt.

"I could try again," he said, then leaned in to infuse her lips with a beer-stained breath. She did not retreat. The canyon between their bodies narrowed as the mill rule about fraternizing with employees intruded. Helena dismissed it in favor of Grace's wise counsel—some rules deserved to be broken, and in any event, a rule introduced for the benefit of Grace at thirteen had no jurisdiction over current proceedings.

Four

December 1966

SKELETON staff in the form of Helena and James managed the mill during the Christmas hiatus: the time from midday on Christmas Eve to the second day of the New Year gifted to all workers, *ex gratia*.

Millie provided limited assistance: coffee, letters, and the post office. Her involvement was more therapy than work as it had been since Robert disappeared and her mind fractured with it. She was a conundrum: still the Millie of old (a masterly homemaker), but at other times, predictable only with regard to the speed of reversion from normal to odd then back again. Such occurrences had waned in frequency as the years had passed, but not in velocity.

Of all the 365 eves in a year, the one before Christmas was the standout for the Wallins, and a fortiori in 1966 due to the return of Grace, her first year away dubbed *annus mirabilis* by James. Success had many owners, and James had claimed a large chunk of it for himself. In truth, shameless self-promotion had been the key. Grace had ennobled her salon by distinguishing herself in the upper echelons of Sydney society, proving that good deportment and name-proclaimed grace had a place anywhere. Her rise, however, came with a price.

The business had expanded in every regard: clients, staff, services, and size. The former dry cleaner from next door was now annexed as The Tea Room where ladies sipped tea with their heads wrapped in white towels while nails were painted a bright red.

Grace was not able to enjoy her success as thoughts of a descent (into Maine), with one hand gripped on the emergency brake, were always in her mind. The scenery on her journey fluttered past, and 'social' came to mean a political ideology rather than the way she used to spend her time. Grace did not rest, not even on the seventh day as it followed Saturday, the busiest day of the week, and that was always a train wreck. Grace Wallin, social butterfly prominent on the Maine scene, had reincarnated as a working dog. A mere five hours sleep each night justified a tear or two in self-pity, and was also cause for concern: her flawless complexion was in large part credited to a good twelve hours sleep every night while resident at Waterloo Street where breakfast was served on fine china at whatever time of the day it happened to be. If Grace had known of this new life before she struck the deal with her father, she might well have chosen the Baden path, and stayed home to continue life as a pampered poodle. In hindsight, the undemanding conditions at the mill seemed more suited to her work ethic, and the smell was not so noticeable after a while, and not so bad at all when compared to coloring chemicals.

Helena, in contrast, was lighter in spirit and body weight. She had taken up Michael Baden's offer, and found time each day to run laps of the Wallin Oval under supervision. The first lap months earlier had caused respiratory distress, and almost caused her to abandon the program sooner than Grace's deportment program. Hypoxia was a grim state she knew from experience; a condition she had managed to avoid since being struck by an atomic football courtesy of her own father at age eleven.

By Christmas, Helena had progressed to a respectable sixteen laps of shuffling, and a non-Sherpa like scaling of the grandstand, one small step at a time. The cool-down, Michael explained, was a critical part of the program, and while five minutes was the norm, they spent twenty minutes together in the confines of the dark space beneath the grandstand. It all amounted to suppression of her appetite and emancipation from Millie's banana mocha tart—its coffee essence now powerless against her. Millie took it personally, her self-worth measured solely by other's enjoyment of her food.

Her father had made no mention of the time she spent with Michael Baden, nor did Helena, but he must know, she concluded, since Maine was not a place that observed the essence of clandestine—if one saw, everyone knew, and lips were never sealed. Her father had mellowed, she believed, evidenced by the fact that he had given Grace her freedom.

The rains had passed by lunch on Christmas Eve leaving behind a quagmire laden with bark and wood chip. A fresh breeze blew off the lake and through the worker's gazebo, tickling the jasmine vine as it braided white flowers in and out of the latticework. Helena inhaled the scent, remembering the day the magnificence birthed.

Millie, garbed in gloves and armed with tools, explained the process as she went about it, while Helena and Grace sat cross-legged on the lawn at Waterloo Street, chins resting in their hands. Millie had extracted clumps of small, eye-shaped seeds from their vine, precise as a brain surgeon. The spores were then transplanted into a plastic bag lined with a moist paper towel, and a light covering of moss completed the operation. Three months later, Grace and Helena participated in the burial ceremony to intern the sprouted seeds around the new gazebo at the mill, "for the workers," James had declared, proud of his contribution to the proletariat.

Michael disturbed the recollection, urging her to eat. Inside the lunch box adorned with Aladdin was a tuna salad sandwich bedizened with a filigree ring. She lifted it from the white cushioning to admire the intricacy of leaves in a platinum band, ably supported by a square-prong central sapphire. When the jewel's bewitching powers receded, panic took over: what to do—place it on the right hand, or left, return the jewel to the issuer, or to the plastic box from where it had risen like a phoenix then shut the lid as if it was Pandora's Box.

"Put it on," Michael said his eyes bright with excitement.

She hesitated.

"Here," he said, taking the ring to slide it down her ring finger, left hand.

She twirled the band, staring at it.

"You don't like it," he stated.

"I do, I do. It's beautiful."

"So?"

"Yes?"

"That's a 'yes' then?"

"Yes," she replied unsure of the question's angle.

Silence engulfed the gazebo while Helena continued twirling the ring.

"I guess we should make an announcement then," he said.

"I guess so."

"What do you think your father will say?"

"Oh, he'll be thrilled," she replied, laughed then gulped. "And surprised...definitely surprised."

"We should tell him first, before anyone else. What about tonight?"

"No, no, not tonight. I don't want to spoil Grace's homecoming."

"What do you mean?" he asked, flinching from the neck upwards.

"Well, you know Grace. She does like to be the center of everyone's attention, especially now. I'll tell him tomorrow, after Christmas Day lunch. He'll be in a good mood then...not that he needs to be...for the news, just...it's always best."

"OK," he said with a shrug, clearly unconsoled.

"It is beautiful." Helena raised her left hand moving its angle to refract shafts of the summer's sun through the blue stone. "Really beautiful. It must have cost you a fortune."

"It's my mother's."

"What!" Helena dropped her arm from its perch, hitting the timber tabletop. She shook her hand to release the pain.

"It's OK," he said. "She wants you to have it."

"I don't know," she replied. "It doesn't seem right."

"She hasn't worn it in a long time. Not for ten years or more."

Helena held her ring to the light again, staring into it. "I'll tell my parents tomorrow. Then I guess it will be official."

Christmas Day lunch at the Wallin residence was consistently remarkable with the annual feast guaranteeing the day would end with the painful afflictions of over-consumption. It was gratifying for Millie, and her favorite time of the year, so long as she did not remember the past.

A highlight every year was the after-lunch soiree held in the air-conditioned privilege of the front living room in armchairs that induced the cognac-fuelled respite, another Wallin tradition.

James raised a tulip-shaped crystal glass filled with the copper fluid. "A toast! To another extraordinary feast fit for the royal family, and three more inches for my waistline." He patted his bulging torso—another Wallin tradition although the girth growth declared varied each year in an arbitrary manner. "To Millie, my love, thank you."

"To Millie," they saluted with staid performances due to the annual repetition.

"Helena, is there anything else we should be toasting?" James asked.

"What? How could you possibly know? It only happened yesterday."

James tapped his temple to indicate omnipresence. "This regime of yours had to have some greater purpose, Lena. You wouldn't be exerting yourself for the sake of exercise alone," he said with a hearty laugh. "And you've lost a lot of weight…well, before lunch you had." More laughter followed.

Helena reached inside her scalloped neckline and extracted the tissue-wrapped ring to place it on her third finger. "You're right, Dad. The insanity has a reason. I…we are getting married."

"*You* are getting married?" Grace gasped. "Who to?"

"To *whom*, dear," said Millie.

"Fantastic news!" James interrupted rising to his feet. "To Helena and my future son-in-law. And about time too, Lena!"

"Who is it?" Grace repeated.

"Michael."

"Michael? Michael who?" James asked. "I thought…it's Greg Allerby, isn't it?"

"Greg Allerby?" said Helena shaking her head.

"Who's Greg Allerby?" Millie asked.

"The young man from the Lodge, the veterinarian…the one Helena has been dating," James replied.

"Dad, I went out with him once, two years ago!"

"It's not Michael Baden?" Grace asked.

"Yes, it's Michael Baden. I can't believe this!"

"No need to shout!" Grace yelled back.

"A wedding—how lovely!" said Millie. "Let's toast Helena and this Michael fellow."

James and Grace raised their glasses with visible begrudging, countering Millie's exuberance.

"Let me see the ring, dear." Millie leaned forward to clasp a reluctant hand. "Just lovely. Look, James, it's an antique," she said, redirecting Helena's hand closer to a disinterested eye. "Gracie, see?" She pulled Helena's hand toward Grace. "You know, in ancient times, they thought the vein in the third finger of the left hand ran directly into the heart, and that's why we wear our commitment rings on that finger. Fascinating, don't you think?"

"Fascinating," said Grace in a monotone.

Oblivious to the sub-zero room temperature, Millie proceeded with a spirited monologue on the pending nuptials. Helena, Grace, and James reached for the Rémy Martin.

"Quicksand," said Helena, thinking aloud.

Five

Christmas Day 1966

MICHAEL would have slept longer, but the familiar stench of potato cakes had exacerbated his alcohol-induced nausea. He loathed the colorless fritters for the destruction of his taste buds, the pervasiveness of their greasy coating, and for what they represented—a childhood subsistence on a determinate nutritional regime in which the edible tuber ruled supreme, and not just any potato, but the humbling Pontiac. At Christmas, his mother massacred the household budget for the sweet ones, hungered for because their orange glow brought life to an otherwise insipid plate. And no one yearned for the habitual emptying of the hessian sack as it promised new clothing for whoever was next in line.

John, an older brother, suffered many a queue ousting as punishment for the improper use of the family's brown gold. The inaugural offence involved a galvanized nail and a hammered piece of copper wire inserted into a potato to generate electricity. While the experiment was a success, the clothing file skipped to the next in the queue, and John was served the electrocuted vegetable for dinner. His hide, indelibly

25

imprinted with a thin metal cord, forced him to savor the shriveled remains in an upright position. Undeterred, he used more potatoes for spudzookas, which occurred whenever his name rose to the top of the hessian clothing queue.

The hour had been a respectable one when Michael returned from The Royal Hotel the night before, seven hours after his first drink to commemorate an unofficial engagement to Helena Wallin. The Royal was deserted by eight leaving Michael alone with Henry behind the bar. By nine, Henry had asked Michael to leave as it was Christmas Eve and he wanted to be home with his family. Michael empathized, notwithstanding he had no personal experience with such a wanting. He accepted the six-pack goodwill offering, and set off in the direction of Park Lane where his mother would be listening to Bing Crosby singing Christmas Carols.

Michael still slept on the front veranda of their house in Park Lane as he had done as a young boy—same bed, same position, and same threadbare sheets.

Two bedrooms formed the centrum of the house, each with two doorways: one opening left to the living room, and one opening right onto the sleepout. At the end of the sleepout, a small bathroom with a basin and a tub cleaned all eight children in one batch of lukewarm water. Next to the bathroom was a room of immaterial size that housed the icebox, potatoes, and everything else. When Michael was born in 1942, it became a bedroom for Alice, Michael's sister, and the newborn. It comprised a bed, marriage chest, a discolored white wicker bassinet, and the icebox and potatoes, all cordoned off by a rose pink shower curtain over the entry.

The master's chamber, the bedroom toward the front of the house, was out of bounds, and any child who dared to step on the chipped, geometric-patterned Linoleum lived long enough to learn that crying worsened the punishment. The three youngest boys shared the second door-less, internal bedroom. John Senior had removed the doors to ensure its occupants did not enjoy a sense of seclusion. One replaced the outhouse door that had fallen off its hinges with dry rot, and for some time had revealed a little too much of its constant visitors.

The two older boys slept on the sleepout in beds lined head to toe along the exterior fibro wall. Alice's bed once headed the line-up, positioned outside the master bedroom to enable interminable fatherly vigilance. The area remained a void of exposed lino when Alice upgraded to the storeroom since neither George nor Harold desired the location, but the space remained vacant for a mere eight months. As soon as Michael could walk, the storeroom returned to its original purpose, and Alice returned to her paramount position at the summit of the bedding row. Michael began his impervious occupation of the new veranda.

The veranda covered the front façade of the Baden family home, encased on all three sides, floor to ceiling, by asbestos-laden fibro louvers. John Senior had removed the front stairs to construct the enclosure then left them where they lay in the yard. In no time, weeds burgeoned between each timber plank eradicating recollections of a once stair-filled frontage.

John Senior had intended that George and or Harold would move onto his veranda, making room on the sleepout behind Alice for Michael and a new baby due in a matter of weeks. George declined: his bed was closest to the back stairs and the outhouse, a necessity given his intestinal lack of fortitude. He also wretched with depression, clumsiness, aggressiveness, headaches, he had a stammer, and walked like a duck. His permanently swollen lips also looked very much like a duck's bill.

Harold declined as well, and suffered an extensive beating for showing a lack of appreciation for everything done to make his life more comfortable. Two days post bruising, Harold was gone, and had not been seen or heard from since. Then George left then Alice, Thomas, Raymond, John, and Edward in quick succession until there was just Michael and the newborn baby, who died some weeks later of unknown causes.

George wrote to report that all of his childhood ailments including the duck's bill had disappeared, the miracle having occurred shortly after he left Park Lane. He had attributed the improvement in his condition to his escape, until a medical practitioner informed him that his symptoms were all potato related. Within days of leaving Park Lane, his health had taken a turn for the better because he had not consumed the "god-forsaken vegetable" since, and by the way, he had married a nice girl.

Michael saw no point to moving into the vacated door-less bedroom: it was not a sign of changed fortune or acquired status, and it was more a part of the main house than his veranda. The room, with its bunk beds, and peeling walls painted before the government reclaimed all green pigment for the war, remained empty. No one ever returned, not when the old man passed, and not even at Christmas.

Lunch on the twenty-fifth day of December at Park Lane was exceptional only with regard to the amount of care and perspiration Dorothy discharged into the meal. She insisted on a roast, and steamed plum pudding with custard and brandy sauce in spite of a scorching summer and a poorly ventilated kitchen that trapped heat to increase the room's temperature by an additional ten degrees or more. The erroneous feast seemed to bestow a sense of penance for her so Michael did not complain or suggest a coleslaw.

Michael retired to the veranda after lunch with a new nylon shirt thrown over a bare shoulder with its market price tag still hanging from a button. Dorothy had also given him a carton of beer, which chilled in the freezer that was as cold as any fridge, and this gift brought him the most joy.

He lit a cigarette and blew rings into the air to measure the velocity of any breeze that may have lost its way on the east side of town, puffing westward before wafting lazily through the fibro louvers. The smoke loitered above his head, undisturbed.

Michael wondered how Helena had fared with the announcement. He thought of Grace, and cogitated about Alice wondering why she never answered his letters. He had learned of his breeding in an educational kind of way, as the recipient of a poem composed by other students when he was eight. The verse penetrated his heart and soul with its disclosure and delivery, and he remembered the words to this day: your mother is your sister and you're a big blister. He was supposed to feel shame from the revelation. He did. He was supposed to feel rejection. He did. He was supposed to feel like an outcast. He did. Containing his bitterness over the years had been a titanic struggle, not won. He was not like Dorothy, his adoptive mother, grandmother, sole speaking relative—she had not capitulated, yet by every account of her life, she had earned the right to swallow the caustic pill. Somehow, she had formed a close relationship with forgiveness, and a peaceful life with what she did not have, but Michael could never accept their poverty.

Through the louvers, he had a clear view of Park Lane and the cricket match in progress. Anyone could join the Christmas Day Test by assuming an outfield catching position, but no one from number 26 ever did, and Michael was not inclined toward a changing of history for no purpose especially on a day that was hotter than Hell.

A cry of "watch out!" caused Helena to cower in a manner that would not have protected anything if the ball had actually struck. She kept a wary eye as she proceeded, keeping to the fence line and out of harm's way, stopping again under the street sign to shake the dust from her shoes. "Park Lane," Michael snickered. He had played enough monopoly to appreciate that the Maine town planner had a vile sense of humor. No one would hope to land on this Park Lane even though everyone could afford to. And while the Lane was deemed a prosaic existence by those on the other side of the railway tracks, it was not absent color: the bitumen was black, houses offered the unmistakable gray of fibro, the soil was brown, and although no grass grew, bindi-eyes added green and bur-like purple flowers. Michael returned his attention to the cricket as Helena continued her descent.

Some minutes later, he heard animated chatter in the living room that drowned out the familiar scratching of the Ink Spots. There was mention of dresses and bouquets, and other such matters of no interest to him. Helena would be some time before she made it to his veranda since Dorothy craved female companionship, and clung to it as if it were life itself.

Michael refocused on the cricket as someone fell to the ground screaming in pain clutching a red brick ball that had rocketed into his groin, but with his bottle of beer still held high with the other hand.

"Merry Christmas," said Helena when she finally stepped through the doorway.

"Merry Christmas."

She bent down to peck his lips before falling into a wooden chair that Michael had restored for his veranda.

"How did you go with the announcement?" he asked, twisting the ginger butt of a cigarette into the side of a soup can and drawing life into a new one.

"Good, good. Yes, good."

Michael laughed. "Sure," he said.

"What? You don't believe me?" she asked wide-eyed.

"How's Grace?"

"She's good. And looking good too although a little tired from working so hard."

He nodded and peered back through the louvers.

"What's that smell?" Helena asked sniffing at the air with a frown.

"Potato cakes, from breakfast." He paused. "She doesn't have to cook them anymore. We can afford real food."

"Maybe she likes the taste," Helena suggested.

"Or maybe her taste buds died a long time ago." He paused. "So I guess it's official then?"

"I guess so. I suppose we should announce a date."

Michael nodded, and smiled as Helena tried to draw cooler air onto her skin by pulling her blouse outward in a fanning motion. He knew it was a waste of time, and the wetness that seeped through her cream silk blouse would soon trickle down her sides.

"I'd better get back," she said, standing to peer through the louvers as a red ball peeled the air landing close to the house siding. She flinched. "Enjoy the rest of your Christmas, Michael."

"Just another day in paradise," he said, not anticipating Helena's kiss.

She cringed and swiped at the smoke. "I hate those things," she said, and made her way to the living room to palaver once more with Dorothy. Michael saw her ambling through the test match some time later. She paused again under the Park Lane sign to wave back at the louvers then continued on her journey to disappear from view.

Six

Boxing Day 1966

JAMES was up at 4:30AM as was commonplace. Mornings with Millie in the kitchen were the belfry of his every day, with the slide downward into the other hours endured because they drew him closer to the next morning. He baptized himself in the wholesome aromas that coursed a way through his flaring nostrils, bringing life to his body. His ears hummed from the drone of the radio, his mind filled with news from his paper, and the daylight's resurrection made his spirit soar.

Millie poured his tea: an Irish blend steeped for five minutes exactly in an earthenware pot kept warm by a colorful homemade tea cosy. The water was not over-boiled and the pot was always taken to the source, never the other way around. James sipped, sighed, and reopened The Maine Times.

"Why don't you like this fellow Helena wants to marry?" Millie asked from her cook's station.

James closed the broadsheet to contemplate the question. "It's not that I don't like him. I feel sorry for him, and his mother—they've had a tough life, but I would prefer it if he married someone else's daughter." He sipped at his tea before adding, "And he's not good enough."

"Isn't it good enough that Helena loves him and she's happy?"

"Michael Baden will only bring her unhappiness. Believe me, I know. It's in the genes." James returned to his paper to signify the end of the conversation.

"Why? Because his father was an alcoholic?" Millie asked. "That doesn't mean he will be."

"I'm telling you, Millie—it's hereditary, and his father was a *violent* alcoholic, beating his poor wife and children to within an inch of their lives. That's the environment the boy grew up in. He doesn't know anything else, and that's what will happen to my daughter if this marriage goes ahead."

"You should give her more credit, James. Helena has never given us any cause for concern. She has good judgment."

"Wrong, my love." He flicked his paper again. "I don't want to talk about it."

Millie placed a plate of scrambled eggs with Christmas ham between the polished silver. James took a deep breath, exhaled, and smiled at his wife as she sat down beside him. He would discuss his concerns with Helena directly, in time, calmly and rationally. There was no urgency since Millie was right: Helena was a smart girl who would realize the mistake of her own accord well before a life was ruined and the Wallin line was infiltrated by a Baden.

Grace surfaced at midday, shuffling her way into the kitchen, a stranger to her alter ego, and settled at the dining room table. Millie rushed over to wait on her. "Just coffee, thanks, Mum," she said, lighting a cigarette. "I'm so tired."

"You need to take better care of yourself," said Millie, delivering the first in a series of coffees brewed in her new coffee maker.

"It's so hot in here," said Grace.

Millie moved the pedestal fan from the kitchen where it cooled her during preparations for their Boxing Day lunch to direct it at Grace's back. Helena came through the doorway and smiled at the familiar scene.

"I'm sorry about yesterday," said Grace. "I was...shocked. It's not like we ever thought you'd get married, and certainly not before me."

Helena sat down opposite her sister. "So it had nothing to do with Michael?"

"Well he was my boyfriend," Grace replied.

"He *was*, until you dumped him. Remember?"

"I had to. It was a condition."

"What do you mean, a 'condition'?"

Grace shook her head. "It doesn't matter. I made a choice. Who's to know if it was right or wrong?"

"I thought you didn't care for him, and I thought you were happy with your city life. You should be—you have everything you always whined about."

"I don't whine."

"You do."

Grace lit another cigarette and inhaled until the end burned bright red. "It's so hard, so tiring, and I no longer do the parts I love, like setting and styling. Every day, it's decision after decision. I'm responsible for everybody and everything, and making sure everyone else is happy. What about me? There's no time to enjoy my life."

"You're whining again."

"It's like I have become you and you have become me," Grace continued.

"No offence taken," said Helena.

"Anyway, Lena, I am happy for you."

"Thank you, Grace. That means a lot to me."

"It's strange no one calls me Gracie anymore. It's as if the old Grace, Gracie, the fun-loving Gracie, has died and been replaced by...me...or you."

"Sounds like you'd better go back to bed, Grace...Gracie."

"No, no, no," Millie interrupted. "We're all going to sit down to a nice family lunch. Call your father, Helena."

"Dad!" Helena yelled from where she sat.

"Not like that, dear. You sound like a fishmonger's wife.

Go and get him. He's in the garage with his new ride-on mower."

Helena returned with her father in tow, who promptly relocated Boxing Day lunch to the back yard under the Eucalypts. "What about the flies?" Grace asked as she carried platters to the garden setting.

"They won't eat much," said James. "And it's a lot cooler out here." He took his seat at the head of the table. "What on Earth are you wearing, Grace?"

"A mini-skirt. It's all the rage in London."

"And it should stay there. What is the world coming to?"

"Have you decided on a date yet, dear?" Millie asked, while passing the homemade mango chutney to James.

"April," Helena replied.

"April is a lovely time for a wedding. The weather will be much cooler by then."

"And your armpits won't sweat all over the dress," added Grace.

"Which year, dear?"

"Next year. Late April."

"Next year!" James erupted, spraying masticated food over the table. "In four months?"

"Ah, yes, no point waiting, Dad. And besides, most girls my age are already married with children, and you know I want four or more."

James shook his head. Silence consumed the rest of the meal with just the whistle of a summer breeze through the gum leaves to accompany the chinking of fine china. James brooded: his empire had collapsed. He was once its undisputed ruler and final arbiter and now, impotent, with his views questioned and often disregarded. Even Millie had challenged his wisdom on the issue of Michael Baden, and it was an ironic fate twisting of mammoth proportions that the girl sitting to his left, with her fashionable thigh exposed at the dining table, had become the sole implementer of his wishes. Four months would not be enough time to rectify the crisis at hand, not without the power to influence which he no longer possessed.

His eldest daughter, most favored, most beloved, was leaving him, and nothing reasonably could be done about it.

"These flies are infuriating!" said Grace.

James sighed.

Seven

June 1967

THE wedding was a somber affair in contrast to the old man's funeral. Michael had worn a rented dark suit on that occasion as well, a mourning suit, which was in no way comparable to the morning version James Wallin had selected for himself as father of the bride, the groom, and sole groomsman, Vincenzo, for the wedding of his eldest daughter.

A moment of almost happiness arose in the gray day when Helena appeared at the entry wearing a stunning ankle-length, full-flowing gown, with no evidence of the aborted training regime and what now grew inside. A silky bow marked the separation of a lacy upper and the off-white A-line silk below. A strip of exposed skin separated the bell-shaped lace sleeves and the long, silken gloves. Michael was less impressed with the bouffant hair and matching veil attached to the head by an Alice band, but the floor-length, coat-like train he loved, and if asked, would have proposed more lace. The regalia made a transpicuous statement: no expense spared. But the appendage that grasped Helena's arm, threatening to remain attached, ruined the vision in off-white. Michael smiled at the irony: the bride's father looked as Michael should have done at John Senior's funeral, and the reverse was true.

The ceremony to inter the Baden patriarch in a plain pine box lined with pink organza and pink satin bows, had been a day of preposterous joy. Michael had removed the pink satin pillow from the coffin to ensure the corpse could not rest comfortably in the confines designed for a much shorter man. The funeral had also made a transpicuous statement: no expense incurred. Michael did not arrange flowers, a wake, or public notice of the passing, the costs assigned instead to his private after party.

Dorothy had remained emotionless from the death to the final goodbye, acknowledging the occurrence only by removing her wedding band and engagement ring to affranchise an almost dismembered swollen finger. Michael had assisted in the process by soaping the congested area. He wanted to use the pliers, but Dorothy had said not, and he was grateful for relenting on the proposed destruction, the ring now on approach down the aisle.

After John Senior's passing, Michael expected Dorothy to warble with her release from a not so gilded cage, but her liberation seemed tinged with a fear of a crow pecking as if afraid to be happy and free. She stayed near to her coop, and perhaps this explained the irrepressible potato cake convention.

They had sent wedding invitations to everyone bar Harold, who had disappeared. A regretful declination came from George: he could not make the wedding for his wife was not otherwise able to cope with their four children. Raymond and Thomas conveyed best wishes in a letter telling of a Nullarbor crossing to work as boilermakers at the Kalgoorlie gold mines in Western Australia. Edward's card enclosed a photo of him standing, hands in pocket, in front of a Japanese vessel at the Woolongong wharf where he worked as a laborer. John sent a card with a letter and ten dollars. He wished he could attend, he explained, but he was laying railway sleepers while waiting for the sugarcane harvest to begin. He had moved to far north

Queensland, staying at a small place called Miriwinni just south of Cairns. He loved the north and loved the harvest: there was nothing quite like the sweet smell of freshly cut cane, and the ceremonial burning of the fields after the sugar cropping. Nothing came from Alice, which hurt.

In the absence of all other living relatives, Dorothy was reliably present for her son/grandson's wedding, bedecked in a cream, boucle wool suit, the jacket buttoned and trimmed on the cuffs and neckline with mink, all courtesy of Helena. Her chic dress was topped with a hat made from large fabric rose petals, and looked more like a well-to-do clown's wig or ice-cream sundae.

The honeymoon was a similarly dismal event, although all expenses had been pre-paid by James Wallin, lifting the stature of the occasion above lugubrious. Their week at the up-market Carlton Ritz Hotel in Sydney was an altogether unpleasant experience for Helena who spent most of every day with her head buried in porcelain while Michael idled from bar to bar.

Matrimonial matters declined further upon their return to Maine on the issue of permanent residency. When Michael suggested to Helena that Dorothy live with them, the proposal was clearly one-directional: she, to live with them, not the antipode. He never expected Helena to leave the right side of town for Park Lane, but she did. And within days of doing so, the misguided and ill-conceived nature of her philanthropic endeavor came home to roost as Dorothy's lard-saturated meals curdled a stomach already incapacitated by other influences. Helena assumed Michael's aversion to potato cakes by osmosis without a single morsel sampling. Without knowing it, Dorothy had delivered retribution, and Michael reveled in Helena's first lesson on altruism: no matter how graceful the dancer, one cannot dance in concrete boots.

The mill vine contributed to the connubial landslide. Michael knew the house on the range that James Wallin had wanted to buy his eldest daughter and new husband. The house was a cliché, a home for dreamers, perfect in its whiteness and picket-fenced botanic. The bay windows invited the morning sun, and cast overawed eyes across a 180-degree view of the lake. It amounted to death by nirvana, causing Michael to think as his father had done about every man's capacity for vengeance.

His wife failed him again on the issue of Michael's request for an administrative position at the mill. She had stalled for weeks claiming a prerequisite "reengineering of business processes," which, in layman terms meant nowhere to sit and nothing for him to do. This Michael knew to be a falsehood: a position, in both respects, had been kept for Grace in anticipation of a failed Sydney venture that never eventuated. James Wallin was responsible, he was certain, and Helena was incapable of making a stand or a scene, especially when it came to her father who she loved more than anyone, and much more than her husband. Embittered, Michael sought relief in an antidotal brew.

Eight

June 1967

THE sky was ablaze with red the night the mill burned to the ground. Tiny embers scrambled free, rising like fireflies in an Icarus-like ascent into the black ozone to extinguish then return to Earth as a scorched skerrick of a once greater mass.

A crowd had gathered at the penultimate hour of June 22 in a sea of flannelette, football socks, slippers, and boots. Helena sobbed uncontrollably while James and Michael united in a jaundiced assault on an unperturbed furnace. James was a man obsessed, unable to accept certain ruination. A flame shroud unveiled images of his father, his grandfather, and his father before him, driving him to fight on in spite of futility.

The burning mill was diuturnal: the night sun would not fall until the subdued winter sun supplanted it to reveal the completeness of its counterpart's devastation. Salt and soot stained Helena's face, anew now with corrugations of wretchedness indicative of a much older woman. She limped home to Park Lane for a tepid shower and an unsuccessful attempt to still the quivering. Her head throbbed, protesting the insatiated demand for tears and unrequited need for sustenance. She dressed in a loose, fleecy tracksuit, not bothering with the usual sensible appropriateness of dress for a workday.

The administrative block at the mill had survived the night with a mere coating of black on the iron roof. The windows had not shattered, and the timber had not been scarred black. Helena unlocked the sliding glass door with her back facing the carnage below so she could deny its existence. She had not seen her father for several hours, not since she cried out to him to pull back from the flames, his otiose blanket like slaying a dragon with a pin.

James arrived soon after Helena, emaciated and damp. He had walked to the mill in the feathery rain wearing his usual short-sleeved, cream collared shirt. He owned a pullover, but never wore it. It was still new, and maintained for prosperity in a box of mothballs. He smiled forcibly at Helena then retired to his office to lock a gaze over the outdoor kiln.

Helena had four priorities: insurance, employees, customers, and suppliers. Reconstruction was not an agenda item—that required courage and conviction, which may or may not arise at a time in the distant future. Within the hour, their people would gather for an official grieving and words had to be said, which ones, Helena did not know.

She pulled the file marked insurance having never questioned the indispensable nature of it despite the horrendous cost. She struggled with the uncomplicated claim form, the most elementary detail arduous without the requisite mental focus. A faint tapping on the glass door interrupted her mindlessness. Charles Baker, their insurance agent for twenty plus years, stepped tentatively inside.

"I'm really sorry, Helena. This is heartbreaking."

She sighed. "It all seems so…unreal."

"I see you have a claim form. I'll help you with it if you like."

"Thanks, Charles, I could do with some help. I can't think straight."

"How's your father doing?"

Helena nodded at the broken, damp effigy still standing at his office window. They stared after James through the open door until another tap on the glass door disrupted the silence.

"Everyone's here," Michael announced.

"I'll leave you to do what you have to do," said Charles. "Just sign the form. I'll fill in the rest and get it away."

Helena handed the signed form to Charles then knocked gently on her father's door. "Dad?" She thought she saw a nod. "Everyone's here," she added when there was no movement. He turned, keeping his eyes downcast. The pride that had once held his shoulders aloft had disintegrated with his mill allowing them to fall forward.

Helena waited for James at the top of the steps that led down to the gathering. Millie bustled among the assembled workers with an impromptu canteen, serving tea, coffee, and an assortment of homemade cakes and biscuits. Helena wondered if her mother's philosophy on life—that home cooked food could remedy anything that ailed anyone at any time, was applicable on a global scale. Lard and potato bouquets rose from the fibers of her tracksuit causing Helena to focus more closely on what Millie served. The consolatory banquet would at least settle her nerves, for the moment.

Two months had passed since the wedding and Helena had cried for most of every day: the unremitting nausea, merciless regret, and the anvil of life in Park Lane. She had coveted the house on the range, the one her father had wanted to buy for her, and she could still see herself in it, living the married life she had dreamed of since the earliest time. And that is where she would be if she had not discussed the house and the move with Dorothy prior to closing the deal. At the outset, Helena had thought Dorothy's uncontained enthusiasm for every detail, especially the way her age-spotted hands clasped as in prayer against her lips, was a willingness to move with them. It was not. The excitement was for the newly-weds and their dream home. Dorothy had no plans to go anywhere Helena learned soon enough, and since the rum had not yet stained the white icing on their wedding cake, it was too soon for a new wife to disregard her husband's wish for his mother to live with them. Helena also cared deeply for her mother-in-law, deserted by seven children and abused for a lifetime by her husband. Her right collarbone still protruded in an unsightly way, broken twice by his callous hands. According to Maine legend, she had continued to function with one break for three months without medical treatment, forcing her to lift heavy, sodden sheets from a boiler to guide them through the ringer with one functioning arm. A neighbor, having witnessed Dorothy struggling with the washing, had invited her to morning tea, with a doctor present. He re-fractured the bone to reset it, and the chores continued unabated and unassisted in a cast.

Helena joined Millie and the buffet on the gathering's perimeter. Beige lace from Burana adorned the pure white Irish linen tablecloth, incongruous against the cindered relics surrounding them. Helena smiled, relieved by the absence of the matching napkins.

James began his eulogy with a raspy throat, and a story of his father and brothers, and a mill for a playground. He had sat alongside his father in the old dozer, the only one then, moving tree trunks from one pile to another. The smell of the mill after the rain endured in his memory, and came to the fore now, in spite of the charring. He talked of family and heritage, stopping at intervals to push back the lumps that rose from his heart. He made promises about a new mill, and thanked everyone for loyalty beyond his comprehension, their hard work, and commitment. If they returned at four that afternoon, their final pay, leave entitlements, and reference would be ready for collection. Helena glanced at her watch in response and shook her head. He wished every one of them the best from life, and suggested no one hesitate to contact him if ever there was anything he could do to help, until the mill restored when he hoped to see them all again, and soon.

The gathering applauded after the last cracked word fell. Their respect was apparent as James circulated shaking every hand, and touching shoulders with a firmness that contradicted the trembling within. Then he and Helena, arm in arm, climbed the one hundred and twenty two steps to the sail that had lost its ship.

"I want to write a reference for every employee," he said. "Can you print me a list with their start date and promotions, and anything else, like names of wives and children? Then ask Betty to take dictation for me."

"OK, Dad."

"And give everyone a week's pay for each year of service to the mill in addition to their other entitlements. That should tide them over, I hope, and you and Michael too, and the office girls."

"OK, so long as you understand it will wipe out our contingency account."

"It doesn't matter, Helena. We have no employees. It's just us for now, just the two of us, until the mill is rebuilt and that might be six months...or longer."

"We still have bills to pay, Dad. All the machinery we bought last year came with a hefty mortgage. We'll have to keep making the repayments. I hope the insurance claim is paid soon."

"There should be enough in the operating account for that...shouldn't there?"

"If we asked everyone who owes us money to pay up, there would be."

"You know my position on that, Helena. People will pay when they can. That's how it's always been done around here."

"This is the sixties, Dad, not the thirties. No one runs a business on goodwill anymore. If people buy, they should expect to pay, and in a reasonable time or no more credit."

"I don't want to operate like that."

"We might have no choice. Money has to come in from somewhere or we can't pay our bills."

"If you think it's necessary, I'll go and see Mr. Chase about increasing our overdraft, but I don't want you calling people begging for money."

Helena nodded, accepting for now. When she assumed

control of the mill, things would be different with strict application of the business textbooks and without qualms.

Nine

July 1967

THREE weeks had passed since the fire, and the last time Helena had spoken to, or heard from, Charles Baker. Desperation was rising: the operating account was still in black ink, but only just with an immutable balance of two dollars and a maxed-out overdraft. The paneling in the exposed coffers confirmed that there was no silver lining, but the apparition of their insurance agent, standing now inside the doorway, brought an allayment and perhaps survival.

A dissertation on the weather fulfilled the requirement for pleasantries. Helena hurried the discussion along, agreeing to Charles' assessment of more rain, anxious for her hands to grip a rectangular piece of paper.

"Anything yet from the insurer?" she asked.

"I'm afraid there is, Helena…and the news is not good."

"What do you mean, Charles?"

"Your premium was due on 4 January and they say they never received your payment."

"No, no, no. That can't be right. I wrote the check myself, and dad co-signed it. There must be a mistake."

47

Helena reached for the insurance file and sifted through its bound pages. "Yes, here," she said, "paid 28 December. See?" She handed Charles the invoice, stamped with payment details hand-written on the four lines.

"Hmm. Interesting," he replied. "Can you check your bank statement and tell me when the check was presented? Maybe there has been a mistake, and maybe they credited the wrong account."

Helena moved to the bookkeeper's station, and extracted the gray board with statements clipped at the top in monthly order. She flicked to January and ran a pen up and down the page in search of check number 0216. She glanced up at Charles with an awkward smile before repeating the procedure for February, March, and so on until June, then returned to January once more. Her agitated movements and mumbling foretold the truth. "That's odd," she said, with labored breath. "It hasn't been presented." She looked up, her face drained of color.

"What's wrong?" James asked, standing at the entrance to his office.

Charles explained the situation in a straightforward and conclusive manner, leaving no doubt as to significance.

"What say we write you another check, now?" James suggested. "We've only had four small claims in decades, from memory. Surely they'll grant us some leniency?"

Charles shook his head and sighed. "I don't know, James. The premium is overdue by six months. If it had been just two or three months, then maybe...but half the policy year has passed. I honestly don't think much can be done now, but I will try. You shouldn't get your hopes up though."

"You're telling me we have nothing left? No mill, no money? Just mortgages for new equipment destroyed in an uninsured fire?"

"I'm sorry, James," he said before disappearing through the sliding glass door.

"How did this happen?" James asked, sitting down on a swivel chair beside Helena.

"I don't know," she whispered.

"The check would have shown up in the monthly bank reconciliation as outstanding...you didn't notice?"

Helena shook her head and closed her eyes tightly. "We follow up on unpresented checks after three months, but—" She paused to blow her nose. "With the wedding, and leaving home, and the house and everything...I just—"

"Come on, Lena, don't cry. No one was hurt." He hugged her and wiped her tears. "We'll sort this out, and deal with it together like we always do."

"I'm going to have a baby," she cried.

James held her tighter, and checked his own tears. He had failed his life's mission to keep his daughters safe and happy.

"Come on, don't cry, love. Your mother and I had already worked that one out for ourselves. We knew you'd tell us when you were ready."

"I wanted to tell you, but I knew you'd be disappointed in me."

"Don't be silly. You could never disappoint me. All we can do is move forward, and besides, it can't get any worse than this." He smiled.

A knock on an inside wall interrupted their discussion, the glass door still open from Charles Baker's hasty exit.

"Morning, James, Helena. I'm sorry to disturb you." The fire chief stepped inside with his hat in his hands.

"Come in, Arthur, come in," said James, standing to offer a seat.

Arthur waved his hand to indicate his preference. "I'm fine, James, thanks. This won't take long." He sighed. "I just wanted to let you know first...before I send in my report."

"What's the problem, Arthur?" James asked.

"The fire...it was deliberately lit."

"You can't be serious?"

Arthur stood still with his lips pinched.

"How, Arthur? Why?"

"I don't know why, but I do know how. We found remnants of beer bottles and cigarette butts down near the wood chip pile. That was the point of ignition."

"So you think it was arson?"

"We do, I'm sorry, although it might have been accidental, but there's no way to know for sure. It's going to affect your insurance, I'm afraid. The insurers will want to do a full investigation before they pay out, to make sure you didn't light the fire intentionally."

James laughed. "Burn down my own mill? You don't think that, Arthur, do you?"

"Of course not, James—I've known you for forty years, but that's what the city insurers might think. It'll help that you still have your records so you can prove the mill was doing well before the fire."

"It's not going to matter," said James, collapsing back into the swivel chair. "We don't have insurance."

"Oh?" said Arthur. "I thought—"

"It's a short and painful story. I won't go into it."

"Maybe you should have locked the gates, James."

"We've never locked the gates, Arthur. We don't even lock our doors at home. No one does, you know that. It's a very sad day if this is what our town has become."

"Bob Dylan says times are a changing. Maybe he's right."

"But who would want to burn down the mill, Arthur? Who?"

Ten

December 1967

WILLIAM arrived 25 August 1967, inconceivably premature as suggested, since he weighed a healthy 7lbs, but Helena had given up caring about arithmetic and who in Maine had concluded theirs. William was everything: the sum of all goodness, the winter of her discontent, and the herald of a new beginning—those were the even days. On the odd days, anxiety, self-doubt, and delirium prevailed, neutralized to an extent by the omnipresent Dorothy. Despite her advanced years, she was a godsend, with a calm control that came from extensive, practical experience. It was enough for Helena to put aside regret: the house on the range was no longer a thing to covet while Helena had Dorothy by her side.

Michael had also undergone a miracle metamorphosis following the birth of his first son. He was employed at last, which lightened Helena's odd days immensely. His appointment though was a perplexing subject for all the tongues in Maine given that he had completed just two years of high school, and was ill equipped for the position with regard to knowledge and experience. Intervention was the only explanation, divine possibly, but most likely James Wallin since

Peter McMurtrie, General Manager of the Maine Shire Council, was to James Wallin as CS Lewis was to JRR Tolkien. The prime real estate that had landed the mill for generations earned a mere pittance from its sale, driven by the microeconomic concept of supply and demand, and a complete absence of the latter. Maine had one speculative entrepreneur who did so as a hobbyist, complementing his career as a criminal lawyer. Richard Keith applied to rezone the land as residential to construct a number of lakeside bungalows for a yet unidentified market. The endeavor would one day pay huge dividends and be declared lawless given the purchase price, which was a steal arising from a literal fire sale.

James divided the proceeds three ways. Grace had no need for her share, but accepted it anyway as of right while James invested his third in the stock market hoping to generate a flow of cash sufficient for the term of their natural lives. Helena and Michael purchased a piece of land one small step up from Park Lane, and akin to moving from Old Kent Road to Whitechapel Road. It was also like decamping to the countryside since the parcel was a good twelve minutes out of town.

A market gardener no longer able to compete with the conglomerated farmers association had subdivided the tree-less area and christened it Woodlands. He retained a manageable slice of land for himself to prolong his only known subsistence.

The agent who sold the plot to Helena and Michael assured them, with his hand placed firmly across his heart, that the cabbage patch adjoining the rear boundary of their property would be re-developed before the paint had dried on their new home. In any event, he claimed, the sewered, mustardy essence that rose from the plot would not infiltrate their new home due to the propensity of the wind to blow a more favorable course. He also assured them, extending his logic, that the nettlesome bush flies would similarly not invade their home due to some implied inability to travel against prevailing breezes.

Helena kept Dorothy apprised of the land purchase and construction in progress, hoping to hear her confirm at some point that she would relocate with them to Orchard Road. When this did not happen, Helena shared her concerns with Michael who was confident Dorothy would budge at the appropriate time. Dorothy loved William, and her son, but Helena feared it would not be enough to incise roots that had coursed through the earth at Park Lane for nigh on fifty years. There was nothing more Helena could do. With another baby on the way, her family came first and that meant a new life away from Park Lane and Michael's stigmata, which seemed inextricably linked to his childhood home.

Michael was pleased with himself having secured a clerical position at the local council in spite of the naysayers so many in number a wiser person would not have ignored their words. For the first time in his life, he wore a white collared shirt, tie, and long socks to his Terylene shorts, and as the exclusive generator of domestic funds, he was entitled to an occasional after-work visit to The Royal without notice. While unemployed after the mill burned to the ground, his plight at home had fluctuated from nail bed to briar patch, and while Helena was opposed to all Royal sojourns for financial reasons, she simultaneously insisted that he remove himself from under either sole of her fatigued feet.

An additional issue arose with regard to cigarettes, which drew nicotine into Michael's lungs and precious sums out of the domestic purse. They were responsible for the stained tongue and groove walls at Park Lane, which were now tinted orange with no evidence of the military green beneath. To protect the fibro and furniture at Orchard Road from similar mistreatment, Helena had outlawed smoking in the house. In support of her argument she had reverted to *The Marriage Book*, which had merely reported that although for grown-ups smoking had undoubted advantages, there was an almost unanimous medical opinion against smoking for children. There was no mention of any alleged pernicious effect on chattels, and Michael retorted that he had no plans to share his Marlboros with William, and so the case closed in his favor. It was not however, a closing of all arguments related to money, which would settle on the marriage like nicotine on timber.

They scheduled William's christening for the third week in December to accommodate the godmother who was otherwise too busy to attend, which brought the selection process into question. The role of godparent was a serious one, their priest had said, and was not suitable for one with a frivolous heart or mind. The appointee must be one who can positively affect the child's life in the areas of faith and morals, be responsible for religious gifts at appropriate celebrations, and make constant attempts to discuss and influence the godchild on ecclesiastical matters. Given the absence of anyone who met the criteria, Michael and Helena settled on Grace due to her experience with celebrations, albeit of the unreligious kind, and her undeniable mastery of influence.

When Grace first cast eyes on William, Michael recognized the twinge, well acquainted as he was with envy, and pleased for once, to be the beneficiary rather than the benefactor. He had not known pride before, and had never understood its controlling until he possessed it, the most enlightening aspect being the way self-importance could devour guilt. He was contrite about the mill, and while he had been incensed earlier on the night in question, by the time he had left The Royal at closing, he had only sought a refuge and a place to drink his beer in peace. He had been careful, he thought, to extinguish the butts, but retrospect told a different story. There was no intent: it was just another unfortunate incident to add to his private collection.

Pride had by-products also, Michael learned, including drive and ambition. The new year of 1968 would be an extraordinary one filled with firsts and seconds: a new house, a first; another child, the second; and night school, another first. Michael was destined now for life as an educated, landowning father of two boys, fingers crossed, since women were inordinately more troublesome.

The pre-christening Wallin-Baden dinner hosted by Millie at Waterloo Street came to an abrupt end when Grace changed to go out. It was Saturday night, and she made no effort to mask her contempt for the sedate nature of the evening, and the exclusionary chitchat about babies. Michael braved consternation from James, volunteering to escort his sister-in-law, and for the benefit of James, implored Helena to join them, her response predictable. The charade failed to settle James, and his unease rose further when Helena endorsed her husband's plans instead of the censure he expected. Still, James could understand why Helena would want to be free of the man even if it was just for one night.

The similarities between this December eve and the last time Michael and Grace were together, bridged the years in between as if mere days had passed. After the dance at the town hall, they strolled in the tepid air, stopping under a lamppost to gather Honeysuckle flowers. Michael placed one behind Grace's right ear, and she placed one behind his left, and they laughed like smitten teenagers. They passed by the neat row of timber shops that were an informal end marker for the misnomer, Central Business District, and Grace pulled Michael into the shadows between the post office and haberdashery. He kissed her neck and earlobes displacing the over-sized sequined earrings that fell like chandeliers. At the top of her chocolate brown dress at the back, above the diamond-shaped cutout, one ornamental button unlocked it all. He released the two parts pulling the fabric down her arms to her elbows then reached inside the exposed black lace. They waited for the passing voices to fade, then consummated what could have been theirs years before.

They leaned against the tar coated siding of the haberdashery to share a cigarette. Grace's back had lacerated from its splintered planks drawing blood. Michael dabbed at it with a handkerchief, and stroked her long hair that had fallen from its gathering at her crown. He had always loved her hair, so much unlike Helena's sensible short bob that did not work with her fuller face. He re-buttoned her dress, and his shirt, tucking it back into his trousers.

They strolled hand in hand down Waterloo Street, stopping once more to collect Honeysuckle flowers to decorate Grace's unkempt waves. Outside the Wallin residence, Michael searched the windows for indicia of life, the blackness not surrendering the silhouette of James Wallin. They kissed at the front door, and with reluctance, Michael turned in the direction of Orchard Road while Grace stepped quietly inside.

Eleven

February 1968

THE house in Orchard Road followed the prevailing design of its time: economical in size and layout, high-set, with three bedrooms at one end, and a kitchen, living room, and dining room at the other. A tiny strip of a bathroom separated the kitchen and one of the back bedrooms. The ground floor was so in name and nature: bare earth sprinkled with construction debris. With the first rain, a muddy river would dislodge most of it. Two rows of asymmetrical posts shaped an informal car space for the new, second-hand station wagon, and a dual concrete washing tub constituted the rest of the underbelly of the timber house.

The furniture, although pre-owned, still exhausted their savings long before Helena was able to contemplate window furnishings and floor coverings. Dorothy donated the threadbare, once-white sheets for the glass panes, but the floorboards would remain uncovered for an age.

Dorothy did not move from Park Lane to Orchard Road, which was not a startling revelation for Helena, but Michael was stunned, and amazed his sphere of influence did not even extend as far as his own mother. The new home, in any event, exuded a level of relative happiness in spite of its scant surrounds.

Helena savored proprietorship of her new kitchen, and added cabbage to her forbidden foods list along with potatoes in any form. Recipes inherited from Dorothy and Millie, and ripped from unattended magazines, ignited a love affair in earnest.

She had not yet divested herself of the weight gained with William, and at four months pregnant, was already comfortably into maternity wear and nothing else. Michael did not object when she insisted on darkness before a naked body revealed itself, and his easy agreement caused some disquiet: with a dark blank canvas, her physical presence could manifest easily into a more covetable someone else. That was unlikely though, she believed, for Michael was many things, but not an adulterer. It was unlikely also since Michael was too tired at the end of every workday to do anything around the home or with the children, let alone muster the creative energy required for the design of a fantasy woman.

The cumulative effect of night school proceeding day work, and a colicky baby, did not warrant the level of asperity Michael dispensed, but it seemed to authorize his solution: time spent at The Royal every Saturday afternoon was 'palliative'. The number of hours of 'care' The Royal rendered was indeterminate since he spent Saturday mornings at Park Lane with Dorothy supposedly until lunch, and only then ventured its way. The impact on the floor-covering budget was similarly indeterminate because Helena received Friday's orange pay packet with all evidence documenting the quantum of its contents removed. She said nothing to avoid the drama that would follow. Michael had already threatened to quit night school if she persisted with queries about his palliative care as if his continued education had been her idea when in fact it was a decision taken unilaterally for the realization of his dream of becoming a defense force pilot.

Not all was lost to those delinquent Saturday mornings:

James, and sometimes Millie too, chose to visit at that time, but unlike Helena, Millie was not yet accustomed to the pervading *eau de cabbage.*

Helena prepared tea and pikelets while William bounced on James' good knee, and squealed and clapped.

"He likes to sit at the table with everyone else," she said, "center of attention."

"He won't like having another baby in the house," said James with a laugh.

"He'll have to get used to it," said Helena, pouring tea with disregard for Millie's ritual pot turning.

"Where's Mum?" she asked.

"Ladies Auxiliary meeting. They're planning to take control of the canteen at the oval, to serve 'decent' food. Problem is, most people I know, me included, would rather have a pie and chips or a sausage roll than an egg and lettuce sandwich."

"That could only happen in Maine," said Helena, sipping her tea. "What's in the shoebox? I do need new shoes."

"No, sorry, no shoes."

"What is it?"

James pushed the box across the laminated table to Helena. She removed the battered lid and peered inside.

"Letters?" she asked.

"Take a closer look at the envelopes," he said, sharing more of his pikelet with William.

Helena flicked through the familiar stationary then stopped at one addressed to the Phoenix Insurance Company. She did not need to open the envelope to know its origins. "It wasn't my fault," she whispered.

James shook his head. "No one ever blamed you, Helena."

"All these letters...she never posted them?"

"Maybe she didn't know what to do with them so she just put them in the box and tucked them away with her gardening things. It was just after Christmas, and you know, it's a difficult time for her..." James sipped his tea.

"It's been hard on you too, Dad."

"I still miss him...and it seems worse now that I'm not

59

working. Your mind decides for itself what you'll waste hours thinking about."

"What about starting a new business?"

"I've thought about it, but couldn't come up with anything I wanted to do, and your mother needs me...more than I realized."

"I'd be happy to offer you a full-time job here, without pay of course."

"I could just imagine Michael's response. He would accuse me of trying to take over his family."

Helena nodded. "Shame really."

"Yes, shame, all right," said James. William bounced his head to encourage James to do more with his knee and released a shrill when James responded. "You're a funny little fellow," said James with a laugh.

Twelve

December 1970

THE first three years at Orchard Road had its highs, and even more lows. Brian arrived 14 August 1968 and Carla, 6 May 1970. She would be the last born since Michael was well and truly over the novelty of fatherhood, the third child having failed to generate the same exuberance as the first two. The pressure of responsibility, of being the sole breadwinner, husband, father, student, man with a dream, and everything else, was taking a toll. He also found the extortionate level of infant noise oppressing. Yet in spite of the centrifugal forces, he continued with his schooling, and marveled at his previously untested capacity for perseverance. One more year would yield a Higher School Certificate (HSC), an essential requirement for entry into the Royal Australian Air Force (RAAF). Michael had already sent his application expecting, and hoping to conclude the recruitment process for military pilots before receiving his HSC in January of 1971. He would enlist the next day.

In the midst of the births, Dorothy passed in June of 1969 in circumstances branded tragic by the informal judgment system in Maine. When Michael left Park Lane for Orchard Road in February 1968, he had set aside every Saturday morning until lunch to spend with Dorothy. Then, without consciousness, the mornings became a couple of distracted hours, then every second Saturday then a random event. On one such irregular act of devotion, Michael discovered her body, the woman he had loved like a mother.

The house was a fortress against the winter, keeping the pure air out and the rancid air within. Even the natural heaviness of chilled air could not repress the insurgent reek that contaminated every oxygen molecule. Michael could not breathe: the stench was far worse than a mountain of potato cakes with a cabbage coulis. He spewed his breakfast over the linoleum, and knelt to pray for the first time since he was three when he learned the uselessness of the practice. For the longest while after the funeral parlor claimed her fragile frame, the smell lingered to remind Michael of his failure. He hoped she had passed in her sleep, comfortable in a flannelette nightgown, albeit all alone.

Michael had gone to The Royal to douse his sorrow and shame until they no longer consumed his mind and body. He failed at that task as well, and was able to hear the newsreader report the lead story on the midday news.

"The decomposed body of an elderly woman was found in Park Lane today after lying undiscovered for six days. Her son who raised the alarm found the sixty two-year-old on her bed. It does not appear she had contact with anyone in the past week."

Chief Inspector Brock appeared on the television monitor to add a commentary.

"From what we can tell, she did not have any medical problems. The frail pensioner just slipped under the radar. It is a very sad situation when someone gets to the end of their life and no one knows they died and no one seems to care. It's tragic."

For the six months following Dorothy's death, a perpetually dolorous expression covered Michael's face, but with night school over, and with Grace's return to Maine, he found reason to set aside his bereavement.

He parked the family station wagon in Waterloo Street, three houses up from the Wallin residence, to wait for Grace. Their planned lakeside rendezvous bore no resemblance to a "poker game with the lads from work", and Helena's gullibility continued to surprise him: he had never shown an inclination for cards nor played a single game of poker before. There seemed to be no limit to the possibilities for deception.

Grace raced down the stairs to the living room, compounding the pulsation in her chest.

"Where are you going, Grace?" James asked.

She laughed. "You *cannot* be serious," and continued in the direction of the front door.

"Have you forgotten something?"

"What?"

"The rest of your outfit? What *are* you wearing?"

"A *dress*, and there's nothing missing, thanks, Dad."

"Looks like the top half and you forgot the skirt."

She shook her head. "I'm twenty-six, and I run my own business. When are you going to stop with all of this?"

"All of what?"

"Telling me what to do as if I'm still a child."

James returned to his newspaper, and the front door closed behind his back.

Grace lit a cigarette, and hurried in the direction of the station wagon. She slid across the vinyl bench seat to sit beside the driver.

"No problem getting away?" Michael asked.

She shook her head. "Not really."

Michael checked the rear vision mirror before driving off. He did not see James Wallin coiled behind the deep red flower spikes of the Bottle Brush, even though his presence had scattered an artillery of screeching Rainbow Parrots.

Thirteen

February 1971

THREE times pregnant, so Helena knew the signs. Michael's reaction was also predictable, and this she anticipated with fluttering nerves and a further dose of nausea. She could hide it for months under her natural bulkiness and free-flowing dresses, which already bore the brunt of Michael's endless gibes as if her size was a choice rather than an outcome. Beneath it all, she was a mere skeleton of a woman with a backbone that could not support the plague of torment.

"I think I might be pregnant," she said, and watched her father's eyes grow round while he continued to calmly chew a pumpkin scone.

"I thought you'd been...you know, fixed," he replied.

"I'm not a cat, Dad, but yes, that was supposed to happen after Carla was born."

James sat back in his chair and sighed. "What a relief. You can't be pregnant then."

"Why is it a relief?"

James sipped his tea several times. "I thought you didn't want more children."

"Michael doesn't want more children, but I do, even though I can't manage with the three I have. I love babies."

"You're probably just imagining it. Must be one of those phantom pregnancies, common in cats, I believe." He smiled.

"And Mary the first, Queen of England, she had a phantom pregnancy." Helena reached for another scone and covered it with cream. "You're right, Dad, and it is a relief. Michael would *not* be pleased."

James nodded.

Carla cried out from her playpen in the living room.

"William!" Helena yelled.

"Whoa," said James. "It's not his fault whenever she cries."

"He pinches her, and she has the marks to prove it. I don't think he's too happy with the invasion of siblings," said Helena. "I really must make more time for him."

"Come here, little man," said James, and lifted his grandson on to his lap. "You're a good boy, aren't you?"

William smiled, and Helena thought she saw a glint of knowing behind the innocence that filled the hazel.

Still spooked by the phantom baby's relentless kicking, Helena revisited Dr. Lange who confirmed that, on or around 16 July 1971, Helena should expect to deliver a fourth child: the growing mass in her abdomen was not an apparition or mere expansion. There had been an administrative oversight, he explained, as he scribbled a script for Helena's high blood pressure, and as a result, the tubal ligation he was supposed to perform following Carla's birth, did not occur. He did not waste time apologizing, but offered to complete the procedure in July without charging the difference in cost, which now arose due to a 1 January price increase. Helena thanked him for his consideration then drove on automatic pilot to Waterloo Street to collect her first three children.

There was no judgment from her father, and only a soulful look that spoke of a heart breaking. She understood how deeply he cared, especially now she had her own, but it was painful for her in both directions: looking upward into her father's eyes, and down at the tiny lives that depended on her capabilities as a mother, which had yet to reach any potential.

Millie did what she did best, lifting wilted spirits with a three-course, home-cooked meal. The effect was instantaneous, with thoughts turned away from the perceived doom toward a belief in the will of God, and a reason that would only become clear over time. No one mentioned the real issues: time was already in short supply, as was money, and the marriage was still problematic, as was the husband.

Helena was rosy-cheeked when she returned home to Orchard Road, high on a regime of comfort foods and parental support, and her cheeks glowed brighter when she checked the mail.

A letter had arrived from the Royal Australian Air Force, and Helena hoped its contents would deliver the news Michael had been waiting for, over-powering any natural inclination to explode when she announced the due date of their fourth child. She opened the envelope, careful not to tear any part of it.

To further his application to join the RAAF, Michael had to attend two days of testing at the RAAF Recruitment Centre in York Street, Sydney. The medical component of the tests required a full medical by a civilian defense doctor followed by eyesight, hearing, and cardiology examinations undertaken by external specialists in Sydney. On the second day, he had to undergo a psychological assessment. Helena shuddered: an inquisition into Michael's mind could not go well, but was likely to be a matter of much interest to the professionals involved. She decided to hold off on the baby news to enjoy the amenable mood the letter would generate, and tell Michael by phone while he was in Sydney, after the assay into his psyche, but before the outcome. She re-folded the letter, added glue to the flap, and placed it on the kitchen bench where Michael would see it the minute he came through the back door.

In the years since James Wallin had asked his good friend

Peter McMurtrie to employ his son-in-law, James had endured a constant disquiet. Peter had never mentioned Michael during any of their regular encounters, and for the most part, that was both desirable and pleasant. However, the absence of feedback had also fuelled James' growing unrest, culminating in an urgent need for information because his daughter was expecting another child.

They met at The Royal in a dimly lit back booth, and James hurried Peter through the usual conversation: golf, the share market, politics, and the shocking nature of all news out of the city. Then turning to the issue of Michael Baden, and feeling confident his son-in-law's absent moral values would correlate with his employable worth, James sculled his whiskey in anticipation of what he was about to hear: cunning, lascivious, and undependable. He ordered another round of drinks before asking Peter to repeat the unfamiliar terms: intelligent, indefatigable, and trustworthy, and James inquired further to be sure the subject under discussion was the same for both. It was, but the report card did not fill James with any sense of pride, just relief, and they had moved on to other more convivial topics when the subject arrived to occupy a stool at the bar.

James watched as Michael ordered a beer then turned to survey the clientele at The Royal. Despite the muted lighting, he spotted James and gestured in his direction. James nodded in response, and checked his watch to record the time of Michael's first drink. He added a second to the count within minutes. "Must be hot out," James mumbled to Peter, but did not explain.

James slowed his whiskey consumption, determined to outstay his son-in-law, and with a keen eye and a temperate glass, he would monitor the hands of man and father time.

Hours passed and James could not continue the exercise, but the conclusion was clear: Helena, William, Brian, and Carla lived an existence more miserly than what a council wage could otherwise afford.

James left with Peter and made no contact with Michael

whose posture over the bar was much less upright. The friends chatted a while in the car park before heading for their respective vehicles.

"Can I talk to you?" Michael called out after James.

James stopped mid-stride. He dropped his head and shoulders, and reluctantly turned to face his son-in-law.

"What was that about?" Michael asked.

"What was *what* about?"

"You, with my boss. You were talking about me, weren't you?"

James shook his head and sighed. "Go home to your wife and children, Michael. You've been here long enough."

White knuckles pierced James' cheekbone, and a full fist cracked his eye socket. James wiped at the blood with a handkerchief then turned in the direction of his Volvo as swelling forced his eye closed. Another strike came from behind knocking him face first into the gravel. James rested a while on the coarse surface, waiting for more blows. He stood gingerly after a while, aware that footsteps had not crunched away.

"Stay away from my daughter," James mumbled, breathing sharply.

"She's my wife. How dare you, old man."

"Not that daughter," he replied, and staggered toward his car.

Up ahead, the red rear lights of Peter McMurtrie's sedan lit up and Peter stepped out of his car. James waved him away.

Fourteen

March 1971

MICHAEL called from Sydney after his tests concluded. It had all gone well, he thought. Helena mentioned the pregnancy, and held the phone from her ear when accusations of trickery caused her heart to pound. Yelling made her shrink: her father had never yelled, not even at Grace. The reproach continued, but the long distance delivery was preferable to having a wrist twisted, and her face sprayed with saliva. When silence finally came, she asked about the RAAF. His response was calmer, as expected, but it allowed for the detection of a slur. Helena knew where he had been, and could only hope celebrations did not continue into the next day when he returned to Maine.

Helena picked Michael up from the Maine Railway Station and dropped him off at The Royal Hotel as requested. He had not yet had an opportunity to celebrate his success, he claimed, and deserved as much. Helena said nothing.

At two the following morning, she woke to find the left side of their bed unoccupied and undisturbed, and the living

69

room sofa similarly uninhabited. She contemplated a 000 call, but had no idea what to report: Michael had not committed a crime, and he would not be in danger anywhere in Maine. She could call her father, but he would conclude the obvious: Michael was asleep, drunk somewhere, and the light of day would reveal his whereabouts, unfortunately. She called the Maine Hospital for confirmation that the night had been a quiet one with no emergencies or admissions. With everything possible done, she returned to bed at 2:30AM with a surprising revelation: she really did not care.

There was still no sign of Michael when Helena woke the next morning. She made coffee then called Sergeant Mackelroth who shared her conclusion: he would turn up eventually. The rest of the morning continued per ritual until William failed to sit down at his cereal bowl, and another ritual began: William had taken hide-and-seek to a new level, primarily as a lone exercise, but also as a gauntlet throw to Helena. She sighed, and started the search downstairs where reward was likely to be fastest, but did not expect the dual discovery: a corpse-like, vomit-stained Caucasian male with the hands of a three-year-old cupped around his face. She pulled William from the scene, and carried him by the underarms to the concrete laundry tubs. Her stomach lurched repeatedly as she scraped a partially digested meal from her son's fresh clothes. William showed no sign of distress, and his early morning swim in the tub would likely encourage more missions of discovery, but Helena envisioned a child psychiatrist pointing at that particular morning to explain William's teenage years of insurrection. It was a call to action.

She packed the station wagon for a day at Waterloo Street to catch up on her crying, and to take a new look at an old subject. As she drove the well-worn route, she resented the punctuation of her day: chores accumulated, and there was no luxury in postponing anything for a later time, and she was confident Michael would not pick up the slack.

Over tea and her favorite banana mocha tart, James proposed a repetitive solution—divorce, and he could see no

70

impediment for a woman three months from a fourth confinement. Millie was more circumspect: a final showdown with Michael was not worth the freedom, and father-less children was worse than the status quo, in Maine at least.

At the end of the day's deliberation, speculation, and calculation, the majority view (James and Millie) was that Helena should retrace the steps she had taken up the aisle and return to her first home, to them. They would support her financially, emotionally, and assume the role of permanent, full-time carers of the children. The solution was idyllic, but flawed. First, Helena was not one for trailblazing except when it had to do with running the mill: she had no desire to become the first young, divorcee with children in the entire metropolis of Maine. Second, the languid state of James and Millie after just one day with two kinetic toddlers and one babbler brought the rest of the proposal to its knees. Still, as suggested, Helena would think on it, a lot, and as she returned to Orchard Road in the snap chill of an early autumn evening, the solution was paramount in her mind.

Orchard Road looked menacing on approach with no light or life emitting through the front windows. Michael could be out, back at The Royal for a dose of dog hair, or lying in wait for retribution relative to the time he had spent fermenting in the midday sun.

She left the children asleep in the car, and ascended the rear steps holding tight on to the railing as she went. The back door was open, and her legs weakened. She should have woken him, helped him out of the sun before the rays burned his skin and caused his head to thump. The favor was about to be returned, and she cowered in anticipation while stepping inside. Silence greeted her, but did nothing to ease the pressure that pushed blood through to every nerve. As she entered each room, she switched on the light from a crouched position in case something was poised for her direction. Only when the house was bright did she encourage calm, returning then to the car to carry each child to bed youngest to eldest.

With William draped over a shoulder, she gasped when she

discovered another form already occupying his bed. It was certainly not Goldilocks or any other auric presence since it snored as a boar might, and was likely to be just as wild if surprised or cornered. She snuck away with William, careful to maneuver around floorboards known to creak. She placed William in her bed, and to her burgeoning chore list, she added more: bleach William's sheets, and disinfect his mattress. She hoped there would be no vomit.

Fifteen

April 1971

MICHAEL received another letter from the RAAF. The Selection Board, which traveled throughout Australia, was convening in Sydney for the final phase of initial testing—the panel interview. There had been delays in scheduling the test due to an influx of applications precipitated by the war in Vietnam, the conflict spawning patriots.

The interviewing panel was comprised of an RAAF pilot, RAAF psychologist, and another officer. Helena tried to visualize Michael in a three-on-one situation, and was certain he would feel threatened. Every question, no matter how innocuous, would be a personal affront, since he was already convinced a conspiracy had almost caused him to fail the medical test.

Regardless, the letter had focused Michael, and he returned home from work the next day not via The Royal, but via the Maine Municipal Library. He had borrowed every book he could on flying and the military, including a novel, Catch-22, which caused never-before scenes of hearty laughter.

The atmosphere at Orchard Road continued with a

tentative level of merriness until Michael left for Sydney, then the stress and pressure of being falsely so, manifested in complete exhaustion for Helena. The time alone would inspire her own solution, and so it was during those halcyon days that Project Alcatraz came to life.

The plan began with a sheet of paper divided into three columns: the first column listed her skills and included bookkeeping, management, and children. She added 'consumption' while chewing on the last of the double chocolate-chip cookies, then crossed it out. A second column titled 'interests', was the same as the first, confirming that she excelled most at what she enjoyed. The final column, 'market opportunities', was not so easy at the outset, and she left the column blank to wash dishes while waiting for inspiration. An idea presented itself as she gazed through the open kitchen window that framed a Van Gogh-like backdrop: an apprentice farmhand was harrowing the cabbage patch beyond their rear fence, scrutinized with some intensity by an older man with weathered skin. Helena abandoned the dishes to add 'honest and trustworthy property agent' to the third column. "How difficult could it be?" she asked herself.

Also under 'market opportunities', she added staffing company, home-baked foods, and clothes for ample frames. On page two of the plan, she wrote 'resources' listing herself, Millie, and James with a question mark beside his name. Constraints on the third page were similarly obvious: money, time, and Michael. On the fourth page, she wrote 'budget', put down the pen and sighed.

On the floor in front of the kitchen sink, she searched the darkened corner of the bottom cupboard for a tin box labeled 'toxic cleaning agents'. She removed the blue bankbooks, and wrote the balance for each on the fourth page of the plan. She circled the total, $123, several times. That was it for start-up costs, which meant certain options were at once redundant, leaving just one opportunity.

A scream pierced the funereal realization, and Helena had to rescue Carla from a Lego-filled nappy. William shook his head before Helena put the question, and Helena did likewise in response. She returned to Project Alcatraz for the final part: actions and deadlines.

A small loan would float the plan, and Mr. Chase, family banker, was the buoy. Helena called his secretary for an urgent appointment, required before Michael returned from Sydney.

Millie arrived early on the morning of the bank interview, to baby-sit, and to assist with crisis management. Helena had one maternity skirt suitable for the occasion, but the waistband was now dissecting mother and child. Another seismic force pulled at the seams challenging the inherent flexibility of the fabric and cotton. It was the same skirt Helena had worn carrying William, but it fitted her best now when un-expectant. Millie undid the side seams and inserted a gusset of stretchy material, and removed the waistband to create a design that was neither fashionable nor maternal, but which enabled Helena to sit in moderate comfort for the shortest period.

Despite the trauma of the morning, Helena arrived early at the bank, and in time for two cups of nerve-settling tea. Promptly at 11AM, she was ushered into the inner sanctum where Mr. Chase stood to greet her.

"Good morning, Miss Wallin. And how is your father?" he asked.

"Fine, thank you, Mr. Chase," she said, not bothering to correct her name or title.

"Please take and seat. And what can I do for you today?"

"I am considering a new business venture, Mr. Chase," she began confidently, until she saw the first brow rise. "And, ah, I require a small loan, sir." She imagined herself as Oliver Twist, much less articulate, but destined for a similar fate.

"And what sum of money do you consider *small*, Miss Wallin?"

"I can't say for certain at the moment, Mr. Chase, but maybe…a thousand dollars…or less, if that's too much." A gulp escaped when the second brow rose.

"I would certainly like to assist you. Your father has been a valued client of our esteemed institution for many years, as you would know. Perhaps when you have a clearer understanding of how much you require, exactly, we can meet again to consider a possible loan for you. Your father would be able to help with that I'm sure, and it would certainly help if you were to bring him with you next time to explain this enterprise of yours. Is that suitable to you, Miss Wallin?"

"Yes, fine, Mr. Chase. Thank you for your time." She stood ready to leave, looking forward to liberation from her clothing and Mr. Chase's brows.

"Before you go, Miss Wallin, there is one other rather sensitive matter I would like to bring to your attention, if I may?"

"Oh?" she said, sitting once more.

"Regarding your mortgage repayments…they are in arrears, you see."

"Mortgage repayments, Mr. Chase? We don't have a mortgage. Perhaps you have me confused with someone else?"

"I'm never confused, Miss Wallin, and I am surprised that you would not recall granting a mortgage over your property to our institution."

"Ah, forgive me, Mr. Chase, but how much is this mortgage for?"

"Two thousand dollars, Miss Wallin—not an insignificant sum, all matters given due consideration." His chin dropped to his neck for his eyes to glare over the top of his glasses.

"And what was the purpose of this loan? Again, Mr. Chase, please forgive my poor memory. I am pregnant, you see," she replied, her muted laugh failing to extinguish the tension.

"Home improvements, Miss—" He stopped abruptly, and a sweat broke out above his brows. A sudden thought seemed to have unnerved him, and Helena watched as he twisted his cufflink. "Would you excuse me one moment," he said then left the room.

When he returned, dabbing at his forehead with an embossed handkerchief, he handed Helena a large green document. "Would this be your signature?" he asked, and

76

pointed to a scrawl beside the words, "Mortgagor, Helena Elsie Wallin."

Helena paused, shook her head, hung it, and whispered, "That appears to be my signature, Mr. Chase. I am sorry for the confusion, and I'll make sure the outstanding repayments are made as soon as possible."

"Yes, as soon as possible, Miss Wallin, please. The mortgage has been in arrears for some time now. I'm sure your father would not approve if he was to know of this."

Outside in the cooling autumn air, away from the austerity and accompanying claustrophobia of the bank, Helena took a deep, much needed breath, and cried all the way to Orchard Road.

Sixteen

May 1971

MICHAEL stared at the form guide. Tiny Dancer in the fifth was a certainty, but he dared not. Since the mortgage issue had revealed itself, life at Orchard Road had degenerated. He was more like a disobedient pet now, and not a much-loved pet either.

When the train had sided into Maine Railway Station, he was still on a high, but that nose-dived as soon as his feet made contact with the platform. He was expecting so much more for his triumphant homecoming, much more than a wife with a silent, cold hostility. It reminded him though, that he had never seen her angry, and he would never have given her credit for having the requisite fire inside. She said nothing, but words were not required. He willed himself to leap aboard the last carriage to wave an Astaire-like farewell as the train rolled out of the station, but turned instead and followed Helena to the car. She said nothing more when he asked her to stop at The Royal on the way home.

He had hoped to win enough on the horses to pay for the floor coverings and window furnishings at Orchard Road, but his motive was not entirely pure: the constant scrambling for every dollar for carpet and curtains, made him feel guilty about his visits to The Royal, and he should not since he was the sole breadwinner.

His system for the horses seemed sure-fire, but when it failed, he had to win more to cover past losses, and that meant betting more. Then the second system went awry at an early stage, and the bookmaker's demands became monotonous and wearisome, so Michael visited the bank, used his father-in-law's name and influence, and secured a loan. The task was easier than expected, and no one questioned the legitimacy of Helena's signature, but the repayments were much trickier. He started out OK, deducting the loan repayment from monies he already creamed from his pay packet before handing it to Helena. The cream, though, was his drinking stash. A single schooner a day was all he could afford after debts were paid, and this made him bitter so he drank more, paid less off the loan, and spiraled into the quagmire that led to the exposure.

Although the detection of the fraud and subsequent isolation had been unpleasant, he was better off for it: the problem now had a new owner, and Helena no longer bothered him with her daily minutiae. William delivered essential communiqués in the back tray of his plastic tricycle, and was so happy with the new modus operandi he expanded his enterprise to deliver food, garbage, toys, and anything else that would fit.

All there was to life was the waiting for something to change. The next RAAF letter was overdue, and every additional day of delay compounded his anxiety. Further complications arose at work, and Michael responded to Peter McMurtrie's changed demeanor with a climactic diminution in attitude and productivity. The risk of imminent unemployment was high, which added more pressure.

The station wagon veered off the usual path from Orchard Road to Waterloo Street to follow the asphalt up to the white house on the range with its expansive view through bay windows. Helena parked across the street and peered inside to imagine herself in another life. Her three fellow passengers were uncharacteristically quiet while she dreamed, but then a sudden cheer from William caused giggles, and three smiles from her babies brought her back to where she wanted to be. She glanced down at the plan for Millie's Home-Baked Treats, her Hobson's choice: the planning process and Mr. Chase having confirmed that this was all there was. Helena stared for the final time at the house she had unwittingly renounced when she thought she was appeasing her husband then restarted the engine to continue the drive to Waterloo Street.

She decided not to mention the mortgage issue when asking her parents for assistance with the new business venture. She knew the response: her father would insist on repaying all monies owed to the bank then a homily would follow that Helena could predict word for word, and did not need to hear.

Millie loved the idea of Millie's Home-Baked Treats, and could not wait to put her talents on a more public platform, but the key to success, James and Helena agreed, was the incestuous market at hand: Grace and her coffee shop in Sydney.

With the plan adopted unanimously in the absence of anything else, Helena and Millie began with the list of foods to bake and sell. They identified ingredients, calculated quantities for each daily bake, and divided the recipes unequally between them according to capabilities. James assumed responsibility for supply chain management: he calculated the time required to prepare, bake, cool, and package, and to transport the output to its final destination. He added ten percent to the total time to allow for the unforeseen, primarily with children in mind, traffic in Sydney, and the likelihood that something in Helena's kitchen might burn.

James would source bulk suppliers for everything from flour, eggs, and milk, to small fridges, cellophane, ribbons and gold stickers that would bear the name of the business. He planned a reorganization of the garage to make way for a storeroom fortified against rats, possums, and cockroaches. In addition, he took on the role of manager, accountant, and messenger. He would deliver raw ingredients to the respective kitchens, and organize the rail consignments. On Helena's original business plan, he transformed the question mark beside his name under resources, into a star.

The new business venture had woken two sleeping giants, but for Helena, it simply meant less sleep.

Seventeen

July 1971

THE last time Michael spent an evening with Sergeant David Mackelroth in December of 1965, he believed the visit would be a one-off, but just as Tiny Dancer had raced to an odds-against victory in the fifth, he found himself a patron once more. But it was not his fault entirely.

While he was in Sydney for the Selection Board interviews a couple of months earlier, Helena had collected his pay packet from the council, and daylight had finally shone on the truth of his net earnings before the cream was removed. Consequently, Michael's drinking fund, the cream, became literally so in the grocery budget. Under ordinary circumstances, he would have defended his right to skim and drink, but he had no hand since the mortgage issue.

And so Michael only came to be at The Royal that unfortunate Saturday afternoon because of Helena: she had acquiesced, and given him money for The Royal to get him out from under her feet. With limited funds though, each drop of ale was precious, and Michael did everything in his power to protect his glass. He had even spread his elbows outwardly to create a physical barrier, harboring his personal space from the ruffians of the visiting football team. Then there was a push, and a frugal sip became an amber river that covered the front of his shirt. A barrage of blows followed, with Michael punching at random from his bar stool, until dragged into the melee that continued on the floor. Broken bottles were the weapon of choice.

Sergeant Mackelroth and his deputy arrived not long after the 000 call reached the station. They pulled at the thrashing layers: three men on top of Michael and an unconscious man below him. Then paramedics moved in to patch four of them while an ambulance sped away with one. They were less quarrelsome on route to the police station in the back of a paddy wagon, and Sergeant Mackelroth bundled them into one cell to allow for more self and collective reflection.

Michael refused to press charges against his attackers and they enjoyed an early discharge with a stern warning. That left Michael alone again for another night with Sergeant Mackelroth, or longer, depending on when the unconscious man woke. Sergeant Mackelroth invited Michael to call Helena. He declined. Helena would already know courtesy of the informal system of telegraphy in Maine.

When the alcohol-induced anesthetic wore off, the depth of the cuts that crisscrossed his body became apparent, but worse pain was to come with a mid-morning release from his cell, and answerability.

Unlike other Sunday morning visitors at the Maine Memorial Hospital, Michael arrived without gifts, and dressed in a bloodied, shredded shirt. The taxi driver had driven directly to the emergency room given the condition of his fare, but continued as requested to the end of the circular driveway as close as possible to the men's ward.

Michael took the stairs up two flights, not wanting a close encounter with others in the elevator and the risk of a nudge. At the nurse's station, he unfolded the ripped piece of paper from Sergeant Mackelroth.

"I can show you where to go," she said, "but only after I've taken a look at your wounds." She steered Michael into a treatment room and turned him into a patchwork quilt. A passing doctor authorized painkillers then as promised the nurse escorted Michael to his destination. She left him at the doorway to the ward, and nodded at the only occupied bed. Thick, heavy curtains stopped the morning sunshine at the glass panes, and Michael was relieved that mounds of surrounding purple skin had pushed the man's eyes together into slits. He moved closer to the patient, and dragged a visitor chair to his side.

"I just wanted to say...that I'm sorry for what I did. I never meant to hurt you. I was just there minding my own business." He paused to take a deep breath. "I don't expect you to forgive me, so I just wanted to say how very sorry I am."

"Fine," the man whispered through bulging, cracked lips. "Just go."

Michael did not want to leave—the darkness, coolness, and having company that could not talk or see him, was comforting. He had nowhere to go anyway, other than home to Helena.

"Just go," the man repeated, and Michael left.

Helena offered no commentary when Michael returned to Orchard Road, luckily for her, since it was all her fault: if she had not provided the funds, he would not have been at The Royal that day, and there would not have been a skirmish or aftermath.

He needed a soothing place to heal, yet despite Helena's silence, he could not find it at Orchard Road. Toys and vegemite-coated bread crusts littered the living room floor, which eclipsed the flour and eggshell scarred kitchen, but only just. The uncontrolled noise that emanated from childish things drove Michael down the hallway into a back bedroom where he rested on William's bed. Three children followed, bringing with them a range of toys including a monkey with cymbals. Michael rose promptly, and headed for the sanctity of the bathroom and a lockable door.

84

Slightly refreshed from a partial bath where only un-bandaged parts of his body could submerge, Michael returned to the living room, zigzagging his way through the debris to the soiled couch where he had slept in the weeks since his youngest son's birth. Matthew, with his fine layer of wispy blond hair and ocean blue eyes, bore no resemblance to any of the other five inhabitants at Orchard Road—mother, father or siblings, or to any other member of the Baden family. The child's bloodline was a matter of question and suspicion.

Michael stretched out on the couch gently lowering his ripped back onto the prickly fabric extending his feet over one worn padded arm. He extracted the letter from the RAAF he had tucked between the cushions the day before, and in an act of self-flagellation, unfolded the letter and read the words again.

He had passed the medical, the letter said, but his stanine score, which combined the results of the psychological testing and Selection Board interview, was four, and a four out of a maximum nine, was not enough for entry at that point in time. He could continue to apply until his score was high enough relative to the scores of other applicants, but Michael knew this meant never, unless applications to join the Force became scant and filled with incompetents, and this was unlikely given the unparalleled benefits of national service.

The first time Michael read the letter, the shocking contents had blocked all comprehension of the latter paragraphs, but he read them then as if for the first time and absorbed the message. There were other opportunities available to him: navigator, air electronics officer, or airman, and he could progress through the ranks to his goal.

He folded the letter, closed his eyes to impede the invasion of infantile gamboling, and focused his mind on what was most important. He wanted to be a pilot, he wanted to be in the Air Force, and while the first goal had aborted, the other had not. The view was clearer once the fog of failure had lifted, and another night with Sergeant Mackelroth had offered some perspective.

Eighteen

September 1971

THE joy of cooking was the title of a much-used book, and nothing more. The thought of preparations for a christening day feast caused vessels in Helena's head to swell, and veins everywhere imitated the knotted, twisted dark blue of her legs. Millie, fortuitously, was unaffected by the unrelenting nature of the weekly bake, and with joy, spent the entire weekend in the kitchen for a post-christening lunch for thirty, and gourmet family dinner to follow.

Grace had returned for the fourth and final baptism with two-fold news: Millie's Home Baked Treats were selling like hot cakes (and she intended the pun), but the gravy, or the soured cream depending on one's perspective on sleep deprivation, was that she needed more, much more. Current supplies were selling by pre-order long before the morning train from Maine had schlepped into Central Railway Station, and clients were taking those supplies home to claim as their own. There was little or nothing left for the dessert trolley in the teashop, which forced Grace to fill it with bought cakes and biscuits no one wanted after sampling what had come from Maine.

Armed with a tray of coffee and a platter of chocolate-dipped fruits, James, Millie, Helena, and Grace, retired to the living room to consider the issue of what, who, when, and how they could meet Grace's latest demands.

The solution was simple according to Grace: double, triple, or quadruple the quantities, but there were logistical complications that could not multiply in relative terms, said James. They still only had two ovens, two cooks, there was just one train to Sydney each day, and they could never send day-old or frozen goods as this was contrary to the essence of Millie's Home Baked Treats.

"Who else could cook for us?" Grace asked, and Brian answered the call presenting his grandmother with a chocolate patty cake. Millie sniffed at it with some discomfort, and asked about the ingredients. The dirt, sticks and leaves were obvious, and the "round brown things" explained the foul air. James confiscated the morsel and went in search of a backyard garden party, hoping Brian had not yet mastered mass production. He tossed the sole patty cake into a garden bed and monitored playground activity for evidence of more resourcefulness involving nature.

Millie escorted Brian upstairs to the bathroom, with wrists fixed in front of his chest, to douse his hands in ample Dettol to kill the microbes and its spawn.

When James and Millie returned to the living room to deal with the 'how' of the problem Grace had created, the think-tank had disintegrated. Helena had fallen asleep in an armchair while Michael had abandoned his Sunday papers, and supposed supervision of the back yard, to entice Grace to The Royal for "a few quiet drinks". James rushed to his drinks cabinet to fill several glasses with cognac.

"You can drink here," he said. "It's a family day."

He locked eyes with Michael and a quiet battle ensued. Grace continued to the front door, ignoring the suggestion, and Michael followed.

James stewed, and woke Helena to unleash an upbraiding

that left her confused. Given his recent incarceration, Michael should not be visiting The Royal, James said, and especially not on the day of his son's christening. He blamed Helena for granting her husband such freedoms. Grace was Grace, he added, and that would always be a problem for any father.

Helena dared not mention Michael's behavior since Matthew's birth, which was odd, even by his standards. He would appear at Orchard Road at the most unusual and unexpected hours during the working day, as if looking for something and expecting to find it. Whatever he searched for, it seemed elusive, for he always left disappointed, but knowing. Helena had no explanation, other than that a lifetime of brawling had caused some damage. She was more concerned about the consequences of his regular absentia from the council.

"What are you thinking about, Helena?" James asked.

"Oh, nothing," she replied then scrambled for a new topic. "Michael has been offered a job in the Air Force."

"Doing what?" James asked.

"As an airman specializing in systems control, or something like that."

"There's no Air Force base in Maine," he replied. "What are you saying, Helena?"

She paused, unprepared. "We'll be moving sometime next year. Melbourne or Sydney, if it all goes ahead, but you know Michael—anything could happen, or not happen. He still has to finish school."

James filled his glass, and they sat in silence while Helena contemplated quicksand. It was mysterious how it sucked one deeper relative to the level of desperation in one's attempted escape. She imagined herself immersed to the neck, waiting for certain death then a child cried out.

"William!" Helena yelled.

James shook his head, and strode toward the source. He returned a short time later with the villain and the victim, handing Carla to Millie, and keeping William for himself.

Matthew was also now favored since he was the only Wallin

descendant to inherit the Swedish looks of their ancestors. Photos of James as a baby and young child confirmed that Matthew was a replica of his grandfather, and that Matthew's fine, fair hair would one day fall to hereditary forces, dropping strand by strand until completely depilated like his grandfather.

"Tell me the fish story!" said William, and James obliged with the tale of the Baltic herring, which was sometimes so fermented that the flat round tins would explode when opened, covering everyone in close proximity with stinking fish. William laughed hysterically. It was the funniest story ever re-told a thousand times.

Nineteen

December 1973

TWO years had passed since the Baden family uprooted and moved to the RAAF base in Laverton near Melbourne. And despite the years feeling like eternity, Helena could not find comfort in her new surroundings. She was only a phone call away from Maine, Michael would say, but a telephone cord was not a hug or a smile, or the smell of a freshly baked banana mocha tart.

She had tried to immerse herself in the community life, but as her mass expanded with each passing month, even the house next door was too much of an effort. She no longer bothered with the hassle of grooming since there was no reward for effort: nothing invented could alter her form to one more pleasing, and no cosmetic mask could hide her despair. She ate more for solace then suffered, as one day's solution became the next day's crisis ensuring she would soon emulate the geographical bulk of China. As her body expanded, the woman she used to know retracted.

Michael's most valued contribution to her dilemma was a diagnosis of 'letting yourself go', and it was not a reference to free spiritedness. There was no malice in his words though, as she would have expected once, because he was happy, and her appearance was of no real concern to him. It was merely a factual observation she could not deny.

Michael had scaled Everest, and the view from the summit, from all reports, was better than the dream. Helena's quest however, was to alight the merry-go-round, an impossible task it seemed despite its slow pace. The barrel organ, calliope, and violin piano tormented her as she circled day after day, yearning for peace and home.

Over a breakfast bowl filled with different cheeses, Helena informed Michael of her plan to return to Maine for Christmas. She expected resistance, but received an "OK."

"OK," she said. "OK."

"What are you eating?" he asked peering into her bowl.

"Cheese."

"I see that, but why are you eating cheese for breakfast. It was apples yesterday."

"I'm on a diet," she replied, surprised he had noticed.

"Which one this time?"

"Israeli Army Diet. Two days of apples, two days of cheese, two days of chicken, and two days of salad."

"Sounds healthy if you ate it all together in one meal."

Helena shrugged.

"You need to stop with all this dieting, Helena. It's making you—"

"Fat? Fatter?"

"Exercise is the key," he said, patting his taut torso.

"Yeah, I'll try to remember that next time I'm sitting on the couch wondering how to spend all my spare time."

He laughed. "Let me know the dates for Christmas and I'll apply for leave."

She watched him strut through the front door, a picture of perfection in his uniform on his way to his perfect job in what appeared to be his perfect life. She still remembered how that felt back when she could not wait to get to the mill for a day's work beside her father, in a time when the miserable spouse who could not get an act together was not her.

The mortgage issue was ancient history and but a blip. The rent from Orchard Road and the profits from Millie's Home Baked Treats had reduced the debt to zero in just twenty months, thanks in part also to James and Millie who had continued with the business after Helena left Maine. When Helena failed to return in a matter of months as anticipated, they sold the business as a going concern.

Helena's bedroom at Waterloo Street had not changed in the five and a half years since 11 April 1967 when she left in a bridal gown. It had benefited from a makeover in 1963 when, after ten years of vacancy, Grace moved into Robert's room at the front of the house. It was a painful time, for Millie especially, as silk replaced boyish checks, and suede, fake fur, leopard and zebra prints displaced everything that reminded everyone that Robert had once lived there.

With Grace and her clutter vanquished, Helena proceeded to paste the walls of her middle bedroom with plain silver motif wallpaper. She covered everything else in clean, crisp white fabric, and only items inherently displayable avoided the closet. The carpet was a soft floor covering once more, and no longer a pageantry of boots, magazines, and the unwashed.

Michael had not taken a single step up the stairs at Waterloo Street until that Christmas Eve, and it felt strange to Helena, exposing her childhood bedroom to her husband for the first time. He scanned every aspect of it, absorbing its richness and unable to hide an invidious comparison with his veranda at Park Lane.

The elongated upper story had three large bedrooms and an alcove, all in a row down the eastern side of the house. The master bedroom at the back was next to the sole bathroom. The alcove between the other two bedrooms, where three Wallin children had once congregated after school for homework with strawberry milk and freshly baked cookies, was still hallowed ground. Robert's desk overlooked the manicured side gardens through a window that fell from the ceiling to the floor. Helena and Grace had desks facing the only two internal walls, which now served as a gallery. Michael studied the photos intently, one at a time, with the same level of vex that had accompanied his survey of Helena's bedroom. It occurred to Helena then, that she had never seen a family photo at Park Lane—not a single photo of Michael, any of his brothers or Alice. The sole image on display was an austere black and white of Dorothy and John Baden Senior on their wedding day.

"Who's this?" Michael asked, pointing at a young boy with fine blond hair and blue eyes rimmed by incongruous dark-framed glasses.

"Robert," Helena replied. "You haven't seen his picture before?"

"No," Michael whispered. "He has blond hair...and blue eyes, like Matthew."

"Wallin ancestry. Dad's father came from Sweden before the First World War. Here's an old picture of dad." She handed Michael a yellowed portrait of a fair-haired youth. "You can see the similarities. Matthew looks just like him."

"Your family is Swedish?"

She stared at him. "I thought you knew that."

"No, I didn't."

"And you've never seen a photo of Robert before? Not even in the newspaper back when he disappeared?"

Michael shook his head.

Grace interrupted the apocalyptic silence with Millie traipsing behind her hauling a bulging suitcase up the staircase.

"A family reunion," said Grace, "How lovely!"

Helena smiled at the pirating of Millie's favorite acclaim. She took Grace's suitcase from Millie, dragging it the rest of the way to the front bedroom while Michael and Grace chatted, and it was not long before the two proposed a night out. Helena declined, happy to be back home, and wanting to stay there for every minute. She had her own plan for the holidays: to generate an abundance of fresh memories to relive in the loneliest hours back at the base. The pain of leaving again shot to the forefront of her thoughts and threatened to overwhelm then Millie suggested a banana mocha tart before dinner, and that single-handedly restored joy.

Michael and Grace returned to Waterloo Street in what was by then, Christmas Day. The Royal had closed at 10PM, but a moonlit lake beckoned, and the hanging willows on its shore had shielded them from its glow.

A moth-ridden bulb guided them through the armada of pots on the front porch. Once inside, Michael clipped his hands around Grace's waist for guidance through the shadows. They passed through the living room, up the darkened stairs, and past the master bedroom toward the front of the house. The procession lacked stealth due to the blocks of cork that were Grace's shoes. She attempted to tread more softly as they crept past the alcove where four children slept on camp beds, but had to stifle a groan when lips kissed the back of her ear. The bedroom door closed behind them.

Michael untied a loose knot from around her neck, which fell to reveal bare skin to the waist. He admired the simplicity of her halter dress as a zip allowed the remaining yellow Georgette to fall to the floor to envelop the cork platforms. He lifted her, and placed her on the bed beneath him.

As the first sign of daylight filtered through the gap between the drawn curtains, Michael sifted through the pile on the floor for his clothes. He dressed in part, leaving his torso unclad, then bent to kiss Grace once more. With his shirt flung across a shoulder, and socks and shoes in hand, he crept toward the middle room, and slid beside his wife onto fresh sheets.

At the end of the hall, a black silhouette watched the morning activity.

Twenty

Christmas Day 1973

CHRISTMAS Day in 1973 was an exceptional one as it rose to greet a house at full capacity with three generations under the same roof for the first time.

James woke in a mood, clearly not filled with the good will of Christmas. He started the day with a shot of rum, adding milk to the dark elixir to give the pre-10AM beverage some pretense of acceptability, but this did nothing to avert Millie's gaze.

When Michael entered the kitchen with an outstretched hand, James ignored him, committed as he was to the hypocritical oath, and on this of all days. The rebuff had witnesses. Helena shifted uncomfortably in her seat, and Millie added an open mouth and raised brow to her stare. Michael was unperturbed.

The rest of the morning proceeded without incident, with the traditional over-consumption of food generating a calmer scene, but if James had thought he had escaped the early morning snub of his son-in-law, he was mistaken.

Millie's tone was one he recognized although its occurrence

was as rare as the day itself. His un-Christian-like behavior would ruin Christmas for everyone, she said, when in reality, he was saving the day by concealing the truth. He could not imagine how she might handle details of the morning's early hours, and much more than a day would collapse. James thought twice about perjuring himself on the Lord's birthday, but resorted to a lie claiming he was unwell. The lameness of his alibi went unnoticed as Millie's concern for his well-being relegated the admonishment, but only an amputation of his right hand could justify the absent greeting, for no matter how ill one might be a hand shaking was still possible.

Grace emerged at midday just in time for the lunchtime gorge that would continue until the regular bean shape of their stomachs had morphed into an over-inflated balloon. The only cure post-lunch was to lie down on one's back to relax a distressed abdomen.

James retired to his outdoor recliner, shaded by the house and passed sun, to monitor alcohol-induced consorting while Millie and Helena sweltered in a kitchen bearing the heat of a 180-degree oven active since sunrise.

Michael and Grace stretched out on the trimmed Paspalum with a respectable distance between them as they watched the children with new toys, and chatted intermittently. James unwound sufficiently at the state of play before him, and laughed at Brian who was busy consigning vegetables from his pockets to the garden bed. For as long as positions remained as they were, peace would reign for the rest of the day. James sipped on his milk-free rum.

Grace returned to the kitchen for another beer for Michael and champagne for herself, repeating the journey several times during the afternoon. On each occasion, the divide between the two narrowed, and James sipped more rapidly as he watched the grassy barrier disappear from view. To the uninitiated, the scene may have appeared harmless: a brushing of a hand or rubbing of arms, but James saw faithless betrayal, impudence, and disrespect on a multitude of levels. When

Michael placed a hand on Grace's knee to whisper in her ear, James launched from his recliner. He pushed Michael onto his back then dragged him by the shirt collar away from his daughter, age, wisdom, and intoxication not evident in the maneuver.

The charge sheet, although not drafted, yet, would signal the end of Michael's military career. He was sorry for all of it, and wished he could banish the new memory of the old man's furrowed face pasted in blood, saliva, and grass, still conscious, but eerily detached. Michael had bruising around his neck and his voice was hoarse from the sergeant's headlock, but it would not console anyone to know of his injuries, which, in relative terms, were insignificant.

The cell was the same as it had been for his previous visits although the purpose had changed. His first stay in 1965 had been for rest and recovery following an altercation with an immovable object: the dressing shed at the Wallin oval, and the second had been more for reflection following a confrontation with four footballers. This stay was for his safety: the Maine telegraph was merciless with every day a workday, and James Wallin, the town's unofficial patriarch, was not someone a prudent man would beat in such a way.

It was not Michael's fault entirely: the old man had started it by ripping his new shirt, but in truth, it was not so much the shirt, but a familiar look of scorn that accompanied the move. Michael had no control when he saw it, etched into his memory as it had been since school days. He conceded though, that the viciousness of his response was not proportional, and he had not heard the screaming of women and children, which might otherwise have caused him to pause.

Grace arrived at the police station some hours later, close to midnight. Michael could not see her from his cell, but heard her voice through the concrete wall as she spoke with Sergeant Mackelroth.

"James Wallin is in a coma," Sergeant Mackelroth said

unlocking the cell door. "I'm releasing you, for now, but only because your wife and sister-in-law have chosen not to press charges. That could change if...when James recovers, but if his condition worsens, it worsens for you too, Michael."

Michael nodded then left with Grace through the front door of the station.

"Michael?" Sergeant Mackelroth called out.

He turned to face the sergeant, but kept his gaze downward.

"You've had all your chances. It's all square now, between you and life. Do you understand what I'm saying?"

Michael nodded.

All was quiet between them as he and Grace returned to the scene to pack, and as he waited for the only train out of Maine at first light Boxing Day, Michael stared at the iron tracks. He had crossed a line: the one that separated justifiable wrong and unforgivable sin. He would never return.

Helena was baffled. Her father was a peaceful man, and as far as she knew, had never before come close to any form of aggression. He was a talker, incessantly so at times, but definitely not a fighter, and not one to ignite an issue, not even one for cause. She did not see the initial act, the push that so inflamed her husband, but Grace had seen it, and was no wiser. Only James knew what had possessed him to do what he did, and he was not talking.

Twenty-one

January 1974

WHILE James Wallin lay in a coma at Maine Memorial Hospital, the white piano at Waterloo Street, not played since 1953 when Robert disappeared, was alive again with ragtime. The trauma of Christmas Day had taken Millie inside to the place she had occupied back then, but strangely, this time she played.

She still believed Robert would return when he realized that he was the boy in the faded posters wrapped around lampposts. For seven years, the posters went up around Sydney on the anniversary of that last piano lesson, until Millie finally gave way to James and tried to heal, but did not surrender her belief.

She was the one who had insisted that Robert attend Scots College in Sydney, a place most suited for their eldest child, only son, and heir to the Wallin sawmilling dynasty. Robert resisted for the duration of his two-year stay, crying for several nights before he had to return each term, until 14 July 1953 when the wasted tears no longer flowed.

While boarding school was a primary point of contention

between mother and son, the piano lessons with Miss Czerny exacerbated the conflict. Robert wanted to play football, as his father had, and with "Liberace" and "sissy" as his nicknames, boarding school became even more of a trial.

The lessons also required travel outside of school, and although Robert enjoyed those moments of freedom, he did not enjoy a second of the time spent with Miss Czerny, who felt likewise since it was clear Robert's heart was not in it.

Miss Czerny was to wait with Robert at the bus stop following each lesson, and her fee reflected this additional irritation, but on the day in question, she left Robert to find his own way so her faltering schedule could return to normal. The 5PM bus did not stop since its congested interior could not accommodate another.

Witnesses were vague about what happened next, with mention only of a young boy seen at the bus stop talking to a man, and a blue sedan parked nearby. The winter sun had disappeared along with its gentle warmth, and Robert.

Millie was with Helena and Grace when the doctors came to deliver the prognosis for James. She showed no sign of emotion, but went home and trimmed her prize-winning garden leaving behind a spiky green mass. While shocking, the scene did not disturb Helena when she pulled into the driveway: she expected the interior was wall-to-ceiling with flowers to brighten the gloom, and that made sense, but there were no floral arrangements on display. The garbage can however, overflowed with a rainbow of blooms.

James had moved his hand on the fifth day of his coma, but it was not a sign of his awakening, the doctor said, for spontaneous movement was common with coma patients. Doctor Pell was concerned though about its duration, and the next nine days were critical with regard to recovery.

Helena spent the most part of every day with her father, until Grace arrived in the evenings. Millie stayed away, and that was for her own good: the holes drilled into her husband's swollen, blood-filled skull left him unrecognizable in any event.

The skull itself, though, had inflicted the main damage on the delicate mass within. Jagged, menacing bones at its front had shredded the frontal cortex as it jolted back and forth during the skirmish. Doctor Pell had seen worse damage from car accidents, he said, but still the fate of James Wallin was set to fall anywhere between full recovery and death. It was all dependent on the extent of the damage and type of damage. Age was also a critical factor with survival and a full recovery more likely in someone younger, and Doctor Pell stressed that the true nature of James' condition might not disclose itself for many months.

Helena and Grace continued to talk to him. Sometimes a reward came with a faint sigh or his chest would rise, suspending hope with it, until it fell once more to its lifeless state.

"I'm coming home for good, Dad," Helena said. "I know what you would say if you could talk right now, so lucky for me that you can't, I guess. No one likes to hear 'I told you so'. The kids will miss Michael, and the base. They do love him you know, and he's been a different father since we've been away." She paused. "I wish I knew what happened that day...what you were thinking, why.

"It's daunting though, the thought of being a single mother, and Brian starts school this month." Helena glanced around the white room, listening to the mechanical confirmation of life.

"If that's not enough, I have other issues to overcome, like for example, I am fat, F-A-T, fat. No point calling that kettle anything else, it is black. I mean, I barely fit into this chair!" She grabbed her thighs and wobbled the surplus. "Look, Dad, I'm oozing out of it." She paused. "How did I end up like this?

"I'm not thinking of another relationship," she continued. "Probably won't divorce either, unless Michael asks for one. I mean, be serious, Dad, no one sees me. I am invisible. It's funny how people used to say, 'oh, you're not *fat*, Helena' or 'you're just strong and healthy,' but now, when I mention my weight, they just nod." She took a green apple from her handbag and bit into it, chewing with a bitter expression.

"I hate apples. Probably because of that diet I went on, the Israeli Army Diet. For two whole days, I ate nothing but apples. Actually, it ended up more than two days. I'd get to the third day, which was the first of two cheese days then I'd break, and binge for a few days. I'd cook up a house-full of cakes and biscuits telling myself it was for the kids, but the kids would barely eat any of it, and I'd eat the rest. You'd be surprised at how much I can eat and for how long." She paused. "I don't stop when I'm full. I keep going and going until bedtime, and sometimes I get up during the night and eat some more and I don't know why. Anyway, then I'd have to start the diet again, from day one, back at the apples. I probably ate just apples for the most part of a month with the odd cheese day here and there, and a few binges in between. I must say, it is a good thing you can't talk right now." She placed the half-eaten apple in a brown paper bag. "It was great back in the mill days, Dad, when we worked together in the office." She sighed. "They were the best days of my life, just the two of us. I loved the mill."

She searched inside her handbag for a Cherry Ripe. "Grace Hand-me-down," she said, holding the Crown Lewis black chenille bag up on display. "Not sure I like the green and red stripes, and these gold handles look a bit silly in the daytime, but beggars can't be choosers. Anyway, as I was saying, my problem is, I have a relationship with food, a love affair actually, and we need to break up, become friends instead, not enemies though—that would make me anorexic, and I love food too much to cut it from my life altogether." Helena stared into the ventilator and took comfort in its steady flow. "How do you end a relationship with something that has comforted you, and been there for you through all the hard times, and brings so much pleasure even though it doesn't last forever, unless you eat all day and all night." She smiled at the self-portrait. "It won't be easy, but I have to try.

"Caramello Koala," she announced after another excursion into her handbag. "Now there's a good, old friend. Where was

I? How do you like my black tent, Dad?" she asked, standing to swirl. "It's comfortable. Goes with the bag I suppose. Michael's not a bad person, you know, he just has a lot of baggage. I wonder what his life might have been like if he had grown up in another family. What do you think, Dad? Does poverty make you who you become? I suppose there are rich kids with issues too, like Christina Onassis, so maybe it has nothing to do with rich or poor. Maybe it has everything to do with who your parents are.

"So, I'm coming home, back to Maine. I'm not sure how it will all work out yet, and I wouldn't usually do something so drastic without a detailed plan—you know me. This time though, I'm starting from a spontaneous decision and working backward. It's petrifying now that I say the words aloud. I'm going to need you, Dad. I can't do it without you.

"I wonder if Michael will sell his share of Orchard Road to me. I'd have to visit our good friend, Mr. Chase for another loan." Helena laughed. "He's been asking after you, by the way. Who hasn't? I should be writing all of this down." She searched through her handbag for paper and a pen. "Can you believe that? I don't have paper with me. There's a bookstore downstairs. Wait right here, Dad. I'll be back in five."

Helena returned twenty minutes later, gasping. "I'm back, Dad, and I took the stairs! There's a new start right there!" She opened the notebook and poised the pen. "Let's begin with worst-case scenario—my particular area of expertise. No, I won't. That's being too negative. Let's start with *best*-case scenario. There, that's another new start! I am on a roll. Let's see…Michael gives me the house for the good of his children. Hmm, that's not very realistic. OK, before I can apply for a loan, I'll need a job. Millie's Home Baked Treats or anything like it is not an option, given my 'condition'. I can't afford to be around food all day if I'm going to lose this weight. What I need is a *real* job where I have to be somewhere at a certain time every day and there's a guaranteed pay packet at the end of the week. I think an accounting or managerial role would suit me. What do you think, Dad? The bank would be great—

they give discounted loans to employees after a couple of years.

"We'll have to live with you and mum for a while, if that's still OK. Then there's school for William and Brian, and pre-school for Carla. Mum will have to mind Matthew while I'm at work at my new job." She paused. "This is already sounding like a burden for you, especially with mum the way she is, but she'll come out of it when you do, hopefully." Helena glanced at her watch. "Oh, it's six already—time for me to be getting home to the kids. I have no idea how Grace is handling it all during the day, and frankly, Dad, it's best not to know. Anyway, she'll be here soon, so prepare yourself for an evening of non-stop, riveting conversation about the latest developments in perms and hair dye.

Helena stood to leave. "Well, it's been a pleasure, as always." She bent to kiss his hand, afraid still to touch his face. "Thanks for listening, Dad. I'll see you in the morning. We'll do some more work on the plan. I love you."

The third step into the hallway outside signaled the tear ducts to release the dammed. The cheerfulness was hard to maintain in the presence of so much machinery that confirmed the dire nature of the situation. If he could hear, he would know that under the buoyant words lay a more melancholy heart. Helena was grateful though, for the precious time she spent alone with him, for he was the mucilage, the cement, the glue, the binder, and without him, she would function like an old envelope.

She cried all the way to the elevator. Behind her, in the clinical, white room she had just left, blue eyes, grayed, had opened unseen.

Twenty-two

January 1974

EXPECTATION by its very nature was a source of discontentment. People wake from comas all the time and life is suddenly beautiful and perfect again, in the movies, but not so in the real world. Grayed blue eyes wide open was just the beginning, not the end. There were new problems for James Wallin to overcome arising from the damage caused to his brain: problems with complex thought, unstable emotions, and a changed personality. All were commonplace. "But will he be himself?" they asked repeatedly.

The brain, Doctor Pell explained, is extremely sensitive to damage, but tough as well. Some neurons die, but amazingly, new ones can grow in their stead. Surviving neurons also come to the rescue, sprouting new lines to patch up damaged circuits, and inactive circuits switch on in a crisis. It was a remarkable creation, they all agreed, and hoped and prayed for new neurons and circuitry.

The damage to his frontal cortex and brain stem could have been worse, said Doctor Pell, and a longer coma would have compounded his current condition, but 'not-so-bad' was a long way from 'good' and the prognosis they wanted to hear. Problems with breathing, speech, balance, and nausea were likely, and some of these were already evident. They were not expecting any memory loss of note since the temporal lobes had survived the trauma unscathed, but there would be changes to the man, in the way he interacts with others, his moods and so forth. The old James was gone, just like the old Millie, but that was not all: damage to the brain can transcend to affect the vascular system and cause a stroke, a cruel irony that arises from the brilliance of the brain's ability to create new circuitry.

James appeared much the same, albeit a lot quieter. "Do not overwhelm him," Doctor Pell had ordered, but it was impossible not to smother him in love and attention. He would regain a sense of his own self and his environment in time and with patience, but for the immediate present, it was foreign to him, like life to a young child. "Do not overwhelm him," Doctor Pell repeated.

Millie returned from lah-lah land to resume daily visits to the hospital. She told James about the demise of her garden, which she attributed to, "that Webcke boy from next door," adding that he was a drug addict, and that this was the kind of thing "those drug people" do. James laughed knowingly, and Helena was certain he had heard her talk of the garden's ruination while in the coma.

Time wanted to dash ahead to the point where life and James were normal again, in spite of Doctor Pell's caution. Helena had to return to the base to pack for her final homecoming, and the salon beckoned Grace, but she would stay to care for the children while Helena tied her loose ends.

The pending charges against Michael did not eventuate, further evidence that James Wallin did not have a single bone of malice in his wasting body.

Michael was remorseful, and for each day of Helena's last week at the base, he brought flowers, listened, apologized, and helped with the packing. He loved her, he said, and thought he always had. His words were sincere, and Helena understood that love was a concept that differed for everyone. She believed he probably did love her.

Helena asked Michael about Christmas Day, but he was puzzled to the same extent. He did not even understand his own action except to say it was in response to a look and he had reacted instinctively.

Their time together sorting through cupboards, talking about the things they found and their origins, was therapeutic. Michael confessed his fear of aloneness: he had never been on his own, not even throughout the lonely years at Park Lane. Helena assured him he would not remain so for long. From her invisible perspective, she saw how women looked at her husband, and flirted with him despite her presence. Time would barely pass before one or more of them offered to console the Adonis abandoned by his un-Venus like wife.

Helena asked Michael about Matthew: why he had rejected his youngest son from birth. He said he did not know, and did not deny it, and Helena was at least relieved she did not have to relive a multitude of examples as evidence. When asked, Michael said he had been faithful for all of their seven years together. He surprised her then by offering her his share of Orchard Road as a sign of goodwill, and gratitude to her father for not pressing charges that would have destroyed his career. The offer was conditional though: he would not have to pay child support, and the transfer of the house they had built together in Orchard Road would settle all matrimonial matters between them. Helena accepted, similarly keen to finalize their separation amicably, and without lawyers they could not afford. She had what she wanted: the house and the children, and no lawyer could do better than that. They discussed divorce, but concluded that there was no imperative, allowing each the time to settle into new lives.

The removal van arrived on that final morning, and within a few hours, was ready to leave, half-full.

They said goodbye on the footpath, aware that eyes peered through blinds in every other direction. Helena had not told anyone she was leaving, and authorized Michael to give any reason he liked. She did not care what anyone in this past life had to say of her. They agreed that it was not a final goodbye for their children would always connect them, and through the rear window of a taxi, Helena stole one last look at her home at the base. She waved back at Michael then disappeared from view.

The journey ahead was daunting: by train from Laverton to Melbourne, by plane from Melbourne to Sydney, then another train Sydney to Maine after several hours of waiting at Central Station in Sydney. Helena could not wait for it to end, to shower away the sweat, grime, and tears, and to see her children once more. She had spoken to them often by phone, and learned through Brian that they ate 'dinner', Rice Bubbles and Coco Pops, from mini boxes without milk. Grace explained the dry evening meal simply: they had run out of milk, and Millie had lost all interest in cooking or had forgotten how. Grace also reminded Helena that she had no experience with cooking herself, and saw no harm in allowing the children to eat whatever they wanted. The stresses of her day in charge of four children and Millie, plus visits to the hospital, were relieved as soon as the sun dropped, courtesy of "Mr. Jack." This latter morsel had come from William who was proud to report that he licked the rim of the bottle most nights as a reward for being good. Even Matthew, according to William, would stop crying after a sip. Helena shuddered at the news, well aware that Baden blood coursed through those tiny veins, and who could possibly know what one sip of whiskey could mean for any descendant of John Baden Senior.

Twenty-three

January 1974

SOMEWHERE between Sydney and Maine, in the middle of the night, James Wallin died from a stroke. Helena had woken suddenly on the train, with an uncomfortable sense of her own presence, and stayed awake the rest of the way while others slept around her. She counted the stops as the train slowed into stations aglow with yellow lights before the rhythmic clacking of railway tracks resumed. Later, when she learned the hour of her father's passing, she knew he had woken her to let her know he was gone.

Helena went alone to the morgue that Saturday morning. Formaldehyde permeated the red curtains that fell heavily from the ceiling panels, a cordon to what or whom, she did not want to consider. James lay still and frozen. She tried to believe he was just sleeping, but a trickle of blood had escaped his nostril and turned into red ice. She dabbed at it with a handkerchief, and placed the bloodied treasure safely inside her dress next to her heart.

"Please, Dad, don't leave me," she cried, screamed. She opened his eyelids and held them apart, willing him to see her standing there broken. "Dad, *please*, I *need* you." She wanted to join him, and would have, but for the incompetence of Grace and Millie, and Michael, as carers for her children. She stayed with him until someone ushered her away as his corpse began to thaw.

Helena rehearsed, "I'm fine," to believe in it, and in the process, came to understand the existence Millie had created for herself after Robert disappeared. Millie had James then, and still needed to escape. Helena had no one.

Hundreds came to the funeral, and the side doors of the church left open for a breeze, filled with genuine mourners instead. They came with words for Helena: time was an eraser, it healed all sorrows, there was a reason for everything, a time to die, joy is as great as the sorrow is deep, the mournful are blessed, grief is a medicine, pain passes, and life goes on. So many people wise about death, even though they had no personal experience with it, for if they knew death, as Helena now did, they would also know that a blade wounded, a stab into the heart was fatal, and time had just two hands, and was not a father. James Wallin, her father, the man she loved more than any other, was gone, and no words could explain that.

Michael did not attend the funeral, nor did Millie. She was not present anywhere in a mindful way, and was exhausted during the day from her nights in conversation with nature, trees mostly.

The 'm' word had never entered Helena's mind until she heard it whispered at the funeral—Michael Baden had murdered James Wallin. The offence was unpardonable, and Sergeant Mackelroth was similarly contemptible for letting the culprit go free, they said.

James was dressed as he had lived, in a short-sleeved, cream, collared shirt—his mill shirt—and trousers. Yes, he seemed peaceful, restful, evident the wise ones said, that someone cherished had met him in the white tunnel, and that he was enjoying his afterlife. Helena wanted to scream. Her father would not be at peace at all knowing that life had unraveled in his short absence.

Grace handled everything for the family, consummate as always when a setting was even remotely social. She circulated, thanked everyone at the church, did so again at the cemetery, and single-handedly represented the family at the wake organized by the Ladies Auxiliary.

Helena went home after the coffin lowered into the ground, needing to be alone, and someone had to relieve Adeline Mackelroth of child minding.

She established a daily ritual for falling apart at 8PM until midnight, devoting the hours in between to keeping busier than ever: washing, tidying, ironing, cooking, cleaning, and taking care of children. Her existence was manageable in this way.

Living arrangements at Waterloo Street were tight with one less bedroom: Millie having locked the door to the master bedroom forced Helena to share her bed with her mother. Helena found the key without looking for it, at the bottom of the laundry basket, and had toyed with it for some time before placing it in the lock. As she glanced down, willing herself to turn it, daylight came through the narrow gap that separated the bottom of the bedroom door and the floor, and with it, a familiar scent. She imagined her father inside, napping under a fan with the newspaper spread across his chest, and his glasses askew across his nose. She staggered away from the door, fell to the floor, and cried. Matthew curled into her lap, sucking his thumb while tears fell into his hair. Helena ran her fingers through the dampened strands to comb it dry then stood gingerly with her little boy in her arms. "Let's have cookies," she whispered.

Twenty-four

May 1974

ACUTE bronchitis saw Millie hospitalized, the winter, having snapped early, caught her wandering the garden in a cotton nightgown and no shoes. The hospital stay offered some respite for Helena, and an opportunity to tackle the mail that had accumulated since February. Armed with a mug of coffee and a tin of still warm Ginger Nuts, she sat down in her father's chair, and held back tears as her body filled the indentations he had made in the leather.

She sorted the mail into three piles: cards, plain envelopes, and window envelopes with logos. The pile of bills was first on the agenda since she could immediately reduce it by a quarter based on the postmark alone. The two piles of cards and plain envelopes were pushed aside for Grace since she was best with protocol for handling sympathies, good wishes, and other platitudes.

Helena stared at her pile of envelopes then shuffled them like cards before opening the one that rose to the top. She used her father's gold letter opener to expose the contents of each, and was shocked to note that despite months of arrears, each page was absent a red sticker, warning, urgent stamp or any other form of demand for immediate payment. She flicked through the pile again and saw her father at the mill the day it had burned to the ground. "People will pay when they can," he had said of those who owed them money. "I don't want you calling people begging for money." Now she understood clemency, karma, sowing and reaping, and unscheduled tears stung her face for even in death, her father had lessons for her.

She wrote checks for each payee then added up the damage. After deducting the total from the balance shown on the latest bank statement, a meager eighty dollars remained, and that was all there was.

Life insurance would have been their savior, except James had cancelled it in retaliation for the debacle over the insurance renewal for the mill, along with the house insurance, car, and health insurances.

James had invested his proceeds from the mill fire sale in the share market in 1967. It was a bullish market at the time due the discovery of oil in Bass Strait, and James had bought his shares at a premium then watched the price zigzag downward to almost worthless. The shares had not improved much over time, but Helena would have to sell them at current values, and that was only a temporary solution. Waterloo Street, family home of the Wallin family and source of much happiness, and sorrow, had to be sacrificed for survival. When the tenants vacated Orchard Road, Helena and her children would return with Millie in tow.

The rest of the solution required a job, preferably full-time. Millie, Helena hoped, would be up to the task of caring for Matthew all day, Carla half the day, and William and Brian after school. Helena shuddered. She sculled the dregs of cold coffee, and wondered if the financial settlement she had reached with Michael had been a mistake. Child support meant food, and perhaps then, she could have saved her childhood home with its memories of her father she did not want to leave behind.

Grace returned to Maine for a long weekend, not because she wanted to, but because Helena had called daily following Millie's discharge from hospital, pleading for help. Millie was a handful, as was William. He had become even more willful, and angry. Brian was clingy, Matthew introverted, and Carla unnervingly calm amidst the chaos.

Other than to say James had gone to heaven, no one talked of him, or explained his ongoing absence in a meaningful way. They were too young to know more, Helena believed, and it was difficult enough explaining why Grandma wore a bathrobe all day long. She could not explain Thorazine, the psychosis it suppressed, nor the sedation it caused, and why the blitz that used to be the kitchen at Waterloo Street was now a retreat most of the time.

Millie prepared French toast for Grace then sat down to watch her eat. Smoke rose from a third Peter Stuyvesant filling the air above their heads.

"Grace!" Helena yelled, as she entered the kitchen.

"What?" Grace yelled back.

"The smoke from your cigarette; mum's had pneumonia you know!"

"Oh," said Grace. "That's all. Sorry, Mum."

"It's OK, dear," said Millie with a cough.

Helena shook her head, and tidied the kitchen.

"When you're done there, we should move into the living room to relax a while," said Grace.

"Relax? You just got out of bed."

Grace pushed her plate toward Helena. "Come on, Mum, to the living room." She guided Millie to the front of the house, stopping at the fridge on the way for a bottle of wine.

"What are you doing?" Helena asked.

"If you expect me to wade through that pile of cards and letters, I'm going to need a little help."

"It's a bit early, don't you think?"

"It's eleven o'clock, Lena, an hour past opening."

Helena shook her head, and followed the procession of

pastel bathrobes.

Grace removed a crystal glass from the display cabinet, and filled it with Chardonnay. "Helena?"

"No thanks," she replied.

"Don't you have something to say?" Grace nodded at Millie coiled into the jacquard armchair.

"Now?"

"I thought you said it was urgent."

"It is," said Helena.

"Well?"

Helena took a deep breath. "Mum, you need to sell the house."

"What happened to gentle and subtle?" Grace asked lighting another cigarette.

"OK," said Millie.

"It's a difficult decision, I know," Helena continued, "but—"

"Helena, she said 'OK'"

"I don't want to live here anymore," said Millie.

"OK," said Helena. "We'll move into Orchard Road in August when the tenant moves out. This place should sell by then, and I'll invest the proceeds in a term deposit. The interest should be enough for you to live on."

"OK," said Millie.

"Wouldn't it be better to invest it in shares?" Grace asked.

"Too risky," said Helena.

"OK, your call," said Grace. She filled her glass and lit another cigarette. "Sure you wouldn't like some?"

"All right," said Helena, "just one glass. It is almost lunchtime."

"So how are the kids coping?" Grace asked.

"In different ways. William is angry with me. I think he blames me that dad's not here."

"He was dad's favorite, and dad did spoil him, so it's not surprising that he's feeling the loss more than the others. Maybe you just need to give him more attention."

"That didn't go so well. When the boys were playing

football in the backyard I tried to join in, but William kept kicking it back and forth to Brian, and he let me know it was intentional. He gets that glint in his eyes."

"What about the others?" Grace asked. "Top up?"

"Maybe one more then lunch," she said passing her glass to Grace. "Matthew plays by himself most of the time, or with Carla. Brian is the clingy one, and he cries a lot. I don't quite understand why he's so sad all the time."

"How are you going to handle a job with all of this going on around you?"

"I don't know, but I'll have to. Michael is taking them for the school holidays, so hopefully I can get on top of things then."

"Oh really? Michael's coming here?"

"He's picking them up and taking them back to the base on the plane, so they'll love that."

"Are you asleep, Mum?" Grace asked.

"Grace, don't, you'll wake her up."

"She seems OK at the moment," said Grace. "A bit slow perhaps, but otherwise fine."

"While she's on the pills, she's OK. She thinks they're for the pneumonia, so I don't know if she'll keep taking them once her chest clears."

"Hide them in her food. More wine?"

"That's helpful," said Helena offering her glass. "Anyway, how did you manage to get away from the salon?"

"I have a prospective buyer who's been working with me for a few weeks. If everything goes smoothly this weekend, I think he'll buy."

"You're selling the salon? What will you do?"

"After eight years, I'm a little weary. I'm thirty in September, and I'd like to enjoy my life again while I still can." She paused, lit another cigarette, and swigged. "I'll stay on as a stylist and employee, and I'm really looking forward to that."

"I'm feeling a little giddy," said Helena.

"After three glasses?"

"They're big glasses, and you're over-filling them. It's a nice feeling though, being numb like this. I haven't slept in so long."

"At last you've discovered the medicinal value of alcohol. It's been working wonders for me for decades." Grace paused to sip. "Helena? Helena?" She reached over to remove the wine glass from a tilting hand. "Good Lord," she said. "Lucky I'm used to drinking on my own."

Twenty-five

May 1974

HELENA rested her forehead on her folded arms, lifting it occasionally to sip a black, sugar-rich brew. "There's a lot to be said for being a non-drinker," she said.

"You should know by now, dear, that you can't drink," said Millie.

"I can *drink*—just not alcohol. I did sleep well though when the bed stopped spinning." Helena shuddered recalling the nausea, which had not dissipated entirely.

"Have something to eat, dear, before the children get up. You'll feel much better."

"Isn't Brian up already?" Helena asked. "He wasn't in his bed when I came down."

"No...I haven't seen him."

Helena sat up, stared at Millie then raced into the backyard. Her head throbbed louder. "Brian!" she called out as she searched every known cubbyhole. She ran back inside. "Call the police!" she yelled at Millie. "Brian!" she screamed. Before tearing up the stairs, she pulled every curtain from its hook and searched the billowing fabric. The fracas woke the children and Grace.

"What's going on?" Grace asked.

"I can't find Brian!"

Sergeant Mackelroth had questions that Helena could not answer: who saw Brian last, where, when, and what was he wearing at the time. That she knew so little of her missing son only served to intensify her suffering, as did the fact that officially, twenty-four hours had to pass before Sergeant Mackelroth could launch a police search.

Sergeant Mackelroth glanced sideways at his new deputy then documented that Brian Baden had been missing twenty-five hours. He left to galvanize troops, and left his deputy to console Helena with statistics: 90 percent of children reported missing return home within forty-eight hours. This had the reverse effect on Helena and Millie, and Grace pointed out that Robert was still missing after twenty-one years.

By mid-morning, most of Maine united in the search, while Helena waited and cried into Brian's favorite t-shirt with the Fern and Wilbur transfer she had ironed on to the front. William, Carla, and Matthew joined Helena in the living room, in her direct line of sight, and for the first time, they ate lunch on the carpet where they sat. William complained that the carpet prickled his legs, and moved on to the clear vinyl runner that flowed from the front door to the kitchen. Once away from the pack and closer to freedom, he moved one butt cheek at a time toward the yellow and brown Marley tile floors at the back of the house. Each time he came close to freedom, Helena returned him to the plastic runner at the halfway point. He retaliated by extracting the plastic teeth from the underside of the vinyl, leaving a trail of destruction in his wake.

Helena did not speak to, or look at, Grace or Millie. She rocked back and forth, and screeched at any precipitous motion or sound, like the oven timer. Grace smoked, drank coffee, made calls, and answered the phone whenever it rang. Millie baked the entire day, not bothered by the remnants of jam drops and chocolate crackles on the white pile. Each hour that closed in on five o'clock and sunset was more volatile than the previous, until a car pulled into the curb and they raced to the front porch.

Sergeant Mackelroth's deputy approached, rotating his navy blue cap with his fingers. "I know this has been a difficult day for you," he said, "but I have some news that has just come to us, and I think you need to hear it." He paused. "I'm sorry to tell you, but weekend hikers have discovered a child's body."

Helena fell to the tiled floor, smacking the side of her face on the edge of an ochre ceramic pot. A torrent of blood flowed, and pooled in her ear and in the ditches around her eyes. Grace pushed Carla and Matthew back inside, crying, while Millie twisted on the spot not knowing who to attend or how to respond. William leaned against the house with his arms folded, and occasionally looked down at his mother with no visible emotion. The deputy called for an ambulance on his two-way radio.

"It's Brian then?" asked Grace.

"Brian? No, I don't think so," said the deputy. "They found a satchel in a shallow grave with the remnants of what looks like sheet music. The initials engraved into the leather leaves us to believe," he paused, "it's your brother."

Millie collapsed on top of Helena, and Grace realized, only then that she missed her father. This moment, always had him at the helm, and no one was less equipped than she was to stand in his shoes. She looked to the skies for his guidance then prayed to the other father who art in Heaven, hallowed in name.

Twenty-six

December 1974

THERE was an eeriness to the night's middle: the blackness, stillness, silence, and knowing you were alone in the dark while the world slept. Helena calmed its disconcerting with sponge cake—orange and poppy seeds or chocolate.

Almost a year had passed since she had lost her father, and the memories had no mercy, wielding a blade that threatened to shred her into pieces that could never reform into a united whole. Another calendar year in any life could not be so devastating, and it proved to Helena that she no longer possessed the mental, emotional or spiritual capacity for forgiveness.

She had not spoken to Grace since May when Brian went missing. If it were not for her sister's influence, Helena would not have passed out on the sofa, and slept until mid-evening when Millie and Grace claimed the children were in bed. She should have checked, but didn't for once, and joined Grace instead for a nightcap to further the release that sleep had brought. If Brian had not come back, reprisal would have been much worse than mere disregard.

Helena loved Brian the most, and only she knew the truth of it because parents did not make such confessions publicly. Brian had the softest heart, was most loving, and showed compassion for all of life: a caterpillar, dog, beetle or a fly. He had once pleaded with her to revive a pigeon, but Helena had said the bird was old and tired of flying. William had scoffed, demanding a fuller explanation as to how she could know, and Helena had pointed at the gray feathers as evidence. Brian named it Snoopy for a formal burial, and Helena provided the requested birdseed for the long journey to bird Heaven.

"That's not birdseed," William had said, staring into the grainy mix then it was Helena's turn to ask how he could know so much. "I know what rice looks like," he responded, forcing Helena back to the kitchen to prepare a concoction more likely to pass William's scrutiny. The new blend of sesame seeds, peppercorns, dried herbs, and pumpkin seeds, received William's tentative approval, and the ceremony proceeded with a few teary words from Brian.

Helena was in hospital recovering from concussion when they found him, and brought him to her. She had curled him into her side as if he were back in her womb, and would not allow anyone to take him away, not even for a much-needed bath.

He was tired from his ordeal, but not hungry having spent the absent twenty-nine hours in the Girl Guides' hut eating his way through their biscuit supplies. A passer-by had noticed a light bulb still aglow through the tiny timber window, and discovered the small mass asleep in a corner with an embroidered pillow clenched to his chest.

When school holidays arrived with Michael, Helena could not part with Brian, or any of her children, and though it made life more difficult, she sent Michael home empty-handed, and he did not seem disappointed. William was angry once more, still, and let her know that he held her responsible for the demise of his holiday that then included the internment of his lost uncle's remains.

Helena bought Basil primarily for William as a peace

offering, but the very nature of Basil meant that he responded to any attention, and Brian, Carla, and Matthew gave him plenty. William watched on from the sidelines, and Helena's heart bled at the sight. He wanted to play, that was obvious, and showed his frustration by yelling repeatedly at Matthew for calling Basil 'toilet brush' instead of Basil Brush, his namesake.

The decision to add another stomach to the household budget had taken months of self-convincing given the immovability of all lines of income, and the ongoing agility of items of expenditure. In the end, Helena was glad she made the decision irrespective of financial imperatives, as Basil was manna: an antidote for sadness, a confidant, entertainer, and companion. During the day, he was the center of the children's world, but at night, late, he sat loyally beside Helena for his share of whatever she baked. He loved cake as much as she did, and his impatience for the oven bell would have his cold, damp, brown nose nudging constantly at her calf.

The photos of Robert conjured up images of their childhood, making it easy to remember a time she did not want to slip away. They reminded her of how he walked, dressed, the things he would say, and how he would say them, and who he was to be as a man and head of their family. He would have been a huge help with Millie, but then, Millie would be the old Millie again if he were alive. Twenty-two years had passed since he stood waiting in the cold, dark dusk for a bus that never came, and now the waiting was over.

A child's hand had broken free from its bushy entombment after decades of reaching for the surface, clipping a hiker's toe as she passed. Sergeant Mackelroth confirmed that Robert had suffered a blow to the back of his head, and his neck was broken in three places. Forensics would one day determine the issue of molestation, but no one ever mentioned it. Other questions went unanswered: did he suffer, was he alive when buried, did he die the day of abduction instantly with a blow or some time later after captivity and torture. Helena wondered why God would take the good son, and leave the errant daughter, and how ironic it was that Grace wanted to live in

Sydney while Robert wanted to stay in Maine.

She pushed the photos aside to finish the Christmas cards to William, Brian, Carla, and Matthew from their father, writing with a backward hand, mainly for William's benefit. She did likewise for birthdays and Easter, placing five dollars in every card, since Michael was consistent in his neglect.

The oven tolled and Basil followed Helena into the kitchen. He pawed at her leg while the cake cooled to remind her he waited, until finally he received his share. Helena placed her slice in a Tupperware container for her break at the supermarket where she would stack shelves until 2AM. She would sleep then until six in the room she shared with her mother before starting work at nine at a local accountant's office. The clock was her life, lived by hours, not months or years, as it would be if there were a future.

PART II

October 1981 – May 1985

Twenty-seven

October 1981

HER father had always said there were doors everywhere opening and closing—a spiritual guiding onto the path that was hers to take. He had not told her what to do if she could not find an open door or if she did not realize that one had already creaked to a close. When it came to William, there were no doors telling her what to do.

The pilfering began when he was eleven, a somewhat courageous enterprise since Helena knew every cent personally and, as Murphy would have it, Campbell Meats was shoulder-to-shoulder with shoppers that Saturday morning when a gray vinyl purse revealed the first discrepancy. A new rich shade of crimson engulfed her face as she instructed the butcher to de-bag the sausages. He did so in a dramatic way, and Helena thought about spontaneous human combustion. She stared straight ahead during the final exchange of notes and coins, avoiding eye contact, and the sign on the wall behind the counter that ordered 'no expectorating', identified the culprit. William had asked her once to explain 'expectorate,' and

127

subsequently spat on the butcher's red concrete floor. "Like this?" he had asked then smiled that smile.

Back at Orchard Road, and still in one piece, Helena made plans to bring Pooh to the honey pot. With her purse in position on the kitchen bench, and the zipper on the coin pouch open so its contents would scatter when moved, she turned away to wash dishes. The ruse almost came unstuck: by the time she responded to the sound of silver on laminate, William was almost out of sight.

She called Michael to discuss the problem, hoping for a solution and moral support, and disconnected with neither. It was a trifling matter, he said, and blamed her for being too austere. Accepting some truth in his words, Helena arranged a spending spree, in Baden-relative terms, taking all four children to the shopping fair for treats of their choosing. She shuddered with each purchase, and made repeated mention of school uniforms and field trips, her words falling into tiny ears that did not care at all for either.

William's earlier capture did not curb his enterprising ways, and Helena learned more of this from Principal Mulder. Visits to his office were so frequent that Helena had good reason to consider him a friend, but for the disdain he did not attempt to hide. Some minor troubles had shadowed William through grades six and seven, growing exponentially to recalcitrant level by the time he arrived at Maine Public High School and the care of Principal Mulder who stated openly that days marked 'absent' against his name were best for everyone— teachers and students alike. It was a quandary, he said, as it would be for any educator, to value truancy in this way.

Principal Mulder had one solution for Helena: boarding school in the city, and one in particular where catholic discipline lobotomized teenage heretics like William Baden. Helena was aware of the school, its reputation, successes, and fees, and raised the matter with Michael hoping for agreement and funding. His response though was predictable: boys will be boys, and she was over-reacting, as mothers tend to do.

Everything would be all right if she did not make mountains from molehills.

But it was Brian who panged her heart the most, under the influence of William now and in as much trouble, although not the ringleader, according to Principal Mulder. Helena had no inkling that such a transformation was in progress—an innocent, doting child of hers one minute then Williams's accomplice and best friend in the next tick.

Matthew's teacher, Miss Orlando, had also called Helena to school for a lunchtime "chat," but unlike Principal Mulder, she began the meeting on a positive, sunshiny note. Matthew was a prolific reader, gifted writer, and talented artist, and all beyond the expected capabilities of a ten year old, she said. Then came the monsoonal rains—he read in isolation never interacting with his classmates, his writing was as dark as Poe, and his art was two-toned, colorless and hollow. Miss Orlando claimed this amounted to an unhealthy predilection for death and suffering. She closed the meeting with evidence, filling Helena's cupped hands with a siege of origami cranes. "They're not black," said Helena, gazing into her palms.

"No, Mrs. Baden. They're not black," she conceded.

Helena left believing the time with Miss Orlando had been a waste of a lunch hour and, relative to meetings with Principal Mulder, unnecessary since Matthew's creativity was at least legal. As she strode from Matthew's classroom to her car, she reeled in the smiles contemplating the progenitor of his artistic talents. She could not identify anyone from recent generations, but perhaps there was a Toulouse-Lautrec somewhere in Wallin ancestry. Her pride did not hold sway all the way to the car as she encountered a scattering of giggling teasers. A "big fat blowfish" she heard them say.

Helena declined Millie's banana mocha tart that night, haunted as she was by images of the toxic fish, and apparent similarity to her own form. She could not deny it, and had to accept that manner-less children were at least accurate with their depictions. Her abstinence though, lived only a short while as new stressors forced her to seek relief in its crusty comforts.

She followed the cussing to the bathroom where Carla and Matthew kneeled against the bathtub. "Basket, basket, basket," Carla repeated, reminding Helena to cease references to Michael's legitimacy in the presence of sponge-like minds. Tiny hands scooped limp birds from their watery grave to place them with care on the now colorful mat to dry. Helena yelled for William who appeared hauntingly within a microsecond.

"Why, William?" she asked. "Why did you do this?"

"They're swans. They should be able to swim," he replied.

"They're *paper cranes*," said Helena glaring. "Get your marbles. Let's see if they can swim."

William stared back, curious, shrugged his shoulders then returned with his treasured glass balls.

"Thank you," she said. "You won't be seeing these again until you've learned to respect other people's property."

The matter did not end at that point as Helena might have hoped.

It was usual for Carla to yell at William to no avail and with foolish regard for the sanctity of her own life. It was usual for Matthew to be involved, though silent, and usual for a rescue to be necessitated.

Helena found Matthew swinging from the clothesline like a carnival paratrooper, painted blue. William did not run, as self-preservation dictated, but stood to account, blue-handed. Helena rushed to unhinge the contraption that held Matthew aloft, her anxiousness elevated by his faint whimpering. Despite her care though, Matthew fell some way to the ground then scampered away to a demilitarized zone under the Rosella bushes.

The spray can, marked 'water-based', brought some relief, eliminating the need for an entirely humorless encounter with turpentine. Helena filled a bucket with warm, soapy water, and headed for the bushes that sheltered Matthew. Carla reached out from the shrubs to take the cloth and pail to re-beige the blue boy. Helena turned her attention to William, meeting his smile and challenging eyes. She wished she could praise the ingenuity of his device, and admire his stoic acceptance of what was to come. She wished she had the power to frighten him into obedience instead of inspiring him to do more, better. If he felt any anger, he did not show it, but his grin was a contradiction: love, rejection, perhaps hatred, game and competition. It was unnerving.

Helena called Michael again, certain of a better reception given William's most recent exploits. He did not agree to her suggestion that they engage a child psychologist: William did not need a "psychobabbler meddling in his head" since he would grow out of his menacing ways if only his mother desisted with whatever she was doing to cause it, he said. Recollections of a three-year-old came to Helena's mind, of William kneeling at his father's drunken carcass rotting in the morning sun. Helena said nothing: confrontation curdled her stomach, and even though she never fired a shot, she was bullet-ridden. On this issue, she also needed Michael's buy-in, whichever solution, as Michael would have to pay: the agreement forged January of 1974 that relinquished his child support responsibilities was now invalid, a *force majeure* was in effect. For the moment, she would do nothing, but allow time for the boys to "grow out of it" as Michael suggested, and to secure that one last chance for redemption.

Twenty-eight

August 1984

HELENA sat behind her two eldest sons and imagined herself reaching forward to stroke long, unkempt locks without repudiation. She contemplated the future for her sons, dire at best, and thought back to when her babies had first cried, coated in blood and vernix. She had not considered the consequences should she fail at the task ahead, but there she was, effectively on trial with her boys.

Michael deserved to be, but she had worked two jobs and fourteen hours out of every twenty-four just to meet the basic needs of her children. In hindsight, she had quit her second job at the supermarket a little too late in the day to guide her wayward sons onto a better path. Millie had wanted to help a long time ago, offering up her savings for any purpose bar boarding school in Sydney. Helena had declined, and she still did not understand why except perhaps that pride had got in the way. It was a fool's lesson: that pride should taint charity in such a way when the consequences were so frightful. Helena would have accepted in a flash if Michael had offered a portion of his burgeoning finances, but he had not made even the slightest overture.

The rapidity of the boys' descent from that last chance to being on trial was shocking, but then there was a catalyst: a soft euphoriant weed they first encountered at school while under the supervision of Principal Mulder who did not accept or acknowledge the dealing that went on behind the sports shed.

Helena had unwittingly supported their illegal horticultural project as an unknowing and gullible baron. She thought their sudden interest in naturalist pursuits was a positive sign, and so she had cared for the 'tomato' plants checking them regularly for insects and red fruit, and had even expanded the boys' enterprise by planting pumpkins and watermelon. Their lack of enthusiasm for her efforts was upsetting at the time, in particular because her plants did not receive the same level of attention as the 'tomatoes' because there was nothing intoxicating about smoking a pumpkin or a watermelon. It was not the new direction for her sons she had thought, but a bogging down on the path already taken.

Helena met Edward Hyde and his less misanthropic counterpart the night of her last shift at Woolworths. She finished early, stacking the final can of baked beans with commensurate pomp, and the hour had gone past two when her old Datsun exhausted its way down Orchard Road. Up ahead in the distance, caught by dim lights on high beam, she saw the silhouettes, and there was no mistaking the tallest gait. She never expected to encounter her two teenage sons in this way, returning home in the early hours from where or what, she could not imagine. Her heart pounded, and conflict-anticipated nausea rose to greet it. She slowed her car to idle, hoping also, to slow the palpitations in her chest, and observed as the two shadows turned into their driveway, as she would a careful time later.

She parked between the rows of carved, graffitied, unsymmetrical posts at Orchard Road, switched the engine to off, and listened to the footsteps above that paced down the hallway to the back bedroom. She closed the car door by leaning against it gently. Her mouth was dry as she crossed the concrete floor to reach the back stairs where she rested against the side of the house for composure before advancing. In her head, a requiem played as she made her way up the paint-flaked rungs, and a dark opera accompanied the opening of the back door. She wished she could go directly to bed, and leave the face-off to someone more skilled, but courage from an unknown source helped her down the hallway to the door to the boy's bedroom. The hallway light broke through to illuminate the masqueraders.

"Where have you been?" she asked, shaking.

William sat up, portraying someone rudely awoken, which would have convinced anyone not apprised of the truth. She repeated the question.

"Nowhere," he replied as if addressing the insane or stupid.

"I saw you. *Both* of you," she said as Brian 'slept' on.

"*Nowhere*," William repeated.

"You must have been sleepwalking then."

"None of your business."

"It *is* my business while you're under my roof!"

William was up, out of his bed and in her face. Despite the gentle lighting, she could see his dilated, red pupils, and a fist poised just seconds from release. Brian yelled, "No! Don't, William!" as Helena's head pierced the hallway wall. William slammed the bedroom door, which woke Millie and Basil. With the discussion terminated, and the showdown won and lost, the victor rested in bed while Helena wiped her blood from the fractured wall. She had to speak to Michael first thing the next morning.

Helena did not sleep as her body refused to still its quivering fibers, and as soon as six o'clock came around, she called Michael to tell him about the hole in the wall, and that there were no tomatoes, and how she, a law-abiding citizen, had played an unwitting part in a criminal enterprise. She was confident of his support under the weight of information that proved there was a calamitous situation at hand.

Michael argued that an occasional late night for teenagers

was surely normal, and William's red eyes was most likely caused by tiredness, and nothing at all sinister was at play just because there were no tomatoes. She reminded him that they were too young to be out until all hours, especially on a school night, and suspected there was nothing 'occasional' about it. He suggested she was the stupid one for watering the plants, and encouraging the venture if in fact, they were marijuana plants, and he remained unconvinced of that much. She disconnected the line in response.

Spiraling seemed to begin at that point, or perhaps it was merely that her awareness had been piqued. According to Principal Mulder, the boys were stealing from the pockets of little children, and their hours of truancy had been devoted to burglary, battery, and possession, according to the charges they faced. They were not alone with two like-minded teens beside them on the defendant's table. It appeared to be a matter of some mirth, and all four pled not guilty in spite of legal advice to the contrary.

Helena was heartened by the day in a strange way: the judge was certain to throw the book on criminal law at them with full force, and a stint in juvenile detention seemed to be the only answer.

Michael had returned to Maine for the trial, said little, but his Old Spice spoke loudly on its failure to disguise the morning consumption of ale.

"All rise. This court is now in session. His Honor, Judge Blackwell presiding."

The prosecution called its first witness, Paul Thorpe, the victim, who swore to tell the truth.

"I had taken the day off work with the flu, otherwise I would have been at work, and they probably knew that."

"Objection, Your Honor, the witness cannot say what the defendants may or may not have known."

"Sustained."

"What happened while you were at home with the flu, Mr. Thorpe?" the prosecutor asked.

"My wife had gone to our store by herself so the car was

not in the driveway as it usually is when someone's home. I heard a noise. I got up to investigate, and I saw one of them coming through the bedroom window."

"Mr. Thorpe, can you please identify who you saw coming through the window."

"That one," he answered, with a stiff finger aimed at Brian.

"Let the record show the witness identified the defendant, Brian Baden. What happened next?"

"I thought he must have been on his own, then, when I turned around to go to the phone, that other one hit me."

"Who hit you, Mr. Thorpe?"

He pointed at William. "That one in the blue shirt."

"Let the record show the witness identified the defendant, William Baden. What happened next, Mr. Thorpe?"

"The other two came out from another room, and the three of them started kicking me while I was on the floor."

"Please identify who was kicking you, Mr. Thorpe."

He pointed at William, the tattooed boy with an inked fly on his cheek, and the formerly sweet, blond boy with ringlets from William's third grade. His parents hung their heads lower as if the finger had pointed at them. Their presence reflected well for Helena, she thought, or better at least since it proved that criminals are borne also of respectability, of a good home, and of good people.

Helena tuned out during the inventory of stolen items, injuries inflicted on the victim, and the police officer's report on the capture. However, she did hear the defense counsel's response that asserted a case of mistaken identity since the victim was too ill, and influenced by medication to know for sure who he had seen that day. And although the defendants were caught with the misbegotten goods, they had merely come across them in the street after the real culprits had abandoned them. The marijuana the four smoked when captured was from the stolen jewelry box, and was thought to be just cigarettes.

It was an unbelievable tale that would not convince the most gullible, Helena thought, since she was the measure of naivety. Detention was imminent, and the system would rehabilitate William and Brian. Michael said nothing, until the outcome.

Twenty-nine

August 1984

GUILTY, with four convictions for three of them: break and enter, theft, battery and possession, and three convictions for Brian since he had not injured anyone. There was no detention for any of them, released instead with good behavior bonds. The punishment was inexplicable, and Helena could only conclude that the justice the judge served had blinded him. It seemed obvious and inevitable to the parents in attendance that the warnings and threats meant to frighten the four into fulfilling the obligations of their bond were futile.

Michael stepped up for the first time in parenting history, claiming that since he had successfully redirected his own troubled life, he would do likewise for his favored sons. He knew how to straighten them out: by treating them as young men, not children, no molly coddling, and he would grant craved teenage freedoms to a reasonable extent. Helena would see from his example, how best to parent sons, and after a short stay with him at the base, the results would speak volumes.

Michael took the boys to the lake to fish and unwind after

the trial. It would be like old times when they were young, albeit, it was just the once.

They settled on the lush banks with rods, and an excess of revelry having beaten the system. A criminal record was of no concern or consequence, but having narrowly escaped prosecution himself on three occasions, Michael sought to explain the ramifications of their convictions on future employment. He told them a little of his own personal pilgrimage, and they laughed. Michael fumed quietly, but accepted that they were too young to understand his lesson. One day, they would remember his words, absorb them, and appreciate his authority to speak on personal reformation.

William removed a bottle of vodka from his jacket, and passed it to Brian who winced with the first scull. Michael warned them about drinking spirits, that it was a serious drink for the seriously afflicted, and urged them to drink his beer instead. They declined, but accepted his cigarettes.

Michael waited a while before mentioning the proposed relocation to the RAAF base, and they wasted no time saying no. They did not want to move to Laverton, or to live at the base, or return to school. They wanted to be free, to drink, to have fun, and to live in another realm away from ordinary consciousness induced by whatever means affordable. They would not live to regret their decision, and William challenged Michael's right to suggest otherwise given the examples he had set, which William claimed to remember.

Helena arrived at the hospital in time to hear Michael relay the circumstances that gave rise to his injury. No, he did not see his attacker who had come at him from behind with his own fishing knife.

"Curious," said Sergeant Mackelroth. "How come the stab wounds are to your stomach, not your back?"

"I might have turned around just as he struck," Michael suggested. "But I didn't see him."

"Hmm," said Sergeant Mackelroth. He flicked his notepad shut, and stared at Michael. "So be it, Michael. So be it," he said then left.

"What happened?" Helena asked. "Who did this?"

"No one," Michael replied.

"Where are the boys?"

"I don't know."

"What happened?" she repeated.

"I don't know. One minute we were fishing, enjoying a few beers, then—"

"You were drinking beer? Have you forgotten so many birthdays that you don't even remember they're under age?"

"They're not children anymore, Helena."

"They are."

Michael winced as he tried to shift his bandaged torso.

"How bad is it?"

"No organ damage, so he didn't mean to hurt me."

"Who?"

"William," he replied after a long pause.

Helena rested her head on the bed's edge to cry. "When did all of this go so horribly wrong?"

"They'll be OK, Helena, don't worry." He reached across to pat her shoulder, but the pain pulled his arm back into his side. He closed his eyes, and fell into a medicated sleep.

Michael woke under the hospital night light. Helena was gone, but Brian sat beside him on the bed. "I'm sorry, Dad," he whispered.

"It's OK, son. It's no one's fault." Michael glanced around the room. "Where's William?"

"He's outside. He didn't think he should come in."

Michael nodded, understanding the Baden way.

"We're going to Sydney."

"What will you do?"

"Just hang out. It's what we want."

"There's two hundred dollars in my wallet. Take it."

Brian removed the notes. "Thanks, Dad," he said then paused. "Where's Mum? I thought she might be here."

"She must have gone home when I fell asleep."

"Oh," he whispered. "Will you tell her I said goodbye?"

"I will. Call her when you get to Sydney to let her know you're OK, and call her every week."

"I will, Dad. Bye."

"Goodbye, Son."

Brian bowed out of the room, and Michael wept.

The day that began in a courtroom seemed endless. Helena drove home from the hospital on automatic pilot, the winter rain reflecting in black pools on the bitumen as she stared at the road ahead. She had stopped at the hospital canteen for a supply of chocolate bars, but only wrappings filled the seat beside her. They did nothing to overcome the exhaustion and complete despair as she pulled into Orchard Road.

Half way up the back stairs, her foot failed to rise high enough to meet the next step, bringing her whole body down on to the damp timber. She cried and cried, and dabbed at the blood on her shins. Light from the kitchen suddenly spilled onto the landing above.

"Come inside, Lena. Dinner's ready, and I've cooked a rhubarb crumble with hot custard."

Only after seconds did Millie tell Helena that the boys were gone, for good. Helena went to see for herself. Their bedroom door was open, and in their wardrobe, tattered uniforms hung freely, no longer pushed to one end by ragged jeans and black t-shirts.

Tears came in earnest when Helena retired to her bedroom. A tiny bird carved from wood rested on her pillow with a note from Brian that read, 'We'll be OK. I love you, Mum.'

"My beautiful boy," she whispered.

Thirty

August 1984

CARLA stretched out on her bed with arms folded above her head. She stared at the poster on the wall, and read it for the umpteenth time: 'I asked of life, what have you to offer me? And the answer came, what have you to give?' It explained everything. At fourteen, between her and life, there was nothing going on either way, although there were two spots of sunshine amidst the bleakness of her existence: William and Brian were gone and at last, she had a room to herself. There would be problems if they returned since Matthew now occupied their bedroom, and had defaced the walls with his charcoal morbidity. That was all there was to Matthew: his art and his writing, which was considerably more than Carla had.

Matthew was a journalist by default arising from a series of detentions that forced him to spend afternoons writing something more palatable about Maine Public High School for the school newspaper, his writings usually shredded by Principal Mulder.

He had made one attempt to fit in by signing up for the school football team with Jeffrey, a fellow outcast, but Carla had defeated that plan because it would cost money for boots, socks and shorts, and there was none. Carla knew this because she stayed up late at night and watched their mother sitting alone at the dining room table with Basil at her feet. On the table in front of her would be the notebook, pencil, eraser, cash, and envelopes. The pencil and eraser worked tirelessly to make the numbers add up. Her mother would insert cash into the envelopes, make adjustments in the notebook, then remove a note from one envelope to insert it in another. It was an endless process as no matter what she tried, she could not make the notes multiply.

Jeffrey was Matthew's only friend. Carla had two: Olivia and Tulip, a perfect combination that made Carla feel average, not inferior, or superior, which was more than a Baden could expect.

Tulip loved her name and its story, which she repeated often because everyone liked to hear it. Her name had nothing at all to do with Holland, but Iran where the flower originates, and where her life as an embryo began. Her parents were travelers, curtailed now to a degree by Tulip's schooling, which brought them to Maine to settle in a rented house with rented furniture. Their house and possessions almost made Orchard Road appear middle class however in contrast, Tulip's house was alive inside with happy pictures and objects from foreign places, and something else unrecognizable. Carla thought it might be happiness if you knew what it looked like, but whatever it was, Carla needed to absorb as much of it as possible before Tulip and her family moved on to somewhere else at the end of the school year.

Olivia Rey did not go to their high school with its green skirt, white blouse, and fake green and red tartan tie. Her school was private, and she had to travel a distance each day by shuttle bus. She could not ride her Malvern Star to school even if she wanted to, for there were onerous rules that dictated how a student should ride a bike, and since her beret could never leave her head, the task was almost impossible. Olivia had two uniforms at her school, one for winter and one for summer. Her classes started earlier and finished later, and they studied Shakespeare.

Olivia had an interesting autonym as well, named after a great beauty and countess of high social standing. Not surprisingly, she portrayed Lady Olivia in a school production of the Twelfth Night, and was perfect for the role. Everyone who saw it said so. Carla's name was not auspicious, not named after anyone of note or for any particular reason.

Olivia's house was special too. They had a fireplace for winter and air-conditioners for the summer. She had two parents, two sisters, and two of everything she wanted including two best friends. Tulip and Carla were her friends because they did not strive to be, for anyone who made an effort to befriend Olivia Rey were of no interest to her.

Carla did not know of anyone else who lived with a grandmother instead of a father, and most of those without a father at least knew the whereabouts of theirs. Hers was a bastard, she learned a long time ago. She had not seen him in ten or so years, not even when he came to town for the trial of William and Brian.

When Brian had run away when he was six, their father had bothered to call then to make their mother cry by saying it was all her fault. He seemed to care a lot about Brian, and why he had run away, but no one seemed bothered, and no one was angry, and no one cried when Carla ran away, three times. No one even noticed she was gone, and walking the streets late at night. When no one came looking for her, she returned home, re-entering the darkened house via the unlocked back door. On one occasion, William had locked the door after she left, and Brian let her in after she threw rocks against his bedroom window. At least William had noticed she was gone.

William was responsible also for Carla's aversion to vomit, since all four of them had to sit through a movie, *No Roses for Michael*, about drugs because there were no tomatoes. The plan did not work on William or Brian, but Carla vowed never to go near drugs since there was so much sickness involved, and because of the movie, she could not witness any form of vomiting whether it be the action itself, stepping around the by-product on the footpath, or the mere waft of it on a breeze. It was enough to invoke extreme nausea.

Grandma was a burden she said, and since she did say so almost daily, it left Carla believing it could be true except there was no evidence to support it and plenty to rebut it. If Grandma was not there, who would feed them, and who would repair their torn clothing, and if she lived elsewhere or died, they would be latchkey kids, and that, according to the playground, was the true sign of abandonment.

It was also strange that Grandma claimed to be a burden when she had so many roles that only she could fill, like when girls phoned to speak with Brian. She always used British politeness: "May I inquire as to who is calling?" or "Who shall I say is calling?" The giggling on the other end did not irritate her, neither did the eternal ringing, and she never disconnected anyone. Carla did so often, and Matthew always. There was so much that Grandma did not include on her encumbrance scales.

She could be a little forgetful and confused though, constantly mixing their names and applying them at random, which was fine for the boys, but Carla did not appreciate William for a name. Grandma also called everyone Robert. He was her son until he died young. There was also another daughter, Grace, and letters came in the mail from her, but she never visited, and no one ever mentioned her name. The Baden children did not have aunties, uncles or cousins. There were no family barbeques or birthday parties to attend. It was just them, Orchard Road, Grandma, and Basil.

They also had real curtains thanks to Grandma and her old black and gold Singer with a slippered foot at the pedal. The boys' room received a fresh coat of blue paint in anticipation of the speckled blue carpet mother had put on lay-by some months earlier. Carla hoped this did not signify that she was due pink for she was as blue as anyone at Orchard Road.

The living room and hallway were the first floors covered, halving the decibels that had ricocheted off every unpadded surface. The carpet was black with green, blue, and orange satellites of coruscating color. It was unusual, unique, and of course on sale at a bargain, basement price.

Mrs. Rey had told Carla and Olivia that education was power, and only the educated can be free, so Carla studied hard. Olivia did not agree—she had always known freedom, and did not need an education for her future life in Sydney as a famous actress, which required something else already in her possession in abundance: talent and beauty.

Although she knew little of herself, Carla had learned in Modern History that freedom was everything. People even died for it. Apart from being free, what else to be was puzzling, other than her list of exclusions: she would not live in Maine, she would not be a Baden, or a wife, and she most definitely would never be a mother. She would not work herself dead for children or any man, and she would not be fat. She would not skip dinner to eat the leftovers then fill up on cake, and she would never cry alone at night when no one else could hear.

Thirty-one

August 1984

KINGS CROSS was not a place to live or die: it was a place for immortals like William and Brian Baden, and the scripting of their journey to this place was in itself spiritual. If they had not broken into the house to steal, they would not have been on trial and convicted. There would not have been a fishing expedition, no stabbing, and their father would not have provided the guilt-ridden funds they needed to make the journey.

As good fortune would further have it, work fell onto their path while they were not looking. A faded sign in a bakery window called out for helpers to apply within. The 4:00AM start was not a deterrent.

A block away from their workplace, there was a room with a view for twenty dollars a week. Most of the rotting steps to the upper story had some worthwhile pieces still intact requiring just a little crabbing to the narrow landing a straight, thin line above. A lone 20-watt bulb cast a faint glow over a long wall with four doors leading to three tenancies, and a communal bathroom of sorts with cracked mosaics on the floor, and a rusty basin for hands and feet where water trickled out of calcium-lined pipes.

Cockroaches and other vermin shared their accommodation, which was inevitable and a minor nuisance given the convenience of Cheap Eats on the ground floor below.

Linoleum remnants covered the floorboards, with its Peruvian tones still evident in the piece intact at the bottom of the cupboard under the kitchen sink. A single-hung sash window framed the white lime, moldy Pollock splattered against the tan brick wall of the brothel next door. Black telephone wires sagged between with only an arms-length separating the two buildings. None of it mattered: they had their freedom, from a monotone existence to kaleidoscope, from languor to life.

At dark, Kings Cross brightened the sky neon, and buzzed, as did its inhabitants including spruikers and other characters you did not look at without repercussion.

Thomas, who occupied the room down the hall, offered the dewy country boys a special introductory price for euphoria that would make them feel Christmassy every day of the year. And Thomas knew the populace of King's Cross, and could open doors into every tawdry settlement in Darlinghurst Road. You did not need eighteen years with Thomas as a friend. Thomas was also an educator: dope was child's play, and more of a purr than a bang. What the new boys needed was amphetamines to be sure bread baking did not intrude on the life they came to the city to enjoy. He offered a free trial, which was accepted.

Michael strayed into Sydney following his convalescence in Maine. He had two days before his medical leave expired for the injury he sustained while "tripping over his own feet with a kitchen knife in his hand". Helena had given him an address in Kings Cross for the boys, from Brian's sole call home, and Michael lingered now on the cracked footpath out front with the piece of paper in his hand. He checked the address again, hoping he had made a mistake then stared upward at the structure. There was no demolition notice as expected given the level of rot and decay that absorbed the two-story building. He shook his head, and focused on the bright side: it would not be long before their new home sent the boys scurrying back to the relative comfort of Orchard Road, or to the base.

Michael stepped inside the open front door, keeping a close eye on what was under his feet and above his head. A steady passage of eccentrics forced him to defend his position on what remained of each timber step. He passed the middle door with 102 hanging over its paint-chipped timber, and avoided the pedestrian traffic that turned left on the top step to a hub at the back room. At 101, he knocked, waited, then knocked some more.

Brian appeared eventually, inert and pasty, and Michael followed him inside despite the lack of recognition. He collapsed from the effort onto a stained mattress on the splintered floor. William did not stir, but life seemed evident.

"He'll regret that when he wakes up," said Michael nodding at William's open mouth. The subdued smile in response was not the infectious laugh Michael remembered, expected, and his heart tore.

Michael inspected the two chairs that surrounded the Formica table then released his weight on the one with the least corrosion even though its four supports spread out at different angles. The inadvertent scraping of the chair across the floorboards disturbed William who rolled on to his side and opened his eyes. Brian had managed to stand again, but disappeared through the still open door down the hallway to the room that was the subject of so much activity. William did not see Michael, or hear him when he spoke. Dazed, he rose, and followed Brian down the hallway.

Michael thought to leave, not knowing how long he would be alone, or if he was likely to enjoy a conversation with his sons when they returned. Then Brian reappeared, bright and talkative, firing three consecutive questions at Michael. Michael understood one word.

"She's fine," he said, "but she's worried about you. You promised me you'd call her every week."

Brian's reply was incomprehensible.

"You don't have a fridge," said Michael after a pause.

"We don't need one," he replied, then said something about rubbish bins at the bakery where they worked, free food, and that bread was a stable, corrected then to apple, and a laugh.

"You need to eat more than just bread," said Michael.

William returned with conversation erupting like a burst water main, and Michael wondered if he had fallen down a rabbit hole and entered a fantasy world. William asked to see the stab wound, his handiwork, and tempered his excitement with apologies. While they inspected his torso, Michael invited them to dinner, and while disappointed, was not surprised when they declined. He gave them two hundred dollars to get them through the winter. In October, he would return to take them home, at which time he expected the novelty of their adventure would have given way to sober actuality.

Michael hailed a taxi for Rushcutters Bay where Grace was attempting spaghetti bolognaise for four in anticipation of a family reunion. She would be disappointed also, or relieved, given her general anathema for cooking.

She opened the door with a glass of red wine in one hand. "Where are the boys?" she asked.

"They're not coming."

"Oh," she said. "I was looking forward to seeing them again after all these years."

Michael opened the refrigerator, and grabbed a bottle of beer. He sculled half of it without breathing then stepped through the sliding glass doors onto the terrace to admire the expanded view from South Head to the city.

"Hungry?" Grace asked, appearing at the doorway in a pair of mauve legwarmers and a headband. He smiled. The mass of teased hair reminded him of sprouting alfalfa, but the comparison did not last long: the forces of man and nature induced a downward cast to her exposed breasts.

Thirty-two

August 1984

MRS. REY called out to Carla through Olivia's locked bedroom door, offering to drive her home since it was dark outside, and a gentle rain had misted the winter air. Carla declined even though a ride in the warmth of their Mercedes was preferred to a walk in the cold rain. There was only one reason for the nonsensical choice: Carla had a job to do along the way, disposing of the empty Southern Comfort bottle in the industrial bin behind the service station. If it had been Saturday night instead of Friday night, there would not have been a problem since the Reys entertained every Saturday night, and it was easy to mingle their empties with the mass of wine and other bottles from the dinner party. An extra empty bottle or two went unnoticed, and it seemed no one noticed either that Olivia had been robbing the liquor cabinet for months. It helped that Mr. Rey indulged every night in varying degrees: from mere cheeriness to passed-out in his armchair in front of Dateline. It was therefore reasonable for Mrs. Rey to presume that Mr. Rey alone was responsible for the declining stocks. She never questioned how much he drank, Olivia said, and never chastised him as some wives did because he was a man with many stresses and pressures as managing partner of a law firm. Mrs. Rey was an excellent wife, Carla concluded, and an excellent mother too for entrusting Olivia with so much privacy, allowing her to lock her bedroom door without interrogation. All doors were permanently open at Orchard Road as a rule, introduced after William and Brian left for Sydney.

The Reys were perfect entertainers, and Carla looked forward to Saturday nights helping with table settings so regal, they were suitable for kings and queens. Plates of gold and cobalt blue Noritake were positioned with a little ruler to be certain of distances. Little square boxes of short-cut roses lined the middle of the table, which Mrs. Rey arranged herself. For each of the ten diners, there were four crystal glasses of varying shapes and sizes. They had crystal at Orchard Road too, in the display cabinet above the kitchen bench, but no occasion ever arose to use it. A man from Weight Watchers had come by recently for dinner, but he drank water from the everyday glasses and chewed on ice cubes throughout. He laughed a lot at nothing in particular, and Carla thought it strange, knowing how little her mother laughed—she had thought until then that happiness and size could not live harmoniously together in one being.

One other man had been to Orchard Road for dinner before the fat man. He was the ugly man, and Carla could tell as much through the front door without even seeing his face. Carla had heard him ask mother for a goodnight kiss, but mother had politely refused. Then he yelled at her, and said she ought to be grateful that he had taken her out as a favor as it certainly was not for pleasure. She would not do better than his charity he forewarned then tried to kiss her again. Mother came inside and cried a lot, alone in the kitchen eating cake before going to bed in the room she shared with Grandma. Carla had listened in to hear her mother say that she had had a lovely night out. Grandma did not ask more questions, and Carla felt sure Grandma had heard it all just as she had.

Carla's head was spinning when she left the Rey residence. She stumbled in a daze for the next eight blocks, liking the world blurred in this way. After throwing the evidence in the bin, she fell to the ground giggling, and tried to stop her body from swaying as she rose to her feet. She checked her wristwatch and thought it said eight twenty—just ten minutes to curfew. "Hurry," she ordered herself. She would take the short cut tonight.

The cemetery was a beautiful place during the day with mature trees forming a canopy, manicured lawns, flowers, and ornate stonemasonry. It was a quiet place, and perfect for reading a book under a tree or for a picnic on the lawn, although no one ever did. Carla struggled over the waist-high, mossy wall, which was a boundary marker only, and not intended as a barrier to keep humans out or spirits in, including her grandfather, James Wallin. She maneuvered her way across the spongy lawn on a diagonal course to the other side, careful not to step on a grave and wake the dead.

Carla's heart paced when she saw the red glows up ahead, eyes of demons, watching, and waiting to possess her. She stumbled over a concrete slab, and landed spread-eagled on a memorial verse. Her skirt ripped, as did the skin on her shin to expose the bone. She rolled on to her side to clutch at her dented tibia, and came face-to-face with a photo of the entombed Kelly Anne Travis. Carla remembered the demons, and saw the red glows moving toward her—they could smell the blood that trickled down her leg. She thought to run, but feared she would fall again unable to see in the dark as they could. She closed her eyes and hoped they might sail past her, and if not, perhaps the spirit of Kelly would protect her.

She screamed when the first demon grabbed her arm. "Don't scream," it said, blowing smoke into her face. She screamed, and a hand covered her mouth, a human-like hand. "Don't scream," it repeated. "We're not going to hurt you unless you scream." It slowly removed the hand. Carla screamed, and another hand smacked her across the face. She thought she heard a zip, then something pushed into her mouth, in and out, with her head gripped at the cheeks forcing her mouth open. She choked. "Don't bite," it said. She cried and retched, but it would not stop, and moved faster and faster inside her mouth until slime from the beast spewed down her throat choking her. It let her go, and she vomited over its shoes, Southern Comfort, ginger ale, chips, and other mush. It slapped her face, hard, and pushed her back onto the slab while another demon sat on her neck to pin her arms above her head. Another demon pulled her jumper from her body. They tugged at her skirt then threw it over Kelly's headstone. Carla dared not scream as it ripped her insides, one demon after another, how many times, she could not tell. One prodded at her face releasing a sticky mass into her ear, and another did so into her hair. She was bleeding to death from every orifice, coated from head to toe in demon ejaculate. Her eyes settled on the headstone, died aged 37, 'Sleep on, sweet mother and wife, and take thy rest, God called thee home, He thought it best.' There would be trouble tomorrow, when they found her naked and dead on Kelly's grave.

"Help me, Kelly," Carla whimpered. "Help me Jesus," she prayed. Silence answered, and then came the soothing rain. She did not move at first, but waited for the white light Grandma had told her about, and for the movie reel to begin that would flash by for a mere fourteen years. There was no white light, and no life passing before her eyes, and only the rain, now heavy on her skin. It washed away the blood, the demon fluid, and salt from her tears. She found her skirt and dressed somehow, panicked because she was still a part of life, and late.

Her watch had stopped at nine o'clock. There would be more trouble because of it: her first teenage birthday present ruined with moisture inside the cracked face blurring the numbers. She dared not think how many cans of vegetables had been stacked in the middle of the night to pay for it.

The rain continued as Carla staggered the last three blocks to home. She waited on the top step outside the kitchen to muster courage before opening the back door to scurry down the hallway to the bathroom. She undressed in the shower, and cowered in the tub under a searing spray with her knees tucked under a quivering chin.

"Are you OK, Carla?" her mother asked from the bathroom doorway.

Carla willed the plastic shower curtain to stay in place. It did.

"Get caught in the rain did you? You should have called me. I would have picked you up."

"I'm OK, Mum." The bathroom door closed, and Carla breathed again. She stayed in the shower until her skin burned red, and the smell of shame had gurgled into the sewer.

Her knees were weak when she finally stood dripping in front of the foggy mirror. She wiped it clear, and saw what the demons had seen. Inside the bathroom cabinet, she found the manicure scissors. Long strips of brown hair fell into the hand basin, leaving behind a jagged aftermath then Carla dragged the blunt edge of the scissors down her cheekbone, repeatedly, until a deep and enduring imperfection emerged. Blood trickled as a tear would have if allowed. "I hate you," she said staring at the image in the mirror. "I hate you."

Carla opened the bathroom door, peered right and left then with her head bowed, dashed the short distance to her bedroom.

"Carla, dear, what have you done to your hair?" Grandma asked, appearing suddenly before Carla in the hallway. "You look like a little boy or one of those rocker people."

"Don't call me Carla, Grandma."

"Oh, what should I call you then?"

"Carl. It's Carl now."

"That's a boy's name, dear. What's that on your cheek?"

"Nothing, Grandma. It's OK," she said then brushed past the obstacle that stood between her and the sanctity of a darkened room. Once alone, she relived every moment, shivering with cold and fear, and cried every tear she could assemble. When the source was dry, she closed her eyes, and recessed the memory by visualizing a box that she bound with string then stored in a deep cavern in the outposts of her mind. When she woke the next morning, she would pretend nothing had happened, with just a scar as a reminder to hate herself with passion for as long as she breathed air. She glared at the poster on her wall, the words she could not see known by heart.

Millie had rushed to the living room to report the gash on Carla's cheek and boyish hair, but in the short distance traveled, forgot she had something to say. She sat down in a worn green armchair to watch Dallas with Helena.

Thirty-three

October 1984

MICHAEL was a man's man. He had no interest in the labyrinthine byways of women. Grace was the exception, although even she now, at forty, wanted more: complication when simplicity had worked well for so many years.

Michael was more consistent in his life, still preferring a pub to a club, the mess hall to dinner by candlelight, football to a movie, and so it was with reluctance that he dressed in compliance of a code for a night out at The Establishment. It was the place to be, his colleagues had said, with beautiful women wall to wall. Guerrillas, Michael thought. He left one collar crooked hoping for rejection by the burley bouncer at the entry, but his wrist bore a stamp without a second glance.

His colleagues were right about The Establishment and the women who went there, and Michael's primary source of entertainment for the night was the misadventures of his peers. They had all tried for the tall blonde who deflected advances like Wonder Woman. A mere strip of cloth across her chest defied gravity and accentuated the positives. They can't be real, Michael thought, but craved certainty.

With the wisdom that came from hours of observation, Michael adopted a circuitous route, which was best against the shield. He collided, 'accidentally' into the least attractive woman in the retinue, apologized profusely for his clumsiness, and offered to refill her drink. She accepted, introduced herself as Caitlyn Robson, and made room for Michael in the inner sanctum. Not once while in proximity to the breasts, did he glance at them, or her. While the task was inhuman, he could see in his peripheral vision that his disinterest had caught her attention. The evening concluded in this way, and Michael arranged lunch with Caitlyn Robson at The Pier the following day.

Caitlyn, a divorcee, had no children from a short marriage. She was a dentist, and daughter of a dentist, and Michael found the phenomenon most intriguing.

Chardonnay from the Yarra Valley flowed freely as did conversation, and Michael was relieved that Caitlyn was willing and able to discuss football in an otherwise dull exchange on subjects more valued by women: relationships, their demise, and why men so consistently disappoint women. There was no mention of the friend until the second bottle of wine, and Michael was not the instigator.

"Aren't you going to ask me about Andréa?" Caitlyn asked.

"Who?"

She smiled. "My friend? The tall, blonde, *endowed* one."

Michael shook his head. "I don't think I met her."

"They're real," she said.

Michael smiled, and realized it was enough to expose the ruse.

"I would have thought there was something wrong with you if you hadn't noticed her."

"How long have you been friends?" he asked.

"Forever," she replied. "I'm not a threat to her social domination if you understand what I mean."

He did.

"Let's talk about something else," he suggested. When it came to a cause like Andréa somebody-or-other, patience would ultimately be the path of least resistance. "Damn those Bombers," he said. "I had quite a sum riding on the Hawks to win the final."

Two weeks passed before Michael next encountered Andréa. Caitlyn wanted to see *Places in the Heart* in the city, and Michael was not at all interested, until Caitlyn asked if Andréa could join them. He agreed.

They waited for her on the steps out front of the Bourke Street cinemas. A curious edginess shook his core, and when she came into view, Michael's nonchalant strategy had to battle it for control. It was absurd that she made such a scene just striding, and Michael struggled to divert his eyes.

They talked for a while on the steps as trams rattled past, and Michael wondered about seating arrangements. Then the reason for the delay came into view: a Ken doll made it four, not three. Michael thought to bail as any spoiled child might, but he could not walk away while a pretty figurine of a man moved in on his woman, and besides, he had invested interminable hours with Caitlyn for this moment. He followed the trio into the darkness, and assumed the position of bookend with just Caitlyn between himself and her.

It was the Depression in *Places in the Heart*. A husband had died, and his widow struggled with the cotton fields and two young children. She hired a black man, Moze, after he stole their silver, then a bitter blind man came to board with them. Michael spotted the Ken doll's hand in his peripherals. It rested at first on her shoulder, flailed intermittently then landed in a deceitful hint of aimlessness on the magnificent cushioning. An urge rose to dislodge it, but Caitlyn nuzzled into him entrapping his upper arm in both of hers. Michael glanced down at her, and recognized the pulpy look as her eyes willed his lips toward her own. Moze gave young Frank his lucky rabbit's foot to ward off trouble, which did not help much as he endured a spanking for smoking behind the school

159

shed. Michael smiled at the scene reminiscent of his own childhood, but was glad when the credits scrolled, and the theatre brightened.

The après movie gathering over coffee prompted another thought to bail: he only wanted to hear from her, but Caitlyn talked most, and the Ken Doll also had a lot to say about everything. They should get together, Michael thought.

The Ken doll and Michael's Barbie were models, which would come as no surprise to anyone at a glance let alone after an endless discourse on the world of modeling. When asked about his career, Michael had a chance to trump his rival, and military pilot always did. Andréa seemed suitably impressed, and for that alone, Michael considered the night a success. There was just one impediment going forward, wearing a white jacket and trousers with a pale pink t-shirt beneath. Michael wondered what his colleagues would think of a man who dared to wear pastel, and so brazenly so.

The group finally split with Michael forced to leave with Caitlyn. She invited him home, and did not accept a parade of excuses, and Michael finally caved in to a reliable upsell: lager substituted for java. He would have one drink then leave first chance.

"What did you think of Andréa's new boyfriend?" Caitlyn asked.

"I didn't."

"Didn't what?"

"I didn't think of him," Michael replied.

Caitlyn retreated down the hallway leaving Michael alone in her quaint living room. He sculled his beer, and was ready to leave when she materialized draped in sheer black. The dim lighting was not dim enough to disguise a body curved like a glass blowing gone wrong. Her hands rose slowly upward from her side as if commanding an orchestra to crescendo, and Michael realized escape was no longer a viable option. Her outstretched arms pleaded, and Michael knew he would have to draw into them with no further delay or the awkward pause would transform into a major discomfort for both of them, but mostly for her. He imagined Andréa in a similar state of revelation, and with this in mind, the obligation would be executable to a satisfactory degree for all concerned, he believed.

Michael woke under a sea of frilly pink hanging from the white four-poster bed. More pink surrounded him on the walls. The furniture was barely visible under a menagerie of plush animals from Paddington to Kermit. Even Dame Edna would cringe at the décor, he thought.

He dressed in slow dread, a precipitous departure unlikely since bacon wafted from the pan down the hallway. The tang of expectation dragged him toward the kitchen.

Caitlyn was much too cheerful for any morning. She filled his cup with coffee, and kissed him with the entitlement that comes from having surrendered most parts of one's anatomy to someone else. When she delivered the bacon and eggs, she dropped into his lap, and kissed him some more. Michael willed her to move away, and she did, but only as far as the seat opposite. She watched him eat with dreamy eyes trailing his fork from the plate to his lips, and lingered there while he chewed. The phone drew her away allowing for a more rapid ingestion, and sculling of the coffee.

"I can't talk right now. We're having breakfast," she whispered into the mouthpiece.

I hope that's not Andréa, he thought.

"Let's just say the movie exceeded *all* expectations, and there were *two* parts I particularly enjoyed."

Oh, please, girl code, he thought.

"I'll call you later, much later," she said with a laugh.

More girl code and he knew what it meant: I'll tell you every intricate detail when he's gone, when I've finished with him, hours from now. Disturbing creatures, women, compelled to share so much of their lives, and with no topic taboo, apparently. There was a greater respect shown in the manhood with conversations restricted to sport and news, with personal issues and emotions locked away in trunks where they belonged.

Michael stayed at Caitlyn's until reasonableness allowed for a departure: an hour after breakfast, and he had suffered for his fairness. He was going to Sydney the following week, he told her, to get his sons. Life would be busy thereafter with two teenagers in his care, and so he might not be around in a while. A woman like her should not sit around waiting for a man like him. She said she was happy to wait, and would call him in a couple of weeks.

"Great," he replied.

The pub opened for communion at ten, and Michael could barely wait for the doors to fling wide to welcome him into its fold. It was a safe house where true providence reigned on any given day, and tortured souls could gather in a secure, woman-free setting for anointing. Michael joined the other life-beaten to convalesce, and the priest for the day served the first ale. The men gathered did not need to speak of unspeakable things.

Thirty-four

October 1984

IN the valley of the shadow of death, evil lurked. William could see it. It taunted him, swinging cross-legged on the telephone wires that drooped outside their window. The motley jesters were multiplying and with it, their jeering became louder. William could stand it no longer. He tried to chase them away, fell fourteen feet to the concrete below, and broke two ribs.

The nurse at the emergency room ordered rest and time for recovery. There was no treatment for broken ribs, and no medication to repair the cracks, only time, and William had ample: he had missed his shift at the bakery again—the absolute last chance used the day before.

The critters were still there when he returned to Room 101 above Cheap Eats. Brian could not see them, but did not doubt their presence. If William said they were there, they were there. It was too much, plus the rent was due, they had no jobs, and Thomas was not so friendly, demanding payment for their accumulated debt, which was beyond their capabilities. They left quietly in the dark. The critters laughed as they made their get-away, and William feared they would alert Thomas. As fast as two broken ribs would allow, William and Brian scampered up the street.

A circle of likeness gathered at the park in Kings Cross, night dwellers with nowhere else to go. A new friend gave William an injection for the pain, and Brian too: they would need it for life on the streets with some minor adjustments required in the beginning. Brian was sick from the new drug that pulsed through his body, but soon after, serenity displaced all other cares, and even William believed he was at last safe from the critters.

Freed of the burden of employment, their day began leisurely at midday with a first shot. Then the serious work began: steal, deal, beg, borrow, whatever was required. Other means, involving old men and slow-moving cars, was not an option, although others made good money from it. They drifted through the streets of Kings Cross for anything unsecured or unsupervised. Begging brought less reward, but filled the hours when energy lagged. The sneers and derogation were just part of the business. They shared the proceeds of their enterprise to purchase gear, which they also shared equally, or so Brian thought. He was sober enough once to see William pocket a hit before distributing the rest 'fairly', and Brian's half share in reality was more like a quarter. Distrust brought about the divide. They agreed to work different sectors, pawn separate brokers, and find their own dealer, but they came together on occasion at night to walk the strip.

William was late back to the park that night, with his pockets filled with hock, acid, and rum. A crowd had gathered around a gray, lifeless mass, with a needle dangling from one arm. They slapped at the boy's cheeks, and rushed as fast as the living dead could, to fill bottles with water from the fountain, the splashing as effective as the slapping. William pushed his way through to the epicenter, and shook Brian around the shoulders. "Wake up, Brian! Wake up!"

A flash of blue and red lit the park as paramedics hurried with a gurney, Naltrexone, and a syringe. The scene was familiar, but still grievous, for anyone's child was a life worth saving. After a short while, the frantic pace died, and calm, methodical processing began.

The ambulance pulled away at a gentle pace, no siren, no lights.

Thirty-five

December 1984

HELENA learned that only the good die young, death is a tragedy only for the living, and life is death, dying is life, to die is an adventure for in the midst of life, we are in death. Brian was in the wind, the rain, the sun, the morning dew. He was at peace, at rest, in a better place, and there was a reason for everything, they told her, although no one was able to say why a child should die in this way, alone on the streets without his mother. Helena wondered why Aristotle came to life at such times when silence was a greater gold than philosophy or a burdensome cliché, for nobody could understand the pain without living it, or know the right words to say when none existed.

Helena met with Janine, her psychologist, twice a week, with concern legitimate that she might take her own life. She thought of doing so every hour, for she could not recover from losing Brian, and time spent with Janine merely tackled a titanic berg with a toothpick. If only He had taken her instead.

She subsisted on a diet of black tea and water, combining her misery with a permanent state of faintness and drug-induced numbness to form a shell of a human being. New impressions lined her face giving the appearance of a woman fifteen years older, and twenty pounds lighter. She slept through the night, but in her restless dreams, her son was alive. In the morning, he was gone again, and losing him every day meant there was no way forward. More pills killed the dreams, her waking hours and everything else, but not the photos, and not the little wooden bird. A single thread of cotton held her together, and Millie was the tailor. There was some mild comfort knowing Carla and Matthew were fine without her, and probably better off if she left them to join Brian, Robert, and her father.

Carl waited at the bottom of the timber stairs for Matthew to emerge from Principal Mulder's office. He surfaced after the longest while with ruffled blond hair, and a smooth pale chest exposed by two missing khaki buttons.

"What happened?" Carl asked.

"Nothing."

"So you ripped your shirt all by yourself? Where's your shoe?"

"Don't know."

"What did Principal Mulder say?"

"He said to stop fighting."

"Anything else? Is he going to tell Mum?"

"Don't know. She wouldn't care anyway. She's always crying, and looking at his photo, and holding that bird."

Matthew ambled toward the lockers to retrieve his shoe from the top shelf, removing sodden sandwiches from inside the toes. "I hate this place."

"Only three days to holidays," said Carl.

"And four more years of school, then I'm going to live somewhere else."

"Where?"

"Anywhere away from here. I hate Maine."

"I'm never going to be a mother," said Carl.

"Me either," he replied, and they managed a smile.

"Let's get some money off Grandma and take Basil to the mall," Carl suggested. "He can chase the pigeons. He likes doing that."

"He'll get in trouble again."

"Yeah," said Carl. "He will."

They laughed, recalling Basil's last excursion into the dog-free zone with a portly security guard in pursuit.

Michael returned to the base after Brian's funeral, returning also to Caitlyn who presented him with three books on grief. He reviewed the biographies on the jackets in search of relevant first-hand experience to confirm the author's right to pen such books. There was none—only mention of a career as a psychiatrist or psychologist, the difference Michael did not appreciate, and did not care to. He threw the books in the bin. Caitlyn would have been more helpful if she had bought him a keg of beer.

He spent nights and weekends with her, not wanting to be alone, and neither did she. She tolerated his melancholy, made excuses for his rudeness, and did not chastise his consumption of beer or the hours he spent on the sofa watching television. The arrangement was satisfactory for both, on most levels.

The front door chimed, and Caitlyn rushed to answer it before the sound disturbed Michael. She whispered with the visitor in a conspiratorial way then returned to the living room with the visitor in tow. Michael shook his beer can to signal that it was empty.

He had not seen Andréa in a while, not since the movies, and although her beauty still captivated, it now threatened his afternoon viewing.

"I'll get coffee," said Caitlyn, disappearing to the kitchen.

"I'm sorry to hear about your son, Michael," said Andréa. She sat down beside him on the sofa with her knees touching his.

"Why do people say they're sorry when someone dies? It's not as if you had anything to do with my son's death, so why *apologize*. What do you expect me to say to your 'sorry'? Thank you? Why do I need to thank you for apologizing for something that didn't need an apology? I don't know why people say 'sorry', but thank you, thank you for being sorry." He placed a hand across his heart and nodded. "That's the etiquette out the way. Anything else?"

"I *am* sorry, Michael, more than you know."

"What could you possibly know about losing a son? Have you lost a son? You don't even have a son so how could you know what it's like to lose one. You have no idea how this feels so don't pretend you do."

Caitlyn returned with coffee for three, and set it down on the table between the sofa and the TV. Michael retreated to the kitchen for beer, and sipped a while on his own. He thought he should apologize—she was just being kind—but he did not want to, and didn't.

Thirty-six

December 1984

WILLIAM understood what they meant by tortured soul. Some passers-by used to call them that when they begged on the streets of Kings Cross, as did the missionaries, and the Samaritans. The vast majority though, simply passed on their saliva, kicked or yelled abuse, junky loser, mostly. They were not tortured souls when they first arrived in Sydney, he and Brian. It was an adventure then with no rules, no nagging or teacher protocols. They did not need the drugs, like the others, and they could stop whenever they wanted, and they planned to leave long before addiction took hold of their bodies—that would take months, years possibly, and only then if you let it.

Brian wanted to go home. He had had enough, was tired and very sick. He missed mum, and wanted to sleep in his bed again at Orchard Road. William had said "soon", it was "too early yet", especially since the weather was warming, and sleeping in the park was not so bad. At Christmas, they would return to Maine and detox themselves. It would be easy together, and by then they would have had their quota of fun and freedom.

They had fought on that last day, over money. Brian had needed some for a hit, and William had said, "Scum for it like I had to". When William walked away, Brian was shivering and scratching furiously at his arms, but William was sure he would be OK. That was the last time he saw his brother and best friend, with pinpoint pupils with life still in them.

William stayed just a short while at the funeral. He thought he heard his mother say, "Why Brian?" and knew she was thinking, "Why not William instead?" Everyone thought that—he could tell by the expanse of private space that surrounded him. No one spoke to him or consoled him even though his body throbbed with grief too, afraid in case he infected them with his toxic life. He was just a junkie now—that was all anyone saw, but he was still human albeit with bloodied cushions for arms.

He knew the dealer, the one who had sold Brian the bad H, and he would not deal again. From unattended purses at the funeral, William stole two hundred and thirty-four dollars. It was enough for a handgun and a box of bullets although he would need just one, or two if his hands shook. In his life, seventeen years of it passed, his defining moment had come. It would be the most satisfying, and easily so since there was not much to choose from other than his time with Brian. Maybe when he was done, Brian, mum, and everyone else might forgive him.

William spent the twilight hours and early evening with a bottle of rum to prepare. He would not run afterwards, just shoot, and wait for arrest or whatever else, and anyway, there was nothing to run to, no one and nowhere. He said goodbye to those he knew as friends—a fickle state for all of them, then set off, ironically or symbolically, for the long, wide street that ran from the Sydney CBD to Kings Cross, William Street.

As he strode deliberately by, a neon blue cross on a small, white timber-clad building caught his eye. It was out of place. He had to stop. A feeble gate, high enough to ward off old dogs and children, separated the church from the street.

William stepped twice from the gate to the patio, and twice more to reach the front door. He pushed the door open, not stopping to read the Outreach hours plastered on its surface.

A crucifix, lit by a mass of candles overwhelmed the small chapel, and William. He shuffled toward it as a man appeared from the shadows.

"Can I help you?" he asked, showing no sign of fear at the intrusion.

"No," William replied, "You can't help me. My brother died. It was my fault."

"Was he a Christian?"

"He didn't go to church," William replied.

"Did he believe in Jesus as his savior?"

"I don't know. We never talked about those things."

"What about you, son?"

"Yeah, I believe in Jesus. My grandfather told me stories from the bible when I was little. Brian too, so maybe he was a Christian. Is that all it means, to believe in Jesus?"

"In essence it is. You need to have Jesus in your heart, but there's more to being a good Christian."

"He was good too, Brian. Everyone liked him. Would he be in trouble with God for stealing? That's the only thing he ever did wrong, and that was my fault too. He can't be blamed for stuff like that."

"God wants us all to be saved."

William nodded. "I have to go. Can I take this," he asked, lifting a bible from the pew.

"Of course, but come back again. What's your name, son?"

"William."

"Make sure you come back, William."

"Sure," he said, smiled and left. He had places to go, things to do, and sooner was best so he could dispense with the sweltering denim jacket, and the metal in his pocket that weighed him down.

He started up William Street and stopped in front of a travel agency, his eye caught by Hawaii in a poster, not so expensive on sale. They should have gone to the beach and learned to ride the waves.

William had never lived a sunrise, although he had seen night become day many times, but not *lived* it or seen the rays break orange on the horizon. He should see one before the iron doors slam shut behind him. He turned to backtrack toward Kings Cross railway station for a train to Martin Place. Ordinarily, he would have walked the distance, but he was dressed for winter on a sultry night, and for once, he had cash to spare in his pockets. From Martin Place, it was a short walk to Circular Quay to catch the ferry to Manly.

After a smooth ferry berthing, William made his way up The Esplanade in search of a bottle shop to buy a six-pack and a bottle of rum. Ahead, on the footpath out front of a news agency, he saw a tower of postcards. He stopped to browse, selecting one with a montage of beach scenes. He wrote on the back, "To Mum, I'm sorry. Forgive me. Love forever, your son, William." He purchased a stamp, and posted the card in the nearest mailbox then continued to the end of The Esplanade to wait.

He settled on a grassy knoll, and removed the denim jacket and his black t-shirt to cool his sticky skin with a sea breeze. He checked the gun was still in place. It was. With everything in order, he popped two wake-ups, and placed the black bible with the embossed gold cross on top of his belongings.

At 5:40AM, the upper glow broke the line of water a million miles away. It was worth the wait. "New day, new day," he whispered as tiredness overwhelmed. He picked up the bible to clutch it against his chest with one hand. "New day," he said then rummaged inside his denim jacket. He found what he was looking for, put the muzzle to his head, and pulled the trigger.

Thirty-seven

25 May 1985

9:10PM A child was born.

PART III

June 1990 – March 1995

Thirty-eight

June 1990

LIFE is a spinning top. It begins in the hands of another who holds it steadfast for as long as possible, winding it and releasing it only when the top can spin on its axis. After launch, the top spins at its fastest, upright, then slows, with precession more and more pronounced, until finally, it topples in one violent last thrash. Helena's life still spun, but barely.

Her children were gone, all of them, and Millie and Basil too. Millie had died from pneumonia at 66, her lungs pushed full with so much bottled oxygen her organs had to move to accommodate it. She did not fight for her life, and it was all over within days. Basil would be the only one to die from old age, and perhaps loneliness.

Michael returned once a year and together, he and Helena kept vigil at gravesites and cried, for they alone understood that a loss was unique for each child to each parent, and no two were ever the same. He did not stay at Orchard Road even though there were vacancies.

Gordon Moore moved into Orchard Road for a while after Millie died in 1987, twenty years to the day the mill burnt down. Gordon was a happy sad man. He laughed a lot, in public, but lived a miserable existence in private. He blamed Helena for his hugeness, which was fully-fledged before they met at Weight Watchers. Before Helena, his ex-wife was to blame, and before her, his mother. Janine, Helena's psychologist, and friend now, said the relationship had to end for even in the Dead Sea one cannot float on a short chain anchored to the bottom. Helena knew exactly what she meant, but living alone required a strength and courage she did not possess, and Janine did not understand that it was better to be with anyone than alone. In the end, Gordon left of his own accord after a row with Matthew, who had no problem expressing the thoughts of others. A 'fat, good-for-nothing oppressor' did the trick. With mission accomplished, Matthew returned to university in Sydney, much less proficient with the aftermath of his actions.

After years of silence, Helena and Grace exchanged words in an awkward reconciliation at William's funeral. Grace shed a few solitary tears, for who or what, Helena was not certain. Then before she left Maine to return to Sydney, the truth of her pilgrimage became evident: the distribution of Millie's estate was not equitable at 50/50, she claimed. Firstly, because Helena had invested the monies from the sale of Waterloo Street in a term deposit, which failed to maximize possible returns during a bull market. Secondly, Millie had lived with Helena at Orchard Road for thirteen years, and contributed significantly in monetary terms and services during that time including child minder, cook, and housekeeper. Helena thought to mention in defense that she had never drawn a cent from Millie's funds during her residency at Orchard Road, but Helena could not be bothered with the conflict: her sons were dead, and Grace was free to take whatever she wanted for a mother lost could not be valued in such a way. Helena agreed to a 30/70 split, and hoped never to see or hear from her sister again.

Helena had never questioned the essentialness of university for Carla and Matthew, and had raised money for it by subdividing the backyard at Orchard Road. From the kitchen window, vegetables were still visible, but on the plates of those who lived where their backyard once was, and where the bones of Snoopy the bird lay buried.

She left the accounting firm after William died, debilitated by her bereavement—ledgers had become illegible, and numbers now baffled, but work was still an imperative for her clover patch had just two leaves: faith and love. Hope was gone, and luck was a myth.

James would not like the vision of his daughter in a navy blue uniform with grayed white cuffs, but cleaning motel rooms did not require mindfulness. The filth and degradation was unfathomable, and Helena might never get used to it, but if nothing else, James would have to agree, she had her independence, and that had always been his vision for her. She was a slave to no man, owned her own home, and supported her family without assistance from anyone. But for the love of a man, she might be someone.

Thirty-nine

December 1992

CARL had been at university in Sydney for four months when Millie died. She went home for the funeral, and almost did not return to the terrace she shared with four other students in Forest Lodge, but Helena insisted: she would be OK, and still had Basil and Matthew for company. Basil died four months later, and Matthew left four months after that. But nothing much mattered anyway from the day the postcard arrived from Manly, one week after William died. If there had been anything of her left to take, the postcard did it, enshrined now with a tiny wooden bird, and photos.

Another lesser blow gusted through Helena's life when Michael returned to Maine for Millie's funeral with a new wife in tow, and invited Carl and Matthew to dinner to meet the second Mrs. Baden. Matthew did not offer an excuse with his refusal, unbothered by the duty of pretense and still governed by a sense of childhood injury. Carl would have done likewise if not for curiosity. Expectations were low, but were in no way a reflection on the first Mrs. Baden.

The dinner was predictably uncomfortable yet genial. Her father did all the talking, and although Carl was only four and a half when their lives separated, she remembered enough to know a modification of history was in play, for Carl's benefit, or for the woman with the French name, Mrs. Andréa Baden. Whichever life was in depiction, wine made it all the more amusing and entertaining, and unlike Matthew, Carl was able to accept a relationship with her father as it was: based on mutual genes.

Olivia was also at the University of Sydney, staying in prestige at Wesley College, and studying Arts. She was still to make a decision on a career having considered most options from actor to psychologist, midwife, nutritionist, linguist, and most recently, television newscaster.

Matthew followed a year later, enrolling in a four-year journalism degree. He would only return to Maine thereafter on an intermittent basis, and made no secret of how he dreaded all such visits. He eventually left for more distant shores as a trainee on the international desk at CNN.

Carl returned to Maine as an Articled Clerk at Rey, Carol & Mendelson. It was not part of her plan since there were no crusades to wage in the world of property conveyance in Maine—city developers having made millionaires out of shack owners around the lake and waterways.

Being back in Maine was the third of Carl's life rules broken: she was still a Baden, and although she cared not to remember it, she was a mother as well. Her return was not choice driven: Helena was all alone, and unlike her brother, Carl was not a runner.

Olivia returned to Maine also, as an intern at the local television station.

In five years away, a lot had changed, but much more had stayed the same.

Forty

February 1993

CARL showed no interest in Nicholas Segher, unlike her work colleagues who found his suave production and designer tastes compelling. This focused his attention, and Carl gave in to his relentless pursuit only to end speculation that she must be gay. Their date though would be a first and last.

In preparation, Carl cut her hair even shorter, and colored it a darker shade of brown to flout his obvious preferences. He liked it. She was sarcastic and rude, and mocked his interests. He smiled. She said he was overly showy for wearing Hugo Boss and onyx cufflinks in Maine, which did not impress anyone. He shrugged his disagreement, and showed her his diamond-encrusted gold ring. "Unbelievable," she said. He smiled, and she laughed.

Carl accepted a second date, intrigued that he would voluntarily seek more of her company, and so it continued. At work, they maintained a professional distance in accordance with the firm's policy, and Nicholas flirted for pretense, but more truthfully, for the sake of image and reputation. He never introduced her as his girlfriend, and handholding or public signs of affection were taboo, especially in the presence of his friends. Carl did not particularly care, uncommitted as she was to the union, but still yielded to months of pressure in the back seat of his BMW. The occasion, filled with some urgency it seemed, reminded her too much of her only prior experience: the pain, sweat, odors, and the repulsiveness of it all. Nicholas barely had time to fall off her before he fell asleep. In the solitude that followed, Carl contemplated her sexuality: perhaps she was gay.

Their relationship was in its autumn when a binding blue line appeared on a white stick threatening to link her for a lifetime to a man she did not love. Nicholas was quick to order the solution, but it was not necessary for Carl had been there before, and knew exactly which path to take this time around.

Olivia had delivered the first mistake armed with four brown towels, a plastic bag, toy dog bone, books on childbirth from the library, and a bottle of cherry brandy courtesy of Mr. Rey and his unlocked liquor cabinet.

Carl's labor had begun conveniently early one Saturday evening, just eight months after the cemetery encounter with the devil's entourage. A movie was the decoy, and the girls hastened instead for a quiet, private place for the birth: the reflecting gardens near the Baptist church. Carl sculled the brandy, and bit hard on the dog bone when the pain came. She made no sound during the three hours it took for the baby's head to appear, with the silence broken only by Olivia whispering, "It's here". Olivia used a washer to clear its nose and mouth as explained in the books then pulled the shoulders gently until the rest of it slipped out. "It's a boy," she announced, cutting the cord. She wrapped the child in a towel and handed it to Carl. Olivia readied a plastic bag for the placenta while Carl held the baby on her stomach without looking down. "What are you going to call him?" Olivia asked.

"Nothing."

"Nothing? That's a strange name."

Olivia placed the bag with the dark red mass and cord into the towel with the baby then wrapped them both in another towel. She stepped out from behind the shrubs and checked for walkers before darting across the lawn to the parish house. She rapped at the door, left the bundle on the doormat, and returned to the shrubs to observe. A collared man answered the call, and rushed the baby inside. He returned a short while later to scan the darkness for a mother while his wife packed their sedan for a trip to the hospital.

The newspaper the following day, front page, had a story about an abandoned baby. It urged the mother to come forward for medical attention with assurances about immunity from consequences. Police visited Carl's high school and interviewed ten girls identified as possible mothers by way of reputation, and or recent weight gain. No one considered Carla Baden, the quiet, studious girl who was not significant on any one's radar.

While Carl had relegated the moment to the recesses of her mind along with the baby's conception, Olivia would not let it rest: she needed to be sure Nothing had found a good home. For the next few months, she monitored the christening announcements in The Maine Times, trying to identify an adopted son then gave up when the task seemed to be absent an outcome. Carl hoped Nothing would surrender with as much ease should he one day decide to find his birth mother for explanations.

Forty-one

June 1993

DESPITE having implanted the problem, Nicholas did nothing to assist with its resolution except to reiterate that there was only one option. He did not travel to Sydney with Carl for the procedure or contribute to the costs, or offer a hand to hold before, during, or after the event. It was Olivia at the Maine Railway Station to meet Carl upon her return while Nicholas surfed on the north coast.

The relationship had died of natural causes, but Carl still found herself naked in the back seat of her Morris Minor clinging to a cardigan. Nicholas had stretched out his six-foot frame with his legs atop the bench seat in front. His jewels dangled between his thighs and settled on the vinyl seat. He lit a cigarette, and blew white rings into the chilled air.

"I think we should break up," he said.

They sat for a while shrouded in smoke, and soothed by the gentle hiss of tobacco leaves burning then Nicholas fell asleep. Carl dressed, and moved to the front seat.

The engine turned after several attempts, and after some coaching, spluttered backward before limping forward for a solitary drive back into town. The windshield wipers struggled as dark clouds released a deluge, sapping the engine of its power, and causing the headlights to flicker. Carl switched off the heating, and took comfort in the rain and the banal scrape of the wipers.

As she approached the railway crossing, the Morris fought hard to challenge the slight incline to the tracks then stopped as required at the sign. Carl looked right and left, and moved forward off the thick white line. The Minor skipped across the first steel track, but stopped before the second. Carl beat the steering wheel with her palms then rested her forehead on the sheepskin cover. They were over, at last.

A bright light in the distance interrupted the accedence. Carl stared into it, mesmerized by the round spotlight of falling rain. A horn blared out, and she hurried to restart the engine. The second attempt failed as did the third, and several more that followed. For the sixth attempt, she switched off every drain on the engine, with no success. Nicholas slept on, despite the repeated warning from the oncoming train and the bright light that filled the Minor. Carl sobbed while forcing the gear shaft into first, and by accident, found neutral. The car rolled backward off the track and down the incline as the train sped past with a high-pitched wail to signify the driver's irritation. Despite being seconds from a crushing death, Nicholas slept on.

Panic faded, and Carl took a full breath. She saw a headline: lovers' suicide pact or murder suicide. They would have interviewed the traumatized train driver. Work colleagues and friends would have commented on the relationship, and many would have presumed to know the source of such a dramatic ending.

Carl cried, alone, in the dark, and another of her life rules broke.

Forty-two

November 1993

FRIDAY nights brought a reason to drink with abandonment as it followed a week governed by discipline and resolve. By Friday, the stress of working too closely with Nicholas Segher, partner-in-waiting, took its toll, and relations deteriorated further when a fiancée arrived from Sydney. The woman had been on his scene for many years, on and off, and there was some ambiguity about the dates for the 'off' period. Carl pretended not to care, and announced a life-long emancipation from the institution of marriage. It was not a revolutionary act as it would have been three decades earlier when a distant aunty had done likewise. Maine had changed somewhat in the intervening years, with liberal views from an influx of outsiders unsettling its staid waters, but marriage and motherhood still reigned as preferred life choices for any woman.

And so she came to be at another function at WTV9 for Olivia's sake, this time to celebrate the departure of Colleen McGlashen, weather-girl, who by fulfilling the town's mantra was making way for Olivia's star. The time spent at the gathering would at least fill the daylight hours until The Casa opened, but when Colleen asked Carl about her plans for motherhood, the evening closed in earlier than expected.

"You won't be complete without one of these," Colleen had replied, rubbing her swollen abdomen more. Before responding, Carl had glanced at Olivia, received a nod, then announced that she had been 'completed' twice and undone on both occasions, and was more complete now without a man or child, and by the way, she added, "I'm gay".

Olivia followed Carl through the function room to the car park, feigning apology while a smile revealed satisfaction as a trail of stupefied co-workers fell in their wake. "I'll tell everyone on Monday that you're mentally unstable," she said, "although they've probably worked that out for themselves."

"I feel refreshed," said Carl.

"And when did you decide to become gay."

"I don't know. Just seemed like a good thing to say at the time."

"You could say Nicholas turned you gay. That might even dent his ego."

"I doubt it." Carl smiled. "It's a bit early for The Casa. There won't be anyone there."

"Perfect!" said Olivia. "You're just not that good with people."

They arrived at The Casa around eight, had their wrists stamped, and charged through the entrance not expecting to find anyone inside let alone on an exit.

"Oops," said Carl as she slammed into a torso. "You're leaving *already*? Early to bed, they say. Makes you healthy, wealthy, and...boring."

The man smiled, and kept on his way.

"No wonder you can't attract anyone decent," said Olivia staring after the man as he stepped into the elevator. "I wasn't expecting him to be so spindly."

"Who?"

"Ethan Marsh, the triathlete. Don't you read the newspaper?"

"Not the back pages and why would you?"

"Pictures, Carl, nice bodies on sporty, successful types."

"He probably *is* going home to bed," said Carl. "That's abnormal."

"Proof that exercise is bad for you. Who in their right mind would miss Friday night in Maine to get up at some un-Godly hour to run and swim and…that other thing they do."

"Who indeed," said Carl.

"This place is pitiful with the lights on," said Olivia. "I need a drink, and look—no one at the bar!"

They sat down in the dimmest of the bright corners. "We're pathetic losers," said Olivia. "And it's your fault, again, Carl Baden."

"Here's to us," said Carl raising her glass. "Never thought I'd say this, but bring on the strobe lights!"

Carl rose late Saturday morning for a coffee-only breakfast and newspaper on the back steps. The Maine Times had a front-page photo of a car wreck with a surfboard atop the BMW eerily still intact. Two had died, the article said, and the driver was most likely asleep when the vehicle veered into a coasty rail. The first victim, a successful litigation lawyer at Rey, Carol & Mendelson, had died on impact and his fiancée some hours later. Mr. Rey, senior managing partner at the firm, expressed deep sorrow, and sympathies for the man's family. The deceased was well respected, well liked, and was soon to be admitted as a partner of the firm. His beautiful fiancée, a successful property lawyer, had only recently relocated to Maine from Sydney. The couple was expecting their first child, and had plans to marry on Valentine's Day.

The coffee mug fell then shattered. Carl had hoped they might reconcile eventually to work more amiably together, although a future friendship was highly unlikely given their disparate views of the world, and the lingering animosity that rose when alcohol induced it.

She recalled that last night with Nicholas as she drove home in the rain while he slept. Fate had intervened, for they did not die on the railway tracks with a car wreck as a tomb. It was a time to die for Nicholas Segher, but it was not a time to die for Carla Baden. Another clock ticked for her.

Forty-three

February 1994

CARL'S preoccupation with mortality following the death of Nicholas had become tiresome for everyone, and debilitating for her. She wondered if it was possible to renegotiate the time and date of death, and if learning a belated lesson could postpone it. People miraculously survived accidents and illnesses beyond all odds, and there must have been a reason they did not go when it seemed they should. Perhaps a guardian angel could intervene on one's behalf, and amend the plan that God had written.

Nicholas, Carl learned after the event, had not kept their relationship as secret as she had thought. It seemed most everyone at the firm knew about the baby and the abortion, and this explained the level of sympathy that came her way. Similar levels of pity had tailed her when the fiancée had turned up, but Carl had not seen it, and this was more a reflection on her than on Nicholas: her ignorance, the power of oblivion, and her total disconnect.

Carl had hoped Matthew would return to Maine after his stint with CNN in Atlanta, but he chose Bosnia instead, telling

Helena he had accepted a desk job in London. On doing so, he immersed Carl in the deceit, and she was the one who had to maintain the lie on a daily basis.

Olivia was in love with Jacob Naylor, the program director at WTV9. Carl hoped it was short-lived, like all the others, and did not try to understand Olivia's interest in a man so shallow his status and wealth were visibly important.

Worse still, Walter Garson had moved into Orchard Road. Helena seemed happy in relative terms to have a man's affection and attention, and clearly, character was not important.

A pile of new files fell into Carl's in-tray from a theatrical height, bringing her back from reflection. "We're in another fine mood today," she whispered as her secretary stormed away. Carl shook her head. At least she could say, in her own respect, that her moods were consistently sullen and did not sway so violently.

Carl opened the first file, *Marsh purchase from Hayes*, and for once, her interest piqued. Ethan Marsh, triathlete, had contracted to buy a bungalow on the shores of Maine's sapphire-colored lake. Carl wrote instructions for her secretary to conduct the relevant searches, and prepare the initial letter, which concluded as usual, with an invitation for the client to contact her at any time. She placed the file in her outbound tray, sighed heavily, and repeated the process four more times, wishing for once, a file might offer a challenge or a fight for justice.

Olivia called again to entice Carl away from the humdrum for a weekend in Newcastle. It was part of her male management strategy for Jacob, with absence, suspicion, and jealousy intended to generate an engagement ring. Carl agreed, also for male management purposes: Walter Garson's presence in her childhood home was driving her nuts.

The girls caught the Saturday morning train to Newcastle, checked into their hotel, and wasted no time suiting-up for a coconut oil basting at Nobbys Beach.

They baked for a while in the morning sun then had lunch at the wharf. In the afternoon, they slept from the excesses of food, wine, and heat, and in the evening, they crawled from club to club, before collapsing into bed at 4AM.

A high-pitched, repetitive buzz from the room next door woke them two hours later, and Olivia ran around the room screaming, "Fire! Fire!"

Carl pounded on the joint wall. "Turn that bloody thing off!" she yelled. With no effect, she called reception, and a hotel employee reported after some investigation that there was no one in the adjoining room, but a prior occupant had set the alarm for six. He apologized for the inconvenience.

"Probably someone's idea of fun," said Carl falling back into bed.

"My head hurts," said Olivia.

"Try sleeping up the other end of the bed," said Carl. "The centrifugal forces aren't as bad there."

Olivia moved as suggested. "I think it's working," she said after a few minutes.

Carl smiled and returned to sleep.

Rhythmic banging against the wall from the other adjoining room woke them a couple of hours later.

"We may as well get up," Carl groaned. "This is ridiculous."

"Oh, my head," said Olivia as the rising cacophony from next door reached its crescendo and died.

They packed their suitcases by throwing everything in at random then dropped the cases at the concierge desk for storage. The foreshore beckoned, where a triathlon was in progress.

"It's the local boy," said Olivia as the leaders emerged from the ocean to sprint along the esplanade to the bike transition.

"Not too shabby," said Carl.

They watched for a while sweating with the masses, until empty stomachs and aching heads demanded sustenance and cover from the sun.

They laughed a lot that afternoon in honor of ten years of

friendship, dining alfresco on the beach with the Pacific gently pushing the last of the swimmers into its shore. Carl recognized the occasion also as a farewell, and the last time they would be together in this way: Olivia was following the mantra, and before long, priorities would change, and a cherished friendship would become a subject for reminiscing, like what had become of Tulip.

It would be different if Carl could like Jacob in the slightest way, but time spent in his presence was not manageable, even though the alternative meant a life without Olivia. The thought was painful, and Carl wanted to cry.

"I know I've said this before," she began, "but thank you for doing what you did for me. If it wasn't for you, I don't know what I would have done."

"Do you ever think about him, Carl, and what you'd do if he came looking for you?"

"No, and he won't come looking for me—he doesn't even know who I am. No one does. I would have to declare myself as the mother, and they would have to connect me to the baby. I can tell you that that is *never* going to happen."

"Never say 'never'," said Olivia. She raised her glass. "To best friends, forever."

"To best friends, forever." Goodbye my friend, Carl thought. I wish you everything.

Forty-four

March 1994

HELENA had wrist burns. Carl said nothing: the problem had no words since nothing would change how Helena viewed Walter Garson. At least the weekend away with Olivia had displaced some of Carl's melancholy, and she tried not to picture what had happened at Orchard Road during her absence.

The poster on her wall was the same, but she was able to see it now from a new perspective. 'I asked of life, what have you to offer me? And the answer came, what have you to give?' At fourteen, Carl had thought the words meant that life was about affordability. Now though, she understood the message: she had to put the past to rest, and live her life rather than exist, and only then would gifts flow her way.

She had been to the cemetery three times since that night she lay bleeding on the grave of Kelly Anne Travis. Each time she had been there—for the burial of Brian, William, and Grandma—Carl had made a point of keeping her back toward Kelly not wanting to remember. The plan, to recess the memory in a box bound with string locked in the outposts of

195

her mind, had not worked indefinitely as Carl had hoped. The time had come to confront the truth, and let it go.

Kelly's gravesite was not so formidable on an autumn morning with the sky blue, grass green, and the air scented by honey. Carl stared down at the concrete slab, and saw her young frame splayed across it, screaming, unable to comprehend what was happening. It was the dominant memory of her childhood, and it had displaced anything good, if there was in fact anything good worth remembering. Ten years had passed yet the smells lingered, and the fear, and it was easier when she believed they were demons, as reality brought shame with it.

She stopped by the graves of William and Brian and felt nothing, as if the skeletons below the well-tendered dual plot did not share her DNA. She could not remember a time before their deaths, just the aftermath.

Helena spent a lot of time at the graves talking to her sons, still giving them life like breast milk for a stillborn. If somewhere on their paths, they had encountered a U-turn, and lived, perhaps then, Walter Garson would not have moved into Orchard Road to wield so much power so easily over a broken spirit.

Their father no longer returned for the deathly anniversaries as he had done for years, because his new wife kept him away from such sorrowful pursuits. Carl knew Baden men better than that, and knew that the rot continued on the inside unabated.

Olivia announced her engagement to Jacob Naylor, which did not come as a surprise, but was still a dagger to the heart. It was worse for Mr. Rey, as the wedding would cost him an arm and a leg, but he accepted this with much love, happiness, and pride.

Carl was not thrilled with the role of maid-of-honor and all it entailed: in particular, the close proximity to Jacob Naylor for nine hours or so, and the gown search. As one would expect with Olivia, the search would not begin in any bridal salon in Maine, but on the stretch in Double Bay where designers presented their creations in glorious showrooms.

Olivia had wanted six bridesmaids, but settled for four, as this was all Jacob could muster for his side of the party. They would wear bronze crinkled organza dresses, and Carl was grateful at least for the absence of pink, lace or fluff, but matching shoes seemed gaudy.

Without giving a reason, Carl left the bridal entourage to visit Mr. and Mrs. Segher who lived in Woollahra not far from Double Bay. She thought to call first to announce her pending arrival, but had no introduction.

A shiny black Victorian door opened to a well-dressed woman with her hair styled, and her face conservatively made-up. She looked as one might if they were going for brunch at a classy restaurant, but was instead just home for the day. Before Carl could find her name, the woman started to cry, and a similarly stylish man came to the door. They ushered Carl inside.

On a classic French provincial buffet, one photo explained the reception: of Nicholas and Carl, and another work colleague who had posed with them for the firm's propaganda portfolio. Carl had come for healing, to confess, apologize, and move forward. She expected hostility and for her news to shock, but Nicholas had been before her, and nothing much needed saying.

She learned though that the fiancée, who was not on display in the silver frames, was not the daughter-in-law of choice since a series of break-ups in a long history painted a grim picture of the future. The pregnancy, not declared until after three months had passed, had forced Nicholas to accede one last time. Her father, an esteemed member of the judiciary, also contributed to the decision. And although they yearned for their son's child so Nicholas could live on, they respected that Carl had not entrapped him in a similar way.

Carl left with the peace she was looking for, and much more, although she could not reconcile the son the parents knew and her own experience.

The Marsh file had been straightforward so no reason had arisen for Carl to call her client during the conveyance. As firm practice dictated, she donned a jacket, and strode to meeting room two to finalize the matter with Ethan Marsh.

It was routine: a handshake, introduction, congratulations on the purchase, here's the final account, and thank you for choosing Rey, Carol & Mendelson.

"We've met before," he said.

"Ah, yes," she said. "I believe so."

"You called me a bore." He smiled.

"Lovely position, the bungalow. You're lucky the developers haven't pillaged that area, yet," she replied handing him the keys.

He smiled. "Thanks."

Carl escorted him to the exit, they shook hands again, and that was that: an anti-climactic encounter at best, and why she felt let down by it, she did not understand.

Forty-five

March 1995

THE marriage of Olivia Rey to Jacob Naylor was imminent, and as chief bridal liaison, Carl had no interest in a primary duty to coordinate a night out for the hens. Fortunately, Olivia, or more correctly, Jacob, was specific on the ambit of the final hoorah: no male strippers flinging G-strings and thrusting pelvises where they did not belong. That narrowed options considerably.

Olivia chose a Mexican night complete with tequila, salsa, and a clothed, yet navel-touching, hip swirling Latin dance instructor who offered far more intimacy than a mere stripper. At midnight, the entourage moved on to the KOKO, a new nightclub in town, to test their new moves on the unsuspecting.

Jacob lurked in the shadows, unnoticed by Olivia, but spotted by Carl who reported him immediately. Olivia responded, cavorting on the dance floor with a bevy of young men in tow who clearly appreciated her hip gyrations. Jacob left in disgust, and Carl strode to the bar for more champagne to celebrate the victory.

At the perimeter of the bar queue, outwards four-deep, she came across Ethan Marsh pressed up against a pillar with a girl in a gold dress hard against his body.

"Oh, *please*," said Carl as she passed. "You have a bungalow, use it."

When she returned from the bar with a tray of champagne and glasses, Ethan Marsh was breathing without assistance albeit still draped in the girl with the gold dress. He nodded an acknowledgement.

"Passed your bedtime, isn't it?" said Carl.

"Retired," he replied.

"And making up for lost time by the look of it," she said flicking a glance at the gold dress.

He smiled, and stepped aside to allow her to pass.

Olivia wore a dress suitable for a princess as expected, with layer upon layer of tulle forcing Jacob to jostle for position next to his wife, keeping him an extra distance away from Carl on the bride's other side.

Walter did not accompany Helena to the wedding: he was away on business, but word had filtered through that he was sporting a black eye arising from a road rage incident in the city. Aaron, Carl's boyfriend, stepped in as an escort.

Aaron was the antithesis of everything Carl thought she might want in a partner: non-lawyer, finance type with a ripped body and power walk that contradicted his lack of confidence. Neither side of him appealed, but Carl had come to appreciate from recent trials and revelations that she needed to reconnect with other humans, and Aaron made himself available.

It was a mistake, but Carl had yet to find a way to end the hapless merger of incompatible beings. Olivia's suggestion had a lot of merit: become uncontactable.

As soon as the bride and groom had left the reception, Carl changed into jeans to join the rest of the bridal party at the KOKO to drown her post-nuptial blues. She did not notice Ethan Marsh as she queued at the bar.

"What's with the hair and Pinocchio face?" he asked when she returned with a drink.

"My best friend just married a penis head," she replied.

"Oh, that's charming," he said with a laugh.

"Where's your girlfriend?" Carl asked.

"What girlfriend?"

"The one you were making out with last week, *in public.*"

"I have no idea what you're talking about, Ms. Baden."

"It's Carl."

"Carl? That's a girl's name?"

She sculled her drink, and fell forward against his torso. He moved a bar stool in her direction. "Here," he said, "have a seat. What are you drinking, Carl?"

"Southern Comfort."

"And?"

"Ice."

"That explains a lot," he said. "Stay on that stool if you can. I'll be right back."

"Are you trying to get me drunk?"

"I think you managed that all by yourself. I'll be back."

Carl woke, sat up in bed, and gazed around the unfamiliar setting. "Oh, oh," she muttered. "Yikes."

Ethan Marsh entered the room. "Coffee?" he asked, offering her a mug.

Carl clutched a white sheet to her breasts, and leaned back into the mass of white pillows that covered the mahogany bedhead with the coffee mug clasped tight in her hands.

He sat down in a dark brown wicker chair filled with more white cushions, and rested his feet on a matching stool. Sheer white curtains blew inward on a cool breeze, the French doors to the timber veranda pushed open to present the lake in its glory. Waves slapped at the pebbled shore, just feet away from the bed.

"Who's Walter?" he asked.

"Walter?"

"Is he your boyfriend?"

"Good God no! He lives at our house, with my mother. Why?"

"Last night, you were begging me not to take you home to Walter."

"*Begging*? I doubt that."

"You were."

"So you took advantage of me."

"*Me*, take advantage of *you*? I carried you in when you fell over on the driveway. I tucked you into *my* bed, then the next thing I know, you're on top of me on the sofa."

"And?"

"You have to ask? I'm not superhuman, and you're actually quite likeable when you're not talking."

They sipped a while in quiet.

"I love what you've done with the bungalow," she said. "You must have had a decorator."

He laughed. "My mother. It's plantation style apparently."

"Very nice. How did you manage to afford your own place when you've never had a real job?"

"Sponsorships mostly." He paused. "How did you get that scar on your cheek?"

"Fell off my tricycle."

"You must have been going pretty fast."

"Yeah, I was."

"How about a morning swim?" he asked.

"In the lake?"

"No, the bathtub. Of course the lake."

"Oh no, I don't swim anywhere I can't see the bottom."

"You're joking, right?"

"No, I'm not...and I'd better be getting home anyway. Mum will be worried about me."

"What about dinner tonight?"

"Thanks, but I don't go out on a work night."

"It's *Sunday*, and what are you, twelve?" He laughed.

"Sunday classifies as a work night."

"What about Saturday night? I'll cook."

"You can cook?"

"*Yes, I can cook,*" he replied.

"OK, OK," she said. "Never had a guy cook for me before. I guess there's a first time for everything."

Forty-six

March 1995

ETHAN Marsh had never cooked a meal, not even for himself. He still dined most nights at his parents, and when he did eat at home, it involved a microwave or a toaster. Preparing a meal with courses, for a woman, and one as querulous as Carl Baden, would be an achievement, if that were the plan.

Mrs. Marsh spent the day on set-up duties for her only son: cleaning, arranging flowers, making the cheesecake for dessert, preparing the lamb and vegetables for roasting, and the tomato soup for blending. Just prior to the guest's arrival, the homemade bread would be placed in the oven, and the heating and blending of the tomato soup would take place with the guest present. Cookery books with the relevant pages tagged, decorated the kitchen bench.

Carl arrived right on seven with two bottles of vintage red wine recommended by Mr. Rey.

"Two bottles?" he asked, answering the door with a tea towel over one shoulder. "Are you going to take advantage of me, again?"

"*One* bottle is for dinner, and the other is a *gift* for you. Anyway, I don't make the same mistake twice."

"No bow, no gift wrapping? Surely, if it is a gift…"

"My grandfather had a rule about dating sportspeople. Clearly, he was one smart man."

Ethan ushered her inside to follow the waft of baking bread down the hallway.

"Take a seat," he said, indicating a barstool right in front of the blender. "Looks like expensive wine. You realize it's probably wasted on me."

"Here, I'll open it," she said taking the corkscrew from his hands. "It smells great in here. I'm already impressed."

He poured the tomato soup from the saucepan into the blender as instructed by his mother.

"Don't forget the—" Carl began, as tomato soup swirled around the inside of the blender rising quickly to the top.

"Have you *never* used a blender before?" she said wiping soup from her eyes.

He peered into the glass crevasse. "Don't worry, there's still some left for dinner."

She shook her head. "I need a shower and a shirt, a *clean* shirt, not something you went running in this morning."

"Certainly, madam, allow me to organize that for you. Shower is this way."

"You're an imbecile," she said as she passed him in the hallway.

When Carl returned to the kitchen in an oversized t-shirt, tomato soup still dripped from his hair, but candles cast a soft glow over a bowl of orange roses in the center of a small, square table.

"It's good," she said tasting the soup.

He smiled. "Wait 'till you see what I cooked up for dessert."

PART IV

April 1996 – July 2005

Forty-seven

April 1996

DIAGONAL rain fell non-stop for six days, but by Saturday, the easterlies had calmed making umbrellas useful again. Carl's bridal gown was plain, champagne silk satin with a sweetheart neckline, an empire waistline, with no sleeves, frill, jewel, embroider, bow, or accoutrement of any kind, initially. The simplicity of the dress and all other wedding arrangements, disappointed Helena, which disappointed Carl, ergo, the bare bodice was subsequently hand beaded, and a Mantilla veil added to cover her bare head. Olivia was also in an empire gown as the matron of honor, but hers was a fuller version with flowing chiffon covering her expansive bulge.

With reluctance, Carl reinstated all other discarded wedding traditions for Helena including the bridal waltz, tiered wedding cake, and speeches, but refused point-blank to spend the wedding night in a bridal suite with rose petals scattered senselessly across a circular bed.

Matthew returned for the wedding, with permanent souvenirs from his assignment in Bosnia: physical and mental. Two members of his crew had died in an attack on their vehicle as they traveled toward Mount Ozren to cover the fighting, and two more lives were lost in pursuit of the truth. He had changed, and Carl was unable to number the many ways how, but the greater burden he had found beyond the perimeter of Maine, seemed to lift him and bring him down at the same time.

Michael and Andréa sent their regrets, having only just moved to the RAAF Support Unit Butterworth in Malaysia. Her father's absence would allow for the dispensation of another tradition Carl did not want: the ceremonial walk down the aisle. She wanted to enter the church via a side door with Ethan, but surrendered again to enter at the egress accompanied by the bridal march. Matthew stepped in for the giving away, also under duress, and together they rushed down the aisle like two bulls at a stampede, amusing only the groom.

The wedding reception was also a subdued affair, particularly when compared to Olivia's gala event the year before. Ethan's friends, fellow triathletes, were nodding off by ten any place comfortable, as were the friends of Mr. and Mrs. Marsh, and when the retirement home bus arrived, the hall emptied by half.

Carl drank water all evening so as not to disgrace the bridal fraternity as she had done at Olivia's wedding, ensuring the evening was a tedious one. Still, they were the last to leave at midnight with no one left to form a human archway, as was the plan.

The newly-weds returned to the bungalow. Carl was quick to strip away the bridal regalia in favor of a tracksuit, and tame her over-coiffed straw hair in a baseball cap. Ethan handed her the Veuve Clicquot and flutes then pushed the dinghy from the water's edge. Oars tapped at the black surface until they eased into the center of the lake. Ethan secured the oars to work on the champagne bottle. A stubborn cork finally burst free, hurtling into the moonlight to land on the moon's reflection causing a mini whirlpool.

"To you, Mrs. Marsh," he said, and held his gold-rimmed glass into the air.

"And to you, Mr. Marsh."

They settled on the dinghy floor with Carl lounged against Ethan's chest.

"I never had a tricycle," she said.

"Oh, what a deprived childhood you had," he said with a laugh.

"It's not how I got this scar, Ethan."

"I figured that."

"You never said anything."

"It doesn't matter."

"I need to tell you the truth."

"OK," he said. "But if you were in a gang or something, I probably don't need to know about the dead bodies."

Carl took a deep breath, exhaled, and nestled further into his chest. She sipped twice then began the recollection.

He stroked her scar and kissed her cheek. "I'm going to buy you a tricycle," he said, "with streamers and a basket. You can ride to work."

"I'd like that."

"Let's go for a swim!"

"Oh, no," said Carl peering over the side. "I can't see the bottom."

Ethan stripped, and star jumped into the dark abyss resurfacing a short time later. "Come on in, baby!" he called out.

"Isn't it cold?"

"No, not at all. Come on!"

"Oh, all right," she mumbled, removing her clothes. She pinched her nostrils, jumped, and screamed on impact.

"Refreshing, eh?" he said.

"Oh my God! It's freezing!"

"I think I've lost my manhood."

"I married a crazy man," she said, and their laughter pealed around the lake.

The honeymoon plans were as simple as the wedding: a week at the bungalow with time for Ethan to develop his new venture as a sports psychologist. His focus was on children, and their coping mechanisms for the pressures of competition and parental expectation—something he had not experienced, but had witnessed often.

His parents had never placed a pressure upon him to be anyone or do anything. They were grateful enough by their mid-forties to finally have a child, and rather than smother, they enabled a free mind and spirit.

Carl woke at two on the third morning of their marriage, and stretched an arm across an empty pillow. She sat up, and found Ethan on the veranda gazing out over the lake.

"What are you doing?" she asked.

"Waiting for you to wake up. Let's go!"

"Where?"

"Coolangatta. If we leave now we can be there for breakfast."

"Oh my God." She resumed a sleeping position and wrapped a pillow around her head.

"Come on, you can bring that with you."

"OK," she sighed. "This marriage thing is harder than I thought."

"Get up, Carl," said Ethan pulling the bed linen off his wife. "We're going for a drive!"

They packed for a few days, loaded up the sedan, and drove away. Carl curled into the front passenger's seat with a pillow against the window and a blanket tucked around her lap. Ethan chattered incessantly, and Carl feigned sleep hoping to encourage a silence that never came. She sat up and stared through the windscreen splattered with insects to see and feel what Ethan described. There were trees topped with the faint glow of a timid moon, and the smell of Eucalypt blew fresh through a half-mast window. The engine hummed, a warmth rose from the floor, and the momentum of tires over bitumen did induce calm. He was quiet at last, but just for a few minutes so Carl could absorb the resplendence. He went on to describe another scene still ahead of them, of sand, still cold from the night, sipping latte from paper cups, and eating bagels with cream cheese while the sun rose on a new life.

Forty-eight

April 1997

THEIR first anniversary arrived as if a month had passed. Ethan was up early to drag Carl from the comfort of a warm bed to the driveway where his gift waited for unveiling.

"Open!" he called out, and Carl removed a stretched football sock from her eyes. "Happy anniversary, baby!"

"A bike? What happened to paper?"

"What did you get me?" he asked.

"A tool box." She paused. "How come there are two of them?"

"One for you and one for me."

"But you already have three bikes."

"*Racing* bikes, Carl. These are *mountain* bikes. Come on! Get changed. I've packed our knapsacks for the day."

"For the *day*!"

"Didn't you hear me? They're *mountain* bikes. They're not for little family fun rides around the park."

"I just wanted a tricycle," she whimpered.

It was not so bad out on that first day. Ethan took her to hidden places with pristine waterholes and majestic waterfalls, and Carl saw Maine as the diamond her mother said it was.

They rode every Sunday morning from then on, setting out at an hour too ridiculous for Carl, but the best time of the day according to Ethan. Each ride was longer than the week before: more intensive, sweatier, and dirtier, progressing from beaten track to path-less terrain where kangaroos roamed and the threat of snakes and other killers increased exponentially. The sixth Sunday would be Carl's last, after an encounter with one such killer.

Her bike came to an abrupt stop as if she had collided with a wall, and when she looked up, a yellow and black mass in a vast web that spanned the distance between two trees, was just a nose tip away. She screamed, causing a vibration in the silk weaving and eight legs shifted aggressively in response. Carl wheeled backwards in haste, lost control, and fell to the ground on top of her bike. She screamed more wondering what sinister form lurked in the grass beneath ready to crawl through the spokes. Ethan backtracked from the higher, rockier ground Carl wished she had followed, pedaling at record speed through the scrub.

"Where are you?" he screamed. "Carl!"

"I'm here!"

Ethan dropped his bike while the pedals still spun, and bent down to lift Carl from the long grass. "What happened?"

She pointed at the web.

"It bit you?" He searched her arm for signs of swelling.

"No," she sobbed. "I nearly rode straight into it."

"You *nearly*?" He stood and inspected the spider more closely. "You *nearly* rode into this harmless garden spider?"

"What if it had *jumped* on me?" she cried.

"Come on, up you get. You're all right." He helped Carl to stand, picked her bike up with one hand and coaxed her on to it. "There's a stream up ahead. You can have a swim while I cook."

"You can't cook! You're a fraud!" she yelled after him, wiping tear soaked dirt from her cheeks.

"I can cook this. It's my specialty," he called back.

"I'm not riding anymore, ever," she said as she wheeled her bike along the designated path. Up ahead, an oasis came into view through a natural archway.

"Cool your feet in the stream," he said as she dropped her bike on the rocky shore. Carl removed her shoes and socks, and waded thigh-deep into the chilled water where she stayed to watch Ethan pander to the needs of a small fire in a circle of rocks. He cut strips from the curve of four bananas and filled the gaps with squares of chocolate before placing them in the fire until the yellow skins charred and the brown melted.

"That was weird, don't you think?" she said. "That I stopped like that, right before the spider's web."

"Didn't you just see it in time?"

"No, I didn't see it at all, not until I stopped. I didn't stop because I saw it."

"Lucky," said Ethan.

"Do you believe in guardian angels?"

"No," he replied. "Here, bananas are ready."

"Wow," she said after a first bite. "Mrs. Marsh, you hiding behind a tree somewhere?"

"Come on, you saw me cook them," he said with a laugh.

Ethan rode off the next Sunday morning, disappointed, but happy all the same: he could go further, faster, and on wilder terrain without Carl. She stood on the footpath and stared after him as he disappeared into the depths of a perfect autumn morning. She thought to ride after him, but returned to bed. If he was not back by one as promised, she would call 000.

The hour between one and two was frantic as Carl paced from the driveway to the telephone ready to lift the receiver each time before checking the horizon once more. She envisioned Ethan lying in the long grass as she had done, but with cause, most likely a snake bite with no one there to hold him as his body convulsed through the pain. Sergeant Mackelroth was on his way, and all she could do was hope, wait, and pray that the hour passed was not the difference between life and death.

An apparition broke through on the horizon, of Ethan running toward her with a bike over one shoulder. Carl gazed at it until the vision finally collapsed on the gravel at her feet.

"Puncture," Ethan wheezed. "Why are you crying?"

"I thought you were dead," she sobbed laying across his chest.

"Water," he gasped

Carl ran to unravel the garden hose and insert the nozzle into his mouth. He gulped then pushed it away. Carl changed the stream to a spray and showered him in a fine mist. Steam rose on impact.

"Nice," he said.

"Oh, oh," said Carl, as a police car came into view.

Forty-nine

July 1997

LIFE has 180 degrees with the nurturer eventually becoming the nurtured. Helena had needed nurturing for thirteen years, since Brian died, or perhaps it was twenty-three years since she lost her beloved father. Either way, it was a life filled with desertion, and Carl worried about how her mother might respond to another: they were moving to Sydney for Ethan's dream job at the New South Wales Institute of Sport.

Walter's heavy hand still had a tendency to flail, and nothing reasonably could be done about it. A rational, undamaged mind would have evicted him a long time ago, but beatings it seemed were better than aloneness. At Christmas, respite came with the summer heat as Walter left each year for Adelaide to spend it with his adult children and their families. He never asked Helena to go with him, which was curious since she had taken him into her home and family, much to everyone's dismay.

In the weeks before they were to leave, Carl spent all her spare time with Helena including Saturday mornings while Ethan held training camps at the Wallin Oval. It was only then that he came to learn of his connection to the name, and that his bungalow occupied land where a sawmill had burned to the ground one wintry night.

The house that Michael and Helena had built in Orchard Road had morphed slowly over three decades, constrained by money and fluctuating enthusiasm. Mature trees now formed an unassuming hedge to hide the façade, and concrete blocks enclosed the rows of unsymmetrical wooden stilts to provide the lower level with some cover from the elements. A concrete floor buried the playing field where young boys had once raced miniature cars in the dirt, and mud when it rained.

Carl stopped halfway up the back stairs to survey the backyard. The lopsided clothesline had never been the same since Matthew's rotation on it in a homemade harness courtesy of William. In the distance, the hillside, which was the wilderness back then, was a sea of shiny iron and tiled roofs.

As usual, the backdoor was open, and Carl stepped inside with a shiver. The house had an aura about it that evoked emotion even if one did not know its history. The walls did it mostly, covered as they were in photos—split seconds of perfection captured to mold future memories. The albums provided a more focused immersion into images of an idyllic past that contrasted with reality, and this is where one could reliably find Helena.

"This is my favorite," she said, pointing at the portrait of four children in a row, book-ended by a parent. Everyone was dressed in their Sunday best with beaming faces for the camera. In the bottom left corner of the photo, the photographer had captured a brown ear, Basil, the source of the smiles.

Helena had other favorites: of her with her father at the mill, of William and Brian, especially those taken when the boys were young enough to say cheese and laugh with it. The albums were her life, but to Carl, remembrance was like injecting poison into withered veins.

In those final hours before Carl and Ethan were to drive away, Helena's stoic pretense of the previous two months dissolved. And while the furniture van was already southbound, the bungalow tenanted, and jobs confirmed, Carl still had no idea how she would leave, but they did. Walter's presence in the frame did not help.

The drive emphasized that a distance grew, and only a discussion on where they might live in Sydney brought Carl's face outside of a tissue. They would buy a townhouse in the inner west, close to the city so Carl could walk to work in George Street via Darling Harbor for breakfast.

"You missed the turn," she said as Ethan passed the northern entrance into Port Macquarie, their first overnight stop.

"We're making a detour for a little wine tasting," he said with a smile.

"I could certainly use a drink," she whispered.

"That's the spirit, Carl."

They passed through a forest with hundreds of flowering rose bushes, flame trees, and jacarandas, and pulled up not far from the Cassegrain Winery's Cellar Door.

"Your recovery starts now," he said. "Let's go!"

The first counter they approached offered samplings of white wines. Ethan swirled, sniffed, sipped, and spat, as instructed, while Carl swallowed every mouthful.

"This one has passionfruit pulp, green apples, and lime zest with lemon sherbert," said Carl, reading a label. "Sounds healthy."

"You'll like this one," said Ethan moving onto the reds. "Ripe blood plums, vanilla bean, and espresso mingled with earthy tones of mocha and blackberry. The palate is rich and ripe, with fine-grained tannins wrapped around a core of mulberries, licorice, and dark chocolate."

"That's a complete meal right there in that bottle. I don't know why people say alcohol is bad for you."

They progressed through the rest of the cellar, and Ethan decided on six cases of premium wines despite the absence of space in the boot of their car.

"72 bottles?" she asked.

"He was a nice old man," said Ethan. "It's sad to see old people having to work like that. He looked tired."

"He's probably the owner and a multi-millionaire, and besides, he probably enjoys being useful."

"You're probably right. Let's get some food, and roll about on the lawn for a while."

They headed back to the Cellar Door to buy a crusty farmer's loaf, cheeses, olives, and nuts then settled on the lawns in the winery's rose garden. Carl opened the additional bottle of chilled chardonnay, and sipped several times before referring to the label.

"This youthful wine has a lemon color with a vibrant green hue. Its aroma is rich and intense showing green nectarines, grapefruit and honeydew melon with a lashing of lemon zest," she read, sipped and continued. "The palate has a lively core of white-fleshed peaches, figs and honey nougat, and a lengthy mineral finish." She sipped again and shook her head. "I can't taste any of that."

"Carl, you have to swirl the wine around the glass like this to release the aromas." Ethan demonstrated.

"I don't think I need to know the origins of the wine. It's not going to make any difference to my enjoyment of it."

"And that's why I bought 72 bottles," he replied. "Ready for Rydges?"

"Rydges? We're not staying at Rydges. We can't afford Rydges."

"We are, and we can."

"We're supposed to be saving to buy a townhouse, remember?"

"Well, we might not get back this way again, so we should make the most of it."

Carl sighed.

"It feels like a champagne and lobster night, to celebrate our new adventure."

"We'll be lucky if we can afford a bed-sit by the time we get to Sydney."

"That'll do me," said Ethan.

After spending the first week of their yet-to-be-earned wages in one night at Rydges, they set south for Newcastle at midday. Two and a half hours down the coast road, they stopped for fuel, Chicos, Jaffas, and Red Frogs. Carl waited in the car for Ethan to complete the transaction, and waited and waited, then went to investigate the delay. She found him in the cafeteria with a white ticket in his hand.

"What are you doing?" she asked. "You've just had lunch."

"It's not for me," he replied.

"Any more information than that?"

He took her hand, and guided her to the expanse of windows at the front of the service station. Two unkempt boys sat on a barbeque table near the roadside with rolled up blankets and a hand-written sign for Brisbane.

"They only had sixty cents for gum," said Ethan. "And they're very thin. They obviously need a good feed."

"What did you order?"

"Burgers and chips, and some flavored milk, Fantales, and Minties."

"We should give them cash as well," said Carl.

"$50?"

"Will that be enough to get them to Brisbane?"

"I hope so. They should be able to hitch a ride. Shame we're not going that way."

"Yeah, like we have room."

Ethan handed the ticket to the waiter and claimed two large brown bags.

Carl returned to the car while Ethan made the delivery, and chatted with the boys for some time as if they were friends.

"You're a good man, Ethan Marsh," she whispered.

Fifty

December 1997

THEIR new life required little adaptation, despite the disparity that was Maine and Sydney. They lived three miles from the city in a brand new townhouse on the banks of Orphan Creek Gully. From their balcony and across the gully, Carl could see the terrace house in Forest Lodge that she had shared with other students while at university. It had not aged well.

Each morning they set out in opposite directions, but at the end of the day they came together to exchange stories, and drink wine from the Hunter Valley. Dinner arrived in plastic containers or in a box.

Helena came to stay for the first Christmas, wearing long sleeves and upturned collars in spite of the scorching heat. When Carl saw what she tried to hide, the plan took shape— over the next two weeks, she would find a way to extricate Walter Garson from their childhood home and from her mother's life. She wished Matthew were there to perform the ousting, much like the one he had done for Gordon Moore. The key, Carl believed, was to help Helena find some level of self-respecting. Without it, Walter Garson had every right to feel secure with his entrenchment at Orchard Road.

The Get-Rid-Of-Walter program, GROW, would die on the vine if Helena knew Matthew was in hospital in London following four weeks in a Rwandan jail. His detention arose from subversiveness—a loud foreign voice lecturing the government on human right violations was fraught with danger, and Matthew had the scars to prove it. When Carl spoke to him by phone, he said he hoped the scars would never fade as the hatred they instilled in him just drove him on to do more. He had died in the muddy gutter where they had tossed his body with other rubbish after days of incarceration and beatings, but as he sensed his soul rising, something brought him back, and he did not know what. He laughed about it, suggesting the angels had not wanted him up there. Several others had died in the overcrowded cells because the guards had refused to open the doors to allow air to circulate in the stifling heat. They made a mistake in letting him go, Matthew said, or dumping his body more correctly, for their crimes would find a voice in his planned documentary. Much of the writing was already complete, thanks to his compulsory convalescence, and a secretarial service CNN had arranged for him. Carl could hear his anger as he spoke, but then Matthew had always been angry. Now, though, the level of angst exceeded anything she had witnessed previously. Whatever had happened to him, then and now, Matthew was strong and not at all broken like his body. He was not his mother's son. He promised to call again on Christmas Day, and for once, he would actually be in the city he claimed albeit he was in a hospital and not a hotel.

Further Christmas complications arose, thanks to Ethan. Helena had mentioned casually by way of information only that Michael and Andréa now lived in Richmond, thirty miles to the west of their townhouse, and Ethan, not understanding that some families are distant for good reason, made contact and invited them to Christmas day lunch.

It was evident at the outset that Michael had enjoyed quite a few nerve-quelling brews before his arrival, and the diligence of Ethan's hospitality both relaxed and heightened the palpable strain, with Andréa's brow rising as each new can of bitter cracked open.

After lunch, Ethan proposed an excursion to see his second love, and despite a lack of enthusiasm for the idea, they crammed into the Fiat with a sober and reluctant Helena in the driver's seat. Michael grabbed two beers to go, and they motored at a tentative pace toward Birkenhead Point Marina.

The closeness endured during the short journey ensured everyone alighted as fast as Ethan wanted, and in no time, he led the motley crew down to the water's edge to where *Eat My Wash* bobbed in its berth. He owned a quarter share of the yacht, bought impulsively one cool, spring morning while they sipped coffee in the coffee shop that overlooked the marina. In the months since purchase, the four co-owners: Marcus, Joseph, Jim, and Ethan, had become the best of friends.

They all joined a sailing club, and Ethan and Joseph signed up for three courses: an introduction to sailing, Competent Crew, and a spinnaker course, then registered for a further two: the skipper's course, and bareboat charter course. It was all part of a greater plan, not yet announced.

Mrs. Rey had always said that golfing wives were widows, and Carl realized soon enough that sailing wives were no different. There was weekend sailing, mid-week twilight racing on the harbor, and time spent tinkering with all its bits and pieces for maintenance.

Carl did not care for boats, the ocean, harbor, wind, or sails. She did not care to have her skin doused in salt so the midday sun could turn her skin into leather. She did not care for the way the craft tilted on its side, threatening to topple into the ocean as it slid across the water's surface. But she cared that Ethan loved every minute of it, and so she resolved to learn to love sailing, and not abandon it, and Ethan, as she had done with mountain biking.

"That went well," said Ethan, as Christmas day hobbled to a close.

Fifty-one

September 1998

ETHAN, Marcus, Joseph, and Jim met weekly to plan their great escape, and had been doing so for nigh on a year. The details were finally ready for presentation, and a meeting convened at the townhouse for the unveiling.

They gathered in the living room with wives on the sofas and husbands in the center of the room in front of charts, maps, and whiteboards, which hinted at the magnitude of the proposed adventure.

The plan was to sail across the Atlantic from the northwest coast of Africa to the West Indies in June the following year. Timing was critical to avoid hurricanes that required warm seas and calm winds to develop. They would fly directly to Agadir in Morocco then spend some time sightseeing, and provisioning the boat before crossing the Atlantic to Nassau. There was one stopover at the Canary Islands, and if the winds blew favorably, there would be time at the end to sail around the Bahamas. In all, they would be sailing for four weeks, but would have sufficient fuel to motor the whole way if calm winds stymied their plans. This was the fear no one wanted to contemplate as it amounted to defeat.

They were not asking for permission. The presentation was for information purposes only. Robyn and Karenna asked about costs, risks, and safety. Jo said four weeks was too long to have a husband away, and received no response, but continued to challenge the self-approval aspect of the scheme. Carl was just relieved her participation was not required, and had already formulated some ideas on how to spend her free time: in Maine on weekends to re-active GROW. During the week, she would devote more time volunteering at the community legal center and at Youths Off The Streets. She would miss Ethan, for sure, but would never try to stop him from living his dream.

June 2001

The great escape did not proceed as planned in June of 1999, postponed for two years because of interventions: Marcus and Robyn had a baby the first year then the Sydney Olympics in 2000 had Ethan preoccupied. By 2001, the seas were ready and so were they.

Carl started missing Ethan from their fifth wedding anniversary two months before the great escape, and she realized then that for the four hundred and seventy-six hours of his absence, she would need strategies to manage the time or it would pass more slowly.

She enrolled in two sailing courses, and planned to present Ethan with her certificates upon his return, but project B would please him most: find the baby born in the churchyard sixteen years earlier. It was important to Ethan for the child, he said, was part of their lives, and he wanted to know him.

Carl prepared a statement for the Adoption Information Unit detailing Nothing's birth: the Baptist church, the police inquiries at school, and the newspaper reports courtesy of Olivia who still kept a shoebox of memorabilia, including the toy dog bone. Carl submitted to a DNA test and left the matter for investigation. Once her maternity was established, and that could take some time, she could apply for a Supply Authority. The child would then be informed. She did not want to think beyond that point, not without Ethan there to make it less harrowing.

The four travelers arrived in Agadir with no sign of weariness from their journey across hemispheres. They spent the first two days on the African continent discovering Agadir, the port city destroyed by an earthquake in 1960. A modern metropolis of contradiction ascended from those ruins: the streets were wide and lined by unassuming low-rise houses of Western and Arabic influence, with luxury and decay, all molded together. The air was unique and scented by pine, eucalyptus, and tamarisk whirled about on a permanent breeze off the Atlantic azure.

Their inspection of the chartered yacht, *Le Maître de Votre Temps* (Master of your Time), took three hours and tested the hirer's patience. He expected them to divide the checklist amongst the four of them for expediency, but instead, they each undertook a full examination with every item checked and queried four times. Provisioning was similarly precise: food, water, fuel, very few non-essentials, and no alcohol—safety was their primary concern, at least, until they reached the Bahamas. At the suuq of Talborjt, they bought souvenirs to commemorate their once-only adventure, as children were a priority for all of them when they returned home.

The long-range weather forecast was favorable with winds between ten and twenty-five knots—perfect sailing for their first day to La Palma in the Canary Islands. That would be their last stand on land for four weeks, a last chance to call home, and a last chance to celebrate before sobriety came into effect.

They formed two teams to rotate the four shifts each day: six hours on, six off. The night sailing was the ultimate: away from civilization the stars proliferated, the moon seemed closer and iridescent; the black was blacker, and the quiet quieter. A week out of La Palma the winds settled comfortably in the projected range.

Ethan was on watch the night the change came through when a breeze whipped itself into a flurry, upwards to thirty knots. It was of no concern—they all had plenty of experience in similar conditions. Fifty knots though, would be a different story.

When five-zero appeared on the wind gauge Ethan dropped the sails breaking personal and world records. The changed conditions woke the two sleeping crew, and all hands were on deck for the sail to the other side of the tempest.

Le Maître de Votre Temps bobbed about on the white tips like a cork. The waves, forty-five-feet higher crashed down on the bow submerging it before allowing it to re-surface. Their starry guides vanished with the moon now harbored behind clouds.

A side stay, one of four, snapped under pressure causing the mast to plunge into the maddened sea. Jim rushed in the blackness to find the bolt-cutters to sever the remaining stays so the mast could float free before the monstrous swell used it as a battering ram against the hull. He was too late. The mast pierced the hull twice below the water line making sizeable holes for water to surge inwards. Jim pressed on anyway. The once great structure that had risen above the vessel to support the weaker elements: sails, signals, rigging, and booms, lilted across the waves like a twig. The pump quit then after a valiant struggle with the motor unable to function immersed as it was in the enraged Atlantic.

Joseph activated the Emergency Position Indicating Radio Beacon (EPIRB)—its GPS receiver would direct rescuers to their exact location, and the unique serial number would identify the vessel and the hired crew. Rescue was on its way.

Ethan and Jim wrestled with the life raft, at pains to keep control of it for Joseph and Marcus to enter. They did not tie the raft to the wire railing so the sinking yacht would not drag it, and its occupants, to an ocean floor to float like an orange flag above the carnage. Ethan fell on the slick decking, and braced his legs against the stanchions to fight the sea as it tried to rip the raft away. The yacht purged as Jim stepped into the raft, throwing him atop Joseph, and rolling Ethan back into the cockpit. He scrambled to return to the raft, but the wind, gravity, and a violent wash pushed him away. He made it, eventually, only to find the raft was gone. He jumped into the water in pursuit. Of all of them, he had the best chance against the current. Jim, Marcus, and Joseph yelled from the raft to guide him toward them and out of the black wall of water. The safety light on Ethan's vest flickered in and out of sight in the undulating waves. They continued to call his name, but with every stroke, the distance between the raft and Ethan grew, until finally, they could no longer see the light.

Fifty-two

November 2003

THE dead can live, Carl knew from first-hand experience. It had been two years since Ethan had not come home, and she had been dead all of that time. Her life was a riptide—pulling her from a peaceful shore out into another ocean, but not the one that took her love, her life, her reason. She held on to the belief that Ethan was out there, alive on a remote island somewhere, and she envisioned the moment they reunited, how she would hold him and cry. He would be weak, drawn, unshaven, but alive.

All four wives: Carl, Karenna, Jo, and Robyn, had received the embassy call that morning in June 2001. The male voice told Carl about the storm, three survivors, and no search initiated for the fourth man given all the circumstances. He made no mention of Ethan as the missing, as he would have, Carl believed, if that were the purpose of his call. Someone, though, one of them, had lost a husband, and Carl was ashamed to be glad that at least it was not hers, not Ethan.

Karenna and Jo had arrived at the townhouse shortly after the calls. Robyn's absence established for Carl that Marcus was the one adrift, presumed dead. While Carl made coffee Jo explained that Robyn was not present because she was on her way to Cape Town.

Carl shook her head. "What a tragedy," she said.

Karenna and Jo exchanged glances then Jo added that Robyn was on her way to Cape Town to be there for Marcus when the freighter docked.

"Marcus?" Carl had asked. "They found him? I thought they weren't searching…"

"They're not searching, Carl," Karenna had said after the longest while.

"So they're all safe?"

"Ethan…" she heard someone say then china fell onto the Sydney Blue Gum floorboards.

Father Paul officiated at the memorial service held in Maine. There was nothing for Carl to inter, nothing to become dust or ashes, for that was lost in the ocean, or perhaps was still intact on an island somewhere. Father Paul was gracious enough not to say, "I warned you," as he had done, back when he had counseled the two before marriage as was required at that time. Their union, he had prophesized, was high risk, not because they were not suited as a couple, but because their identities had fused already when in marriage, each part must continue distinct and independent of the other. Oneness, he had said, was idealistic and dangerous because when one part dies, the remainder cannot exist alone. Father Paul, Carl concluded, was a prophet, for she would never exist again.

Suicide should not be a sin, she told him after the service, and asked for proof that it was since there was no commandment that said as much. Only God knows how long your life will be, he had replied. It was God's decision, not hers, and it was not for her to play with mortality. It did not matter: she had died though she lived and Sophocles had once said that this was worse than death itself.

Carl finalized the closure of her life: she quit her job, sold the townhouse with the first offer and left Sydney for Maine.

She sold the bungalow to the tenants, and settled back at Orchard Road with Helena and Walter. In the wardrobe, where green skirts, white blouses, and fake tartan ties had hung decades before, she hung Ethan's clothes. Each time she opened the door, she could smell him, and it brought her comfort. She kept his comb and toothbrush on the bedside table, and she touched them every night before sleep hoping to connect with him in his spirit world.

She had no need for her clothes, which stayed packed in a suitcase. She chose instead to live in a white dressing gown in summer and a tracksuit in the winter. She went nowhere, did nothing, and even Walter became invisible.

There were no occasions to break the cycle. Baden family Christmases were historical events and Carl started to remember them as her father did as a cherished time of family unity and happiness—time was a remarkable modifier. Matthew spent all of his in any non-Christian country, preferably one at war, and one with a religious war even better. God was a fiction he said, and the Baden family was cursed. Carl had not subscribed to either theory in the past, but now believed in the curse. There was plenty of evidence through the generations, like the disappearance of Uncle Robert, the burning down of the mill, the death of their grandfather, Brian, William, and Ethan.

The poster on the wall still talked to her, 'I asked of life, what have you to offer me? And the answer came, what have you to give?' She had nothing to give. Everything had been taken.

Carl did not bother to ask God, "why?" for he was not about to descend with an explanation, but she knew Ethan was there, with Him, and not on an island or in a wardrobe in Maine. She had to reach him, and then she might find some healing, perhaps.

Leaving Helena would not be so difficult the second time around—she had chosen Walter and accepted her life for what it was, unwilling or unable to change any part of it.

Carl arrived at the monastery with one suitcase, her life condensed into a single moveable object and half of it taken up with Ethan's clothes. She stood before the decorative iron gates like Orphan Annie, but more abandoned. The cloistered existence she craved was ahead of her, away from the life that persisted even though Ethan had died and no one seemed to notice that he had once walked the Earth. If they had known him, they would understand the futility of it all— the price of fuel and the shortage of bananas.

Sister Mary Catherine ushered her in from the rain. Carl was oblivious to the cold, wet spikes that pricked at her face causing no pain, only relief. The day was late to darken in the summer sky, and Carl was weary with its duration. She would write home when her heart and mind were less fragile.

15 November 2003

Dear Mum

Well, here I am at the monastery, settled into a modest room without trappings, which suits me just fine. I have no need for material things that only make life without Ethan seem even more futile. I feel strange, but then I don't know what normal is, but I do remember pure happiness. They are not the same.

They say it is better to have loved and lost than never to have loved at all, but I don't know – if I had not loved Ethan, I would not know this pain, and it's hard to imagine living the rest of my life feeling this way. If I could end it all, the answer would be different – then yes, it is better to have loved and lost, but what if my life goes on for another fifty years like this? Can there be any way to bear it? I guess I know the answer because I have witnessed your life, twenty plus years of it since Brian and William died. I do not know how you find a way to go on every day, but I understand now, what it has been like for you.

It's been two years since I lost Ethan, and I do not know where the time has gone. I still miss him as if it was yesterday, and I'm sick every time I think of him in that ocean. I try to focus on the good times we had together, but that does not work. All I can do is remember the times that I could have been a better wife, like when I stopped riding with him on Sundays because of a spider. It doesn't seem so big or scary now, compared to my life ahead. Why couldn't I do that for him? I would now. Regret, regret, regret – I hope I never have to regret another thing in my life.

I am glad to be here though, away from civilization, away from stupid people who pretend to understand how a ripped heart no longer feels anything. They do not understand yet they judge me because I cannot go on. Why can't I give up? Don't I have a right to quit my own life? I don't have children who need me, you do not need me – you have Walter. No one is dependent upon me, but life must go on they tell me, like a show. Repetition goes on, rituals go on, routine goes on, but that is not life. I guess this proves the world is full of the living dead and most do not even know it has happened to them.

What seems stranger to me is that every single person will experience losing someone they love more than life, and come to wish they had been a better person because of the pain. If only they could know now, how bad it will be then perhaps their lives now might change. I am ranting again. Maybe I will find peace here, from myself.

We did not talk much these past two years, but I knew I did not need to tell you what was happening in me. It was more to do with him, I think, and here I go again even though I am chastising myself as I write. Why do you need to be with Walter? He treats you so badly, and try as I might, I cannot find a good word to say about the man. Maybe the nuns can help me discover something, anything. Who goes through life saying he, or she, does not need to change? Is this not the purpose of life, to be a better person at the end than you were in the beginning? Does he believe he is perfect in every way? He must. Surely, we are all in need of change. Ethan changed me – I lived in his goodness and wanted to be just like him. I was so calm with Ethan, with no sign of my once mighty Baden temper. Now I have to change again, in another way, to be someone else I don't yet know. The nuns have their work cut out for them, putting this broken soul back together.

I wish we had been able to say a better goodbye, but as usual, he was lurking about, not giving you a second alone with me, or anyone for that matter. I expect he is reading this letter before you get it, if you get it.

I almost did not leave – you looked so sad. If I had one wish, no two, my second would be to put you back together again. Now I feel guilty for putting you second, but no guessing what my first wish would be. Without a wish or two, I cannot begin to think how we might repair ourselves, but I do know you would be better off on your own than with him. It is a shame you cannot see it, and that you are so afraid of being on your own.

I should explain a little about monastery life. My being here must seem odd to everyone who knows me, and I heard it said on the Maine grapevine. It is true I have not been a religious person at all during my life, although I have always believed, so I guess it's fair enough for them to say this is a peculiar decision, but I could not think of what else to do other than more of the same.

Life here is monastic, naturally, which is what attracted me to this place. It is beautifully humble, intensely quiet, and no one is absorbed with the ordinariness of mortal life and its minutiae. I love the seclusion and the people, and I do feel closer to Ethan. I will not recover from losing him, but I hope to find a way to exist without him – I have to, there is no alternative.

Before you ask, no, I do not wear a habit, and I am not a nun and may never be – that is one path too far down the road for me to contemplate. For now, I am a resident, a 'live-in' and going through what is expected to be a lengthy discernment process – not just for me to decide if I belong here, but also for the nuns to decide if I am right for this life. Time will tell, but the fact that I have not yet mentioned God in this letter is somewhat telling. I should have said I feel closer to God being here, and I do, but Ethan as well, mainly.

Anyway, a little more about the life here...we pray in the chapel seven times a *day* – not seven times a *week*! I have prayed more in one week here than previously in my whole life. Holy Mass is the highpoint of each day. There is also a daily exposition of Blessed Sacrament, two hours of contemplative prayer, and we pray the entire Liturgy of the Hours. In between, there are chores – working in the kitchen, infirmary, general cleaning, laundry and sewing, office work, and the part I enjoy most, the gardens and acres of forest and open fields. There is also a lake here, which reminds me of home, although this lagoon does not compare with Maine's gem.

It might all sound quite hectic, but it's not. There's plenty of time for relaxation. It's quite a sight to see the nuns playing volleyball and riding bikes in their habits. There is only one communal television here, which I do not watch – I spent two years stuck in front of one, and would not be bothered if I never watch another minute of it. Study and learning is encouraged, so I plan to get involved helping others learn if I can.

I must go now to evening prayers. Do you have a current address for Matthew? Is he still working for CNN? It is sad that we have all gone to different corners and each living such solitary lives, even you with Walter. I will make an effort to contact Matthew and stay in touch this time. I would like to try to keep what is left of our family intact. It has taken quite a battering over the years.

A plaque hangs above my bed, which says, 'I will lead you into the desert and there I will speak to your heart.' My heart is waiting to hear from God and I hope you hear from Him too.

Love
Carl

30 November 2003

Dear Mum

I was so relieved, and surprised, that you received my letter. I should not be so derisive of your Walter. I do pray to end the thoughts I have of him, and look forward to hearing from you that he has changed for the better, or moved out.

To answer your question, no, I am not angry with God for taking Ethan. I am angry because Ethan is gone and because the world goes on without him, but I do not blame God or anyone. I blame myself for words I wish I could take back. Anyway, it's easy to understand why God would want Ethan. He was such a good, good man. I wanted to be like him and still do – he still touches my life. I used to ask myself, "What would Ethan do in this situation?" and this always led me to say something positive or to do better when I might otherwise have done nothing or worse. I guess now I should be asking, "What does God say I should do?"

I hope the ink does not run on this letter – it is still so hard to speak or write about Ethan and not cry. I must be grateful though for our years together. I was lucky to have had my life blessed in that way. When someone dies, they take something from you, so you can never again be the person you were before they left. You would understand this better than anyone would, and I suppose this is why I am here – to find the person I am with the piece missing. It probably depends on how big the missing piece is. I am trying to learn this much – I am not the only one who has ever lost someone precious.

Mum, you do not become a nun simply by living in a monastery. There are a number of steps in the process and you must be able to show a calling from God into this life. I am still a long way from basking in the glow of that candlelight. I know it, and Sister Mary Catherine knows it too. She is trying to help me, to guide me, but it is so hard when you do not even recognize what is inside of you. I feel an overwhelming emptiness nothing seems to fill. We talk of broken hearts, but the heart is not injured – it does not shrink or scar, as far as I know. The emptiness is not the heart, but the mind for it knows to think incessantly about what has been lost.

I must go to prayer now, but before I go, something has bothered me for the longest time and I need to ask for your forgiveness – when I was in grade six, you came to pick me up from school one day and I walked straight past you directly to the car. I remember you smiled at me and bent down to kiss me, but I strutted past pulling away, not wanting anyone to see me with you, because you were – I have to say it – fat. I'm ashamed that I treated you that way, ashamed that I was ashamed of you, and ashamed that I cared what other kids said about you. For this and anything else I cannot recall, I am truly very sorry. You were, are, the best mother anyone could ask for. Please forgive me.

Good news to hear Matthew will be home soon for a break. It has been a long time since he was back in Maine. I hope I will get to see him and will certainly try to be home at that time. Please let me know the dates as soon as you hear more from him.

Love
Carl

14 December 2003

Dear Mum

I tried to call you yesterday, but you were not at home. I left a message with Walter – I hope you received it.

I continue to work toward settling into the life here. I still feel distant and an abstract part of all that goes on around me. It is as if I am on auto-pilot, just going through the process, attending prayer etc., but I am not really here, if you understand what I mean. Perhaps it will come with time, a sense of true belonging.

I've been working in the monastery office doing administration. It has been two years since I worked, and I must say it is good to be back doing something that requires brain activity although it is not that taxing. I like the routine and organization, but I doubt I could ever be a lawyer again – when I think of myself as such, it is as if it was some other person not me, and such a long time ago, another lifetime. I guess it was.

What are your plans for Christmas this year? Are you going to Adelaide to spend it with his family again? To think it took eight years for him to ask you, and for you to meet his children and grandchildren. I can understand it if you do not want to go after last year, the way his children treated you – as if you are to blame for the dissolution of his marriage. Now I must resist the temptation to think and write why his first wife would have left him, and why you should similarly find a way out. I wonder how long it will take, living here, until such thoughts do not even enter my mind. I wonder if the nuns ever think ill of others or if their thoughts are completely good and pure all the time.

What is the latest with Matthew? Have you heard more from him on when he is due home? If it will not be until after Christmas then perhaps I can arrange for you to come here for a few days should you decide not to go to Adelaide? It would be good for you, a time to think of your own life.

You really should get yourself a computer and email. You are not too old, as you say, and you are still the intelligent businesswoman you were when you were younger. You were quite a trailblazer – getting a business degree back in those days. That was an amazing achievement and you should feel proud of yourself. You should not be afraid of learning something new – you need to keep your mind active, which is fine for me to say after the past two years doing nothing at all. Learning new things is the best way to keep dementia at bay, so they say – not that I think you need to worry about dementia. You've always been so clever with numbers and words.

Each day I go for walks in the bush around the monastery to find a place to read, or attempt to read I should say. I lose concentration so easily, sometimes after a few pages, but often after just a few paragraphs. My mind always turns itself on to Ethan, torturing me with my own loss. I try to dismiss the thoughts and concentrate on the words, but with little success possibly because I do not want to abandon any thought of him in spite of the pain. I guess until I can overcome my mind's power over me I will not recover or perhaps I have not yet found the right book – the one that will take my mind away, absorb me in its story. Maybe I should re-read the books that have absorbed me before like Angela's Ashes and April Fool's Day. If they can capture my mind again, then I'll know the problem is not within me and it might just be the selection of books available in the library here.

I have nothing else to report. Life is uncomplicated. I am happy to be here even though in reality, not much has changed in me. I will call you Christmas Day.

Love
Carl

1 January 2004

Dear Mum

Happy New Year! I hope and pray the year ahead brings you everything you deserve and is one of new beginnings.

I am so sorry to hear about your Christmas in Adelaide and agree – you absolutely should not go again. I cannot understand how or why they could be so cruel. It must have been uncomfortable for you, sitting there while everyone exchanged gifts, ignoring you. Did they at least thank you for the gifts you gave to them and their children? And as if you could afford to spend so much on them, but you did. They could have bought you something small, a token gift, but I guess that was their point. How can they still blame you because he left his wife and moved to Maine long before he met you? They are setting a poor example for their children on how to treat others, but I guess that is the example that was set for them by your Walter. Still, it does not matter how you grew up, but how you grow up.

Christmas here was quiet, and mostly spent in prayer, but it was also a day of celebration.

Have you thought of getting another pet? Another Basil might be all the company you need then you can get rid of Walter. Doctors should prescribe pets for loneliness and depression instead of drugs. If I do not end up staying here, I will definitely get myself a dog, one from the shelter so we can start out on an equal footing. I was not able to care for myself before, let alone a pet, but I have made some progress. Getting away from the real world has helped. The nuns have life in perspective unlike most of us who are just swimming around the goldfish bowl going nowhere in particular. Life with Ethan was not like that. I was soaring on the wings of an eagle before the fall to Earth. I do not expect to fly so high ever again.

Love
Carl

8 January 2004

Dear Mum

I'm sorry to hear your news, well not sorry about the news, but sorry that you are so upset. You are better off without him. Sorry for the cliché, but it happens to be true. I wish I could think of something to say that might console you. It would be nice to be home again with Walter gone, but he will probably be back again soon so please do not cry over him. I pray that you might find the courage to turn him away the next time he comes back – he cannot keep coming in and out of your life as he pleases. How many times can you do this, once a year, every year? It's not healthy, and definitely not good for you. You should have the telephone re-connected so I can call you, and put the account in your name this time so he cannot disconnect it again. It's crazy that he would do this just to stop you talking to people. It is not a sign that he cares for you – possessing someone is not caring, it is not love.

I'm not sure that I'm suited to this life here. I'm finding it hard to establish a deeper relationship with God when I still feel so disconnected, and this obviously sets me apart from everyone else. They know their God, trust and love him, with their lives surrendered to him. I am numb. I want to feel normal again, feel something, but do not know how. Perhaps this is normal and I will not feel a connection anywhere with anyone ever again.

Not much else to write about – I have another session with Sister Mary Catherine shortly to discuss progress. She is an angel, but I know she doubts my motivation and commitment just as I do, but I do not want to leave here. I wish I could stay on my own terms in this sanctuary away from life. Some days are better than others, but at least I do have good days now and again.

Love
Carl

17 January 2004

Dear Mum

Happy Birthday! I hope you had a great day and did something special.

I was surprised to read that you are back working again at that motel. Do you need the money? If you need money, you should draw what you need from my bank account. That is why I had you added as a signatory, so you would have access to funds whenever you needed it. I hate to think of you working because you need money, and worse that you are cleaning motel rooms. Your stories are awful – people really can be so disgusting. Please take the money from my account and do not worry about how long it will last. When it runs out I will be forced to find a job and that might be the best thing that could happen for me.

It really frustrates me at times like this, to be away from you. I know I was not much help to you after Ethan died, but I am better than I was. I can function. I think I should come home, especially now he has left and not returned. Let me know what you think, but PLEASE stop working at that motel. What would Grandpa say? Sometimes I wonder why God does not seem to respond to my prayers, or maybe he is, and I am enduring the life I must for some purpose I don't know yet.

Have you heard from Matthew? Is he coming home?

Must go now – I have another session with Sister Mary Catherine. At our last meeting, she asked me to think over a few questions and I have not yet found a way to answer them. This will be rather telling and may well be the only answer there is.

Love
Carl

A commotion outside the monastery's administration office caused Carl to stop work with the letter opener and stare out the open window. She laughed aloud. Sister Mary Paul and Postulant Collette had collided on their bikes with habits flying in unacceptable directions to expose stocking-covered legs. She did not hear Sister Mary Catherine enter the room, and only knew she was present because of the tsking. She stood beside Carl at the window and shook her head as the giggling nuns rolled around on the lawn. Carl thought she saw a hint of a smile.

"Come, let's sit." She took Carl by the hand and held them firmly in her clasp. "So, child, how are you progressing with your discernment? Have you come to an understanding? Is God truly calling you to this life?"

"I don't want to leave, Sister. I feel safe here, but…" Carl sighed. "I know I don't belong the way everyone else does, and I don't know if that will change with more time or whether I just don't belong, but I love it here."

"The sisters and I have come to the same conclusion. The problem is your motivation, child. You are running away from something, not running to God and I, we, do not think He is calling you to this life. He has other plans for you, and through your prayers you will come to learn what those plans are."

Postulate Josephine arrived with a tray of tea and biscuits, placing it on the small, round coffee table. Sister Mary Catherine turned the ceramic teapot three times anti-clockwise and smiled. "Jasmine," she said, breathing in the steamy aroma. "Smells lovely, doesn't it? Father Sebastian at Saint Anthony's says it helps prevent cancer. I'm not so sure about that, but there is something wonderful about drinking flowers."

Carl nodded.

"Novice Imogen told me you've been more distressed these past few days and she has been unable to console you. What has you so upset?"

"I had another dream about Ethan. When I woke up, I was crying. I had been crying in my sleep. Since the dream, I've been filled again with the pain…as if it was only yesterday."

"God will ease your pain. You must pray, keep praying and He will be there for you."

21 January 2004

Dear Mum

I will be coming home sometime in the next few weeks. Sadly, the monastery is not the solution to my problem, even though this is the only place where I have found comfort. I came here looking for peace and isolation, believing that this is all I needed, but I at least now know, definitively, that this pain will never pass. Sister Mary Catherine says it will, one day, but I cannot see how. Nothing is going to change in my life.

Sister Mary Catherine has been so kind. I will never forget the way they have treated me, so full of caring and compassion, not judging me, and not telling me to stop feeling sorry for myself or to "get on with my life", as so many others have done without any understanding of what this feels like. Sister Mary Catherine said I should stay until I feel ready to leave, no rush, she said, and I am grateful for that. I will take the time to think through what I might do next.

I am looking forward to seeing Matthew. It will be great for the three of us to be together again at Orchard Road after all this time. Knowing that I will be seeing you and Matthew soon will help me to step through the gates of the monastery.

I am waiting for the rain to pass so I can hike again through the bush – I go there in search of my guide. There is something about the rain. I have always found it comforting. It makes me feel warm even when it is cold. I love the way it smells, especially the way the bush smells after the rain. I love the way it tastes and I love the way it feels on my skin. Rain is life – everything grows from it. Maybe I should go now while it is still raining, and tempt fate. Maybe I can catch the proverbial death of a cold. Maybe a dose of pneumonia is all I need to set me free. I wonder if that would be suicide, dying of intentional pneumonia. There is nothing quite like the rain.

Love
Carl

Fifty-three

March 2004

CARL and Matthew huddled in a window alcove at The Caffeine Fix, ten years since they had last talked.

"So you've been living in a monastery? What was that all about?" he asked.

"I was looking for something."

"Did you find it?"

"No," she replied with a sigh. "It can't be found."

"And what's that?"

"Peace."

"I could've told you that. There's no peace on this Earth, and no goodwill to men either, if the truth be known."

"You sound bitter...more bitter."

"Occupational hazard I guess."

"Where exactly have you been? Mum was a bit vague on the details—said you were in Europe somewhere."

"After Rwanda, I went back to Atlanta to finish my documentary. Then I went to Afghanistan and I've just come back from the Sudan."

"You must have a death wish."

"It's all I know."

"What's it like, in the Sudan?"

"Not for the faint-hearted. Human slaughter and nobody seems to care enough to stop it. It's absolute lawlessness. Like the days of the Vikings."

"You've survived so far. God must be protecting you."

"God? I don't think so. I *survive* thanks to good management and good luck." He sipped pensively from a white mug. "I spent some time in a Congolese prison."

"What for this time?"

"We were covering a story on the disappearance of a French journalist who had been kidnapped and murdered. Certain people didn't appreciate the direction our story was taking, and thought we should spend some time in custody to think about it."

"Were you charged? Did you have a lawyer?"

"Unfortunately the Rule of Law doesn't exist in these places. They have something else—personal law—that's the law of the person holding the gun. We were lucky to get out— that's what it all comes down to—luck." He picked up a teaspoon to add more sugar to his coffee then waved it at Carl. "Did you know there are over a hundred journos stuck in prisons throughout the world with no hope of release? Abdullah Ali al-Sanussi al-Darrat—heard of him?"

Carl shook her head. "Could you put that teaspoon down? It's rather threatening."

"He's been in prison in Libya since 1973. No one even knows where he's being detained or if he's still alive." He dropped the spoon from a height onto the unclothed table.

"Why do you do it, Matt?"

"I don't have an interest in anything else. It makes me miserable and cynical, but it's also very rewarding, like when we help a family or make a change in someone's life. I mean, *real* change—change that is the difference between eating and starving, life and death."

"Aren't you afraid?"

"Every single time we head into a war zone. We lost a member of our film crew in Afghanistan. That's where I got these new scars." He lifted his shirt to reveal an abstract cluster of ill-formed scar tissue. "I have them on my legs as well. I was lucky."

"Don't you think God might have something to do with your luck?"

"Don't go there, Carl, you know I don't believe in any of that, but tell me more about your monastery adventure. I am curious."

"I wouldn't call it an 'adventure'. That demeans it."

"I'm sorry. Go on, I really am interested."

"Nothing much to say really—it was just a place to go to get away from the rest of the world and all the noise insignificant things make. I didn't realize it at the time, but it has helped me move forward. Maybe I can even see my new reality now...maybe...I'm not sure."

"So what's next for you since becoming a nun didn't work out?"

"I sent an application to volunteer with Doctors Without Borders. Sister Mary Catherine suggested I get into volunteer work. She seemed to think it would help."

"Medecins Sans Frontieres. I take it you didn't somehow manage to get a degree in medicine these past few years?"

"I've applied for an administrative role. I am a lawyer—not entirely useless."

"I wouldn't have put it that way. Some would say—" He stopped. "We should order lunch."

Carl scanned the one-page menu. "I'm really worried about mum. I wish I could convince her she'd be better off on her own, but she keeps taking him back."

"I hate that he's living in our house."

They stared outside, and watched a procession of sensible sedans pass by.

"How are you coping, Carl, seriously?"

"I really don't know yet. The memories...he was such a good man, and a perfect husband."

"He really was a top bloke. I liked him a lot."

"He tamed me, calmed me, and I no longer had a temper."

"You had a temper? No, really?"

"There's that Baden sarcasm again. What about you, Matt? Anyone in your life?"

He shrugged. "I've been in relationships. Nothing meaningful. It's not possible with my work, and anyway, I'm better on my own. I can go anywhere I want when I want and…that's enough on that topic."

"Avoidance—another Baden trait lives on. That one is male-specific, though."

"Back to mum," he said. "Have you noticed how she flinches whenever he speaks to her? I was wondering if it's because he hits her."

"It's been going on for years, Matt."

"What have you done about it?"

"What could I do? She lives the life she thinks she deserves. Anything is better than being alone."

"She's so small now. Has she shrunk or is it an optical illusion because she cowers?"

"I don't know. She is very subdued, and never has an opinion on anything. Have you noticed she's always losing things, like the keys—how many times have we had to search for the keys in the past week alone?

"Did you see how flustered she was preparing dinner the other night? It was as if she was learning something new. I had to walk away," he said.

"Maybe we should take her to the doctors for a check-up."

"It's probably nothing. Just stress related from living with that imbecile."

Carl moved the cutlery to accommodate an oversized plate, and stared into the pasta.

"Haven't seen proper food in a while?" Matthew laughed. "I'll leave it to you to persuade her to go. There must be some lawyer left in you."

251

"She's had such a tough life, and made so many sacrifices. Can you imagine how much it must have cost her to send us both to university in Sydney?"

"I never really thought about it, but whenever I wanted something she always made it happen somehow, even if it was second-hand."

They ate for a while in silence.

"Have you noticed she still has the same clothes she wore in all the photos of her and dad before they were married, and they only take up half the wardrobe?" Carl shook her head. "Motherhood is just one momentous sacrifice."

"We should head home and rescue her from that idiot."

"As soon as I've finished my lunch," she said. "This is good."

Watching Walter strut around Orchard Road like a rooster ruling his roost, was like yeast on dough, and Matthew did little to hide his rising unease. He would leave any room Walter entered, and sat in his immediate vicinity only when dinner forced it. It would not take much. A bellow would do it.

"I haven't finished with that!" Walter yelled as Helena took his plate with the knife and fork lined side by side. Matthew hurdled two dining chairs to get to Walter at the table's head, fists flying for any contact. Walter fell backwards to the floor still seated in his chair, and fought back as best he could. Helena cowered in a corner facing inward while Carl watched, did nothing, and wondered what the nuns would think of such a scene, and her inaction. Matthew had Walter around the throat, and the fight for desire and conscience was visible on his face. He stepped back and stared down at Walter before walking away.

"You'll live to regret that," Walter said as he crawled onto his feet. "I'll be pressing charges, and you can get the hell out of my house!"

Matthew stopped, turned, and raced back to within a breath of Walter. "This is *not* your house! This is *our* house. *You* get the hell out!"

They stood there, nose tip to nose tip, with fists poised and willing, until Walter took his turn to step back and away. "Pack your bags, and don't come back this time!" Matthew yelled after him.

Helena cried softly into the corner.

Several days after the Walter showdown, Helena emerged, happy in the comfort that came from having her children home again and without the tension. The reunion though, would not last—the quiet ordinariness of life at Orchard Road pricked at the soles of Matthew's feet.

"No luck getting mum to the doctors?" he asked Carl.

"I'm afraid not. She says she's fine, and she seems a lot better since Walter left."

"Is that because he has left or because we're here?"

"Both, I'd say."

"I have to be getting back."

"*Have* to or *want* to?"

"Have to, but I want to as well. Can I leave though if he's going to press charges against me?"

"You don't need to worry about that. He won't be pressing charges."

"How do you know? He's not the type of man to let something like this go by without retribution."

"I went to see him at his shop, in front of his staff and customers, and encouraged him to press charges so that his decade of mental and physical abuse could be made public, and everyone would finally know that he's not the upstanding business man he pretends to be."

"What did he say?"

"Not a lot, possibly because his lips were quite swollen. I told him you were leaving for Rwanda, and it would be in his best interests to let you go. Since Sergeant Mackelroth hasn't knocked on our door, I think it's safe to say he agrees."

"I take back everything I've ever said about you lawyers."

"I'll send you my bill."

"What are you going to do now?"

"I'm not sure. Mum saw the letter from Doctors Without Borders. I told her I wasn't going to accept, and stay with her instead, but that upset her—she said she didn't want me giving up my life on her account. I don't want to leave her on her own—I've done that twice before—but I also don't want to stay in Maine. There are just too many memories here."

"So you're a runner too," he said with a smile.

"It's self-preservation. If I immerse myself in other people's misery, maybe I will be able to put my own into perspective. While I'm here, living this life, I can't help but feel sorry for myself—everything tells me that I'm the only one who has lost anything significant."

"If you need to go, then you should go. Mum will be OK. She's a survivor. Look at what she's been through and she's still standing."

"Maybe I'll go for twelve months, and see how she is after that. It would make it easier if I knew someone was watching out for her. It's a shame she lost touch with her sister."

"She wouldn't be much help in any case. Grace lives with dad in Sydney."

"What? Grace has moved in with dad and Andréa? I didn't even realize they had stayed in touch."

"No, not with Andréa—they're not together anymore. He's with Grace."

"Oh, *with* Grace." Carl paused. "Mum doesn't need to know that."

Matthew started to pack while Carl watched from his bed.

"Where would you be stationed if you join Doctors Without Borders?" he asked.

"Angola."

"We'll be neighbors!" He paused and sat down beside Carl. "Are you sure you're ready for this? Nothing can prepare you for what you'll see, and—"

"And?"

"You're not as strong as you used to be. The things you'll see…you need to be strong."

"I don't know what I'm capable of anymore, but I need to do this. What else is there?"

"When will you leave?"

"In a couple of months, but before I go, I'll get mum involved with the church. I'd be happier knowing there were people looking out for her."

"I've got a better idea. We should get her a dog."

"What were you doing, visiting dad in Sydney?"

He shrugged. "I honestly don't know for sure. Looking for answers I guess, just like you."

"Did you find them?"

"Yes." He sighed. "It wasn't my imagination. He really does resent me, but the feeling's mutual."

Fifty-four

April 2004

Journal Entry: 22 April 2004

Sister Mary Catherine suggested I keep a journal—it would help me, she said, to write it all down. Reading your own thoughts is apparently therapeutic so here goes with my first entry.

I arrived in the Angolan capital, Luanda, three days ago. We flew in from London after ten hours on a plane packed with a diverse group of people—from beautiful, statuesque Angolan women in long, brightly colored wraparound dresses, to business men in gray suits headed for the comfortable compounds of the foreign oil companies.

The pilot did two loops around the city before landing at Luanda International Airport, so I had a good view of my new home. There is a beautiful bay, dotted with containerships and oil tankers, and surrounded by shanties. Office buildings mark the core of the city and industrial development encircles it.

In Russia, red means beautiful, so I guess this place is very beautiful. Red is also the most common color in national flags—I learnt this from the in-flight magazine. The magazine was well worn; the article was not. I guess people just aren't that interested in flags.

You can tell a lot about a country by its airport so I knew then what lay ahead. There were a lot of restless people in the customs queue waiting for unhurried index fingers to tap everyone through, but not me—a benefit of being permanently numb and immune from the unimportance of everyday life.

I was picked up at the airport by Lucas Tanner, a volunteer from Australia. Lucas is the logistician—a man who likes to get people and things to wherever they need to be, and so it was fitting that he was the welcoming party for the latest influx of volunteers—there were three of us.

Lucas herded us into the Land Cruiser, also red although there was a hint of white paint under the dust. The interior was much the same. I have decided to keep a list of everything that might take some getting used to—mum would be proud—she is the Queen of Lists. At the end of my time here, I will go back over the list and see how far I have come, if anywhere. First on the list will be red—red is not my color of choice, then dust. I might even go so far as to say I prefer salt on my skin to dust, and that's really saying something.

The journey from the airport was interesting, and red. Lucas drove us 'home' where my heart will rest for the next twelve months. The MSF houses are scattered throughout the city intermingling with the real world, unlike the oil people who live in compounds in another foreign, western, world. I guess that is the fundamental difference between a volunteer—people about people, and employees—people for prosperity.

I am sharing a room with a Polish girl, or woman, I'm not sure which. She looks very young, but could be much older. Her name is Ala Nowakóna. Her surname lets everyone know she is single and available. If she were married, her surname would be Nowakowa. It seems like a complicated system to me, but I guess they know what they're doing. Ala tells me her name means truthful.

I haven't shared a house, let alone a room, since my uni days and that wasn't a particularly good experience, but having met Ala I'm sure this will be different. I've spent a lot of time on my own since Ethan died so it will be good for me to try the alternative since solitude didn't work out so well.

I share the house with three other volunteers. In total, there are two doctors, two nurses, and one administrator—that's me. It's not a bad place to be if I get sick.

The house is not as nice as the monastery, but it is pleasant enough with pale blue walls and colorful curtains tied in knots to allow the air to flow through. The concrete walls and floors are better than air-conditioning—it's almost arctic in here (that's quite an exaggeration and I don't have an eraser).

There was not a lot of time for getting settled in after we arrived, but it was not needed anyway—it's not as if there are resort facilities to check out. We went straight into orientation sessions until the sun set then Lucas escorted us to dinner.

We drove to the peninsula, the *Ilha de Luanda*, which used to be an island, but is joined to the mainland now by a causeway. There were restaurants lining both sides of the road, catering for every taste bud, and many with discos, bars, casinos and or local singing and dancing. We went to "Coconuts"—a bistro where you can drink, eat, or swim in the rolling surf. After a few drinks there, we moved on to a restaurant which served national dishes including palm oil beans, dried meat, corn funge (sort of like mashed potatoes) and chicken muamba. We wondered then if the pre-dinner alcohol was medicinal—a necessary pre-requisite before sampling the local cuisine, but in Lucas we trusted. He surely would not throw the new ones into a furnace on the first night.

At the apex of the curved bay, we could see the Marginal, a wide pedestrian sea walk lined with coconut palms and rose-colored Portuguese colonial architecture highlighted by the terracotta of the earth. And from the beachfront restaurant with its views of the African Rio, it was easy to believe you were on an island paradise anywhere in the world.

Several others from the MSF community joined us for dinner and it was a fun night. The life of a volunteer is not all work, it would seem.

The potholes on the way home seemed even bigger. They are everywhere and unavoidable. I would not attempt to drive in Luanda in a car—it is four-wheel drive territory, especially during the rainy season they say. In fact, I would not attempt to drive in Luanda, period—the streets are a maze and I have never been one for puzzles. My mind is too linear when it is operational.

So that was my first day in Angola, my first day in Luanda, my first day as a volunteer, and the first day, I hope, of a new beginning.

Journal Entry: 23 April, 2004

Breakfast on the first morning caused a gush of stupid tears. The stale bread did it. It reminded me of Ethan—he loved bread. He would eat stale bread, pick the mold off it if he had to, and he would have stolen it from the geese at the park if allowed. I was sad because I wanted to give him my bread, like I used to, and I was sad because he was not here to witness the first time I actually ate dough that was not just out of a baker's oven. Ala put her arm around me and everyone rushed to see if I was OK. They all thought I was suffering culture shock and I really didn't want them to think that of me—as if I was too precious for the conditions, because I'm not. I had to decide whether to correct their misperceptions or to tell them about Ethan. I didn't want these new people in my life seeing me as a pathetic little widow, which I am. Precious or pathetic were my options and I did not want to be either. I went with the truth because Ala was looking into me with those doleful blue eyes and her name means truth. I was surprised that I felt better afterwards, and the incident seems to have shortened the bonding process between us.

After breakfast, there were more briefings until lunch. Then there was an afternoon tour of Luanda courtesy of Lucas. He greeted us with, "Welcome to the Paris of Africa." Jan, our housemate doctor from Denmark, said he had read that Luanda was also known as the Rio de Janeiro of Africa. It seems that Luanda could be a lot of places, but from what I've seen, it is uniquely Luanda. I have not been to Rio de Janeiro, but I did stop off in Paris before coming here and this most certainly is not Paris.

I like Jan a lot—he has a great sense of humor, and won't hesitate to tell you what he thinks. I like that trait in people, but I guess it's not so successful with sensitive types. He asked me, "What are you doing calling yourself with a boy's name?" Karl, with a K, he says, is a very popular name for boys in Scandinavia. I suggested to him that he has a girl's name, but he said, very matter-of-factly, "No, it is not," as if that was conclusive on the issue. Ala said she thinks Karl means strong man, but was not certain, to which they both laughed a mixture of amusement and embarrassment, for me.

Gisele, the French doctor, has a room to herself and she enjoys her solitude. Jan shares with Thomas, a male nurse from Berlin—they have been sharing a room for two years and still like each other. It is early days yet but I wonder if it is coincidental that everyone who lives in this house can get along, or if it is an inherent trait of volunteers. I'll answer that question in months to come—as I said, it is early days yet.

Luanda is divided into two parts, the old city (the baixa) and the new city (the cidade alta). The old city is next to the port and has narrow streets with colonial Portuguese architecture. We went to the São Miguel Fort perched on a hill above the city. From our vantage point, I could see a place that may well look like Rio de Janeiro with high-rise buildings gracing the foreshore of a beautiful bay. The views were breathtaking, so long as I did not look down, although that perspective was also breathtaking but in a negative way. I wonder how long it will be before the displaced people will have somewhere permanent to live—how long before they can move from their sheds, garages, and chicken coops. People elsewhere would pay a fortune to live by the ocean like they do, but life in a musseque (shantytown) is not a dream come true for these people. The shantytowns are called musseques after the red ground on which they are built. The red dirt turns to red mud in the wet season, which lasts for six months. There are millions of people living in the musseques and probably more to come.

The fort was once a Franciscan monastery, but now it is the Armed Forces Museum filled with rusty relics of the civil war that lasted thirty years. There is some irony in that—that an army museum commemorating war would be housed in a monastery, a place of peace. The people of Luanda have only known peace for three years and many of them have not known a life other than one mired in bullets. It's not comprehensible for a girl from Maine via the monastery.

Many Angolans still live hiding in the jungle not realizing the war is over—there are no telephones or internet to alert them. Masses of Angolans made the treacherous hike to Luanda during the war—it was the safest place to be back then. Five million people live here now, in Luanda, in a city built for four hundred thousand. Imagine if every person in Sydney went to live in Canberra. I do not think there is a city in the world that could cope with a population surge of that magnitude. You can't judge this city for being what it is and the fog of war lifts very slowly.

I'm exhausted. Tonight will bring sleep, I hope, uninterrupted by a two o'clock waking from dreams that remind me of what I want but cannot have. Ethan is gone.

Journal Entry: 6 May 2004

I never thought it would be possible to be so full of hatred as I am, to hate with a passion another of God's creatures, but these wretched mosquitoes are driving me nuts. We are protected in our beds by a shroud of netting, but nothing can stop the incessant squealing as they press inward trying to break through to get to me. It is without doubt the most excruciating sound—worse than fingernails scratching a blackboard, and relentless. Only the female bites, Jan informed us suggesting also that this was expected of any female of any species—they are "the aggressors" he said. We threw various accoutrements at him to which he calmly replied that we had proven his point. He is very courageous, living in a house with three women, four counting Thomas (he is one of us) but Jan obviously thrives on it.

Simeon Baptista is another doctor with MSF, but he lives in his own place. He called in early this morning and took me and Ala to the famous Roque Santeiro market, one of the biggest markets in Africa. The drive to Roque Santeiro was an experience in itself. Miles upon miles of squalor I could not have imagined even though I had read plenty about Luanda before I came here. It sounds clichéd to say nothing can prepare you for it, but that is probably because it is impossible to conjure up an image of the desperation of the people who have no choice but to live like this, their huts indistinguishable from the vast rubbish dump they surround. The smell is Hell. It is distressing enough to pass by in our air-conditioned, fly-free Cruiser, but to live this life, from day to night and then back to another day. I wonder if the people who live here have any hope that their lives will ever change, or do they wish for it to end as I have done, but for a reason that fades somewhat by comparison. It is hard to envision them as world owners as they will be one day, blessed by God to inherit the Earth when it is free of war, famine, and poverty. They will be deserving owners. I hope they forgive me for passing them by today.

You can buy anything at the market from bananas to spare parts for armored personnel carriers. I bought fruit and food to give to the children when they come to our door with their tiny hands stretched up above their heads, pushing each other for prime position. We were told not to give them food from our door because hundreds or thousands would come each day. It was good advice and Ala and I soon regretted our actions—we have been under siege ever since, and we spend endless hours at markets buying food and clothes.

I was even able to buy bananas today with only a few quiet tears behind my sunglasses. I gave up on bananas after Ethan died—unable to escape the memory of him crouched down by the fire cooking his chocolate-stuffed treat. I still see how he looked up at me and smiled so proud of his cooking—it is clear in my mind as if it happened moments ago. I can see the blue of his eyes and the colors in his shirt. I don't want to lose the memory, but I wish it didn't come with so much pain. Contrary to Sister Mary Catherine's advice, it is also painful to write about it. When I stood there today, at the market in front of the mountain of bananas, I had an epiphany—they say you can run but you can never hide, and it is true—there is no place you can go to escape what is inside of you.

Jan and Thomas cry a lot too, but they cry because newborn babies die in their hands, and they cry when they mend broken bodies torn apart by a mine. They cry because they see the faces of the walking dead and know, as the last bastions of hope, that there is nothing they can do to honor the trust in the eyes of a mother. They cry because of what others have lost and what they must suffer. There'll be no more banana tears from me.

Journal Entry: 14 May 2004

Today I joined a convoy of MSF volunteers, mainly doctors and nurses, headed back to Camabatela in the Kuanza Norte province to treat more patients for sleeping sickness.

Sleeping sickness is spread by the tsetse fly, which bites. Without treatment you die, but only after suffering excruciating pain. Most people only seek treatment when the disease has already advanced to the second stage. I guess because the first stage symptoms, fever and weakness, are so like their 'normal' day-to-day sufferings that they don't realize they're sick. The second stage is easier to diagnose when the parasite has invaded the brain—confusion, convulsions, and they find it difficult to eat, speak or walk. Some become violent or show signs of insanity. At night, they cannot sleep, but during the day, they do. That makes for a lonely existence. It is yet another curse of the war—they fled into the bush away from the bullets, only to discover swarms of flesh-biting tsetse flies and a certain death. You have to wonder what was worse: a quick death by a bullet or this insufferable suffering. They shoot horses don't they?

The treatment used to be as cruel as the sickness, Jan said. And it is the only treatment he has administered in his entire career as a doctor that filled him with dread and shame. The drug they used for the sleeping sickness contained arsenic and killed some patients outright. He said it was so strong they had to keep it in glass vials because the plastic ones would melt. He said that whenever he placed the syringe on his patients' arms he would picture the melted vials, and he could almost smell burning flesh as he injected the drug. Injecting the children was the worst, Simeon says—when the arsenic entered the bloodstream, the children would squirm in pain, and clench their eyes shut like vices, but no one ever complained. Simeon said there is a safer drug—the resurrection drug, so called because it brings people back to life from a coma. It was not a profitable drug and the people who need it, those who are susceptible to sleeping sickness, are poor, so the drug company stopped producing it, but resumed after pressure from the World Health Organization. Jan said they still needed to buy intravenous solutions, catheters and syringes, and treatment of those infected required two weeks of hospitalization. Jan fears they might one day have to revert to the arsenic concoction unless another solution presents itself, one that could be administered orally. The disease will never end, he says, unless they find a way to kill every single tsetse fly and that would cost too much money.

The way to Camabatela was littered with bullet-ridden dwellings. I wondered what had happened to the occupants when the bullets struck—were they killed inside their homes or did they escape to the bush with the tsetse flies and nothing else, no food, no shelter, no clothes. What did they trade? Eternal life (the bullet) for a living death (the flies)? I wondered what choice I would have made without hindsight as a guide.

We had to make a detour on the way because a Land Cruiser, not one of ours, was billowing with smoke and flames from a land mine that was detonated by the stream of passing vehicles. No one was injured, this time, but another metal carcass was added to the landscape left to rust in the vegetation. I once read that a truly happy person is one who can enjoy the scenery on a detour. I think we disproved that philosophy—no one amongst us was even remotely happy, not even the effervescent Ala.

We went to a local hospital in Camabatela. It was a derelict hall with no running water, no electricity, and no ventilation. The walls were as sick as the people who lay expressionless on the scant bedding that lacked the antiseptic quality ordinarily found in a hospital. There were more people than beds so some lay on the floor on mats. Imagine what the cost of thirty years of guns and ammunition could have done for this place—it could have been the Taj Mahal of all hospitals.

It dawned on me, pun intended, that millions of dollars are spent each year on New Year's Eve. Maybe we could ditch the fireworks, pool the money and do something positive with it instead of blowing it into the air and watching it disintegrate. That would be a good way to start any year. It would bring new meaning to city pride, and there would be no losers other than the firework companies.

We went to dinner to "*really* experience the local food" so it seems I had not been adventurous after all with the corn funge. There were no menus when we sat down at rickety tables in a permanent makeshift construction, although 'construction' implies some sort of structure, which is not accurate. Simeon and a couple of other local doctors did the ordering, which was a relief and a concern.

The food did nothing to appeal to my senses, not by look or smell, but at least there were no sounds coming from it. I did not eat the calulu, which is a dish made with fresh and dried fish, and I could not even contemplate the cabidela—chicken's blood eaten with rice and cassava dough (made from the leaves of the cassava shrub—which looked somewhat illegal to me). I had to endure a lot of pressure to try the cabidela. Everyone said "You have to try it" and I said "Why?" I don't understand why you would eat something that you know you are not going to like and certainly not for "the experience," which was the popular answer to my question. I don't need to experience chicken blood, not now, not ever.

I hope the bed bugs leave me alone tonight. Ala and I are covered in red dots. Jan has taken to drawing lines between Ala's dots to make animal shapes. He thinks he is quite clever, but I think he just wants to be closer to Ala and to touch her pale skin.

Journal Entry: 12 June 2004

I have been in bed for the past week sick with a stomach virus. Perhaps I swallowed a bed bug in my sleep. At least I can't blame the chicken blood. Simeon has been very caring, calling in regularly to check on me even though I live in a house with two doctors and two nurses. He came by this evening declaring me fit to eat and to take me for a "real meal"—fruit, bottled water, and dry bread do not count as real food according to Simeon.

From the street, the restaurant looked like any other house in Luanda with planks crisscrossing the exterior defensively. The approach was like an episode from Get Smart—we entered via a metal doorway then passed through a long, narrow hallway through to a small room with a brick oven and finally, we arrived in the dining area.

The owner himself, a Portuguese man, waited on us and I had thought Simeon was receiving special treatment, but he assured me that, even though he was a regular, the owner or his wife waits on everyone. I kept it simple, not wanting to end up back in bed. I would like to return to that restaurant another time, but would never be able to find it without Simeon or a compass.

Simeon is an interesting man. He has seen and done a lot in his thirty plus years. I had assumed that he had always lived here—he was born in Luanda—but he has only been back these past five years. His parents sent him to England when he was eighteen for an education. He stayed on after his internship and worked in a London hospital in a casualty ward. He came back, he said, driven by guilt—there is only one doctor for every fifty thousand people in Luanda, and the ratio is far worse outside the capital. The needs of the people didn't end with the war since sickness is a correlation of poverty and poverty reigns supreme in this country.

Simeon said he was working in Kuito when the war ended two years ago. He said there were thousands of people walking in a single line, coming out of nowhere—old people, sick people, malnourished children, and disabled people—all walking with everything they owned strapped to their heads or to their backs. They had lived on leaves and raw manioc for decades. They came from nowhere and they were on the road to nowhere else.

Thousands of villages were destroyed during the war, and along the way 'home' many more of them would die one way or another. To this day, there are one and a half land mines for every Angolan, just waiting for that foot or hand, or passing vehicle, to set them off. That, he said, was how so many children lost their faces—picking up a mine. Seventy thousand have been maimed by land mines—that is twice the entire population of Maine. I pictured the main street of Maine on a busy Saturday morning filled with stumps and prosthetic limbs and missing faces. It was even harder to imagine that no one would be complaining. The image was surreal like a horror movie, but it is very real here.

Simeon said the worst smell in the world is the smell of a

rotting bandage with maggots in a pus-filled wound. It is not uncommon, even now, and he said he would never get used to it.

He asked me about the scar on my cheek and I told him it was from a childhood accident. He pried further and I said I had fallen off my bike. I didn't want to lie, but I also didn't want to explain my life to him. I could tell he didn't believe me, and it was a stupid answer considering his experience with a scalpel—he knows what sort of scar is made by the infliction of a sharp object or a blunt pair of scissors, but it is not the sort of issue you share with people, other than the person closest to you.

We had not spent any real time alone together until then, and it was very comfortable until the realization struck me that we were on our own then I felt decidedly uncomfortable. I looked up at one point and noticed how intently he was watching me. I wonder what was in his mind or perhaps he was contemplating the scar and my story—when someone suspects a lie, their mind will pursue another truth that is often worse than the reality. That's the risk of being secretive.

When I arrived home, Jan and Ala were having a quiet dinner together. They make a nice couple even though Ala constantly says they are just friends. Me thinks she doth protest too much. I went to bed and wrote a letter to mum. I hope above all hope, that she is OK on her own. What a failure I am as a daughter, to leave her that way.

Journal Entry: 23 June 2004

A new volunteer joined us in the office today. She will help us with HR. We have eighty or so volunteers at the moment, and about a thousand locals working with us throughout Angola in various capacities: helping in the nutrition centers, digging latrines, uploading supplies, or housekeeping—cleaning, washing and ironing for our volunteers—not an easy task with just a scrub board and hot charcoals to heat up the antique irons.

Thomas is leaving tomorrow, and as is the custom, we sponsored his farewell party. Parties are a common occurrence—someone is always coming or going. It seems like a lot of socializing, but it is necessary for the equilibrium of the heart, mind, and soul.

Thomas is quite fond of the semba, a sensuous belly dance popular in Luanda, even though he has no rhythm. For the rest of us, watching Thomas on the dance floor is entertainment at its best, and doesn't cost a cent. Whenever I am feeling sad, I will picture him dancing the semba with the locals.

It's late. More tomorrow.

Journal Entry: 10 July 2004

It has been a month since my last entry (that sounds like a confession—it is not meant to be). I just have not had anything to say. Life goes on—what seemed extraordinary then is ordinary now. I'm not sure if that is good or bad—probably both.

I processed a number of reports this morning from MSF teams in southern and eastern Angola. Children treated for malnutrition months ago have been readmitted with acute malnutrition. It's like winning a case then losing it on appeal, but worse because there are lives at stake, not riches, profits, or assets. Forty-five percent of children under the age of five are chronically malnourished, a condition that can irreversibly impair learning ability if they survive long enough to learn anything. Like I said—it is an ordinary life.

A group of us took a Saturday afternoon boat ride up the Kuanza River to a restaurant, *Varanda dos Mangais* (Restaurant of the Mangroves). It stands alone in the middle of nowhere surrounded by lawns sprouting immature palms and dotted with white umbrellas. The restaurant veranda hangs over the water's edge. The décor inside is distinctly African, but done tastefully in muted colors of white, creams, and brown. It was perfect for a celebratory afternoon in honor of Gisele's birthday. Unfortunately, the atmosphere was conducive to the consumption of crisp, chilled, white South African wine and platters of fresh seafood. Even Gisele was a little rowdy, which is really saying something—she is the yardstick of reserve and maturity upon which we all try to base ourselves, unsuccessfully most of the time.

My guard was disarmed by the wine and I found myself ensconced in a D&M (deep and meaningful) with Simeon. I don't talk about Ethan, not even with Ala. It does not mean he is forgotten—I love him still, more than life itself, and there will never be anyone else. It wouldn't be fair to subject any man to Ethan's flame.

Simeon asked me why I wear my wedding ring and I said because I am married. He gave me one of those knowing looks and then, without realizing it, I told him everything about Ethan, the sailing trip, how he died, the monastery, and everything up to this moment in time. It all came out like a torrential storm, and just like a storm, a beautiful calm followed. The calm may have been alcohol-induced—I will know tomorrow, if it is replaced with regret.

Our conversation was not all one-sided—I learned a lot about Simeon as well. I had wondered how a man like him could still be single, and now I know. He was living with an English woman in London for eight years when his conscience pricked, forcing him home. He said the woman did not want to leave London for Luanda, understandably, or to leave her high-paying surgical position at one of the most prestigious hospitals in the United Kingdom to enter a war zone, not even with the man she supposedly loved. I would have—if that is what Ethan had asked of me, I would have gone in a second. She must not have loved him for if love is true you can make such a sacrifice because it doesn't even feel like a sacrifice. It's a Catch 22.

So Simeon lives alone and says he is happy enough, which left me thinking about my own state of mind—I think I can safely say that I am no longer completely miserable, which is another small step forward.

Journal Entry: 11 July 2004

I went to the markets this morning with Ala, Jan, and Gisele. We stocked up on food for our own private feeding center that we have set up as a stall along the roadside—it lasts mere minutes before the food runs away, but at least we have found a way to relocate the masses from our front door. It was causing problems with the neighbors.

Afterwards we met up with Emelie who is volunteering for the Red Cross. Gisele has been working with her to find the family of one of her patients. Emelie works with the Tracing Program and her stories are as bad as ours—orphanages filled with children separated from their families, and children kidnapped by rebels during the war and forced to work as slaves for soldiers and their families.

She told us about the schools she has been to with no roof, no desks, and no equipment. When it rains for the six months of the wet season, the children 'study' under plastic sheets that pool with water. However, she also had happy stories of reunions like one little girl who was separated from her parents when she was three and reunited after eleven years. I must write to Matthew—I haven't heard from him in months.

The discussion with Simeon yesterday over lunch has been playing on my mind. I feel awkward and vulnerable, but I don't want it to affect our working relationship or our friendship so with a racing heart and sweating palms, I ventured down to the Centro Medico where he works on Sunday afternoons.

The medical center is a decrepit concrete building surrounded by red dirt and a lengthy strip of knee-high garbage. Suburban garbage tips are everywhere and it makes a mockery of the medical center. I was hit by a blast of antiseptic when I entered and was not sure if it was a good sign or if it disguised something more sinister. The latter, I would suggest.

I could see Simeon's smooth, black head in the distance and I watched him for a while, admiring him. There was a shadow following his every move—whenever Simeon's hand dropped to his side a little black hand would slide into it. I watched how Simeon looked at the child, the way he smiled at him, and it was clear for all to see that Simeon Baptista was a good man.

When Simeon finally turned around and saw me, he seemed happy, surprised, and flustered. I hoped he wasn't feeling as I was, and that he would be able to smooth things over like he always did.

Simeon introduced me to John Paul, who looked like a three-year-old, but was probably much older. Simeon said he turned up every Sunday afternoon and would not leave his side, but would then disappear at the end of the day.

We were uncomfortable together and I regretted going down there. I think I made matters worse. It seems to have affected our friendship, revealing aspects of our personal lives to each other. I don't understand what goes on between us, but it turns me into a moron. I'll resort to a tried and tested Baden strategy and do my best to avoid him until this blows over. I hope that things between us will settle like the red dust of Luanda.

Journal Entry: 23 July 2004

It is Friday night and we are off tomorrow for an excursion to the place where the Congo River meets the sea. There are nine of us going, captivated as we were by Simeon's tales of Sir Henry Morton Stanley. He tells the tale as if he is a distant relative of Stanley, who, by the way, is American and white. The Point is where Stanley began his historic trip into the heart of Africa in search of Dr. Livingstone who had not been heard from for several years having previously been a prolific reporter of his every move.

When Stanley finally found the pale, wearied Dr. Livingstone living with an African tribe, he wanted to run toward him and embrace him, but driven instead by cowardice and false pride he walked deliberately, took off his hat, and said, of course, "Dr. Livingstone, I presume?" It is a relief to have that famous question put into context. According to Simeon, Livingstone replied with a simple "Yes," a kind smile and doff of his hat. Dr. Livingstone was surprised that Stanley was sent to find him because he did not consider himself lost—just temporarily weakened by disease and short of supplies. Perhaps that is me also—not lost, but temporarily weakened.

While we are up that way, we are also going to the Maiombe Rainforest in the Cabinda Province. It is famous for its butterflies that are prized by collectors.

Simeon and I seem to have moved past the awkwardness we were experiencing, no thanks to me though. I had successfully invoked the Baden avoidance tactic for a week, feeling like an eight-year-old in the process then Simeon turned up unexpectedly Sunday morning to take us to the markets. He seemed determined to interact with me whether I wanted to or not.

After the markets, we went to Mussulo, one of the palm-fringed islets on Luanda Bay. We usually avoid touristy places believing ourselves to be above them, but it was worth the exception. We had a chance to talk, and he asked me why I had been avoiding him. I wanted to say I wasn't, but I knew he was too perceptive to believe it, and I'm not a convincing liar due to my neurotic hair twisting, which gives me away every time. We talked about work and life generally, keeping away from anything personal, and managed to reinstate our friendship on terms similar to how it was, but not the same. I don't know why I am not able to let anyone get close to me, or why I react this way when I share pieces of my life. Maybe I need to keep my memories of Ethan sacred, for me only, maybe I don't want people to see how vulnerable it makes me, maybe my heart is full of rain and I like it that way, maybe it is broken and I don't want it repaired. I don't know. I just know I'm afraid, whatever it is.

Journal Entry: 16 August 2004

Tomorrow, it will be three years since Ethan died, since he was lost in the darkness of the Atlantic Ocean. It is an image I cannot erase, a pain I cannot relieve. If only I'd been more selfish. If only I had scorned his dream and forbidden the great escape. If only—the worst two words in the English language. They are killer words.

For the first two years I lived in my pajamas, I drank to numb the pain, and I slept to escape it. At the monastery, I prayed. What do I do here? It has been three years, and I still do not know how to handle it. I have been miserable for days now, and it has not gone unnoticed, but no one knows why. I wish mum was here, or Matthew.

I don't want to wake up tomorrow.

Journal Entry: 17 August 2004

I went down to the beach to stare at the Atlantic Ocean— somewhere out there was my love, my Ethan. Maybe the current had brought his body to rest here, and maybe his soul is the wind that blew against my face. I felt an affinity with the ocean, as if I was as close to him as I could be, but I also felt something else—as if he wanted me to let him go. I cried at the thought—I did not want to say good-bye. How do you say good-bye to the meaning of your life?

When I returned to the house, Simeon was there waiting for me. Jan had cooked dinner and lit some candles. I was grateful no one asked questions or tried to make me laugh. They knew something of my state of mind, and respected it, and I was happy to be here this day, with these people, my friends. I feel like something has changed in me. I don't know what. Maybe the acorn has finally fallen from the tree.

Journal Entry: 17 September 2004

It is National Hero's Day today, the day Angolans celebrate the birth of António Agostinho Neto, their first President. The government statement says he was "an acclaimed doctor, humanist, intellectual and poet, who always fought against all forms of obscurantism and prejudice." I had to revert to the Oxford for 'obscurantism'—it means the opposite of free speech. Jan was way off target when he suggested 'absence of light', but we think it was another futile attempt at humor, which we all laughed at.

You can see Neto's Mausoleum from just about anywhere in Luanda. It is not in the same league as the Washington Monument although similar in shape. It was funded by Russia and was never completed due to the collapse of the Soviet Union. I guess that is the story of Luanda—full of promises that never realize.

I won't be joining today's celebrations as I am recovering from yet another stomach virus. Getting sick is par for the course here, despite our best efforts.

I received a letter from Matthew. He is still in the Congo, but planning to visit me soon. I am not sure if he is coming specifically to see me or if the primary purpose has something to do with Angola's World Cup qualifier against Zimbabwe next month. Simeon is organizing tickets. It will be stinking hot in the Citadel in October, like a cauldron.

I need to talk to Matthew about mum. Her letters are confusing—she uses words that do not make any sense. I can't help but worry that he is back there and the duress is causing her thoughts to fragment. She has not mentioned him in her letters so maybe it is something else. Matthew might have a clue.

Journal Entry: 18 October 2004

Matthew has been and gone—his visit has disturbed my equilibrium, and I've found it hard to settle again. He is going back to Maine early December to check on mum. I'll wait until then to decide what I'm going to do next year. I would like to stay here for another twelve months although the permanently gridlocked traffic is testing my patience. There is no traffic in Maine to speak of, so I'm not used to sitting for three hours in a heated car locked into position by thousands of other rattling exhaust pipes. It's a wonder we don't gas ourselves to death with the air-conditioning being what it is.

Simeon took me out for dinner to cheer me up, and I needed it. He told me about his family and the sacrifices they had made to send him to the UK for an education. He had earned good money while he was working in London and was relieved, more than anything that he could help his parents and brothers and sisters—all eight of them, toward a better life.

I asked him if he was planning to get married, and he said that there is a woman in his life and he wants to marry her, but it was "complicated". He did not elaborate. I have to admit I was a little green at hearing this, to know that when he wasn't with us, when he wasn't working, he actually had someone in his life and in his heart.

He asked me about Matthew—if he was my only sibling and I hesitated for a while before telling him about Brian and William. I left out the details, just as he had. While we were on the topic of families, I asked him about mum's strange letters, if there was a medical explanation for it. He was reluctant to answer—it would barely amount to supposition he said, without examining her. His reluctance made me nervous and I pressed him to give me his best guess.

It could be dementia he said, or normal changes from aging. There's no clear-cut line between normal and the warning signs for Alzheimer's, but he did say, with caution, that people with Alzheimer's often forget simple words or substitute unusual words. He then quickly retraced saying that it is perfectly normal to have trouble finding the right words from time to time, and that depression can cause similar symptoms. He would make a good lawyer.

It was easy tonight, talking about our families, albeit there was not full disclosure—maybe that is the secret, to hold something back always.

Journal Entry: 24 December 2004

It has been almost three months since my last entry—I do not know where the time went, work, play, and rain, lots of it, turning the roads to mush.

It's Christmas in Luanda tomorrow, promising a new experience. In Luanda, on Christmas Day and New Year's Day, friends take turns giving gifts to each other. One offers a gift on Christmas Day and the other returns the gesture on New Year's Day. I think it is an excellent system and saves those embarrassing moments when gifts are completely inequitable, for example if one friend buys a box of soap and receives a diamond-encrusted bracelet, or one receives lingerie and gives a toaster. With the Luanda system, the Christmas giver establishes the gift parameters viz-a-viz cost and personal versus practical, so the New Year giver has some guidelines for the reciprocation. It really is pure genius. My gift buddy is Simeon, and I am relieved he has assumed responsibility for the Christmas gift. I can follow his lead.

I am really missing Ala since she returned to Kraków last month. Jan is missing her even more, but he will be leaving in March so not much longer for him to pine before they meet up again in Copenhagen for Easter. He has invited me to join them, but I would feel like an intruder. Apart from which, I may have to return to Maine when my twelve-month stint ends in April. Matthew is at home for Christmas on a reconnaissance mission to check on mum. Until I wrote that last sentence, I was feeling fine about Christmas away from home, but suddenly, I'm not.

There has been an outbreak of Marburg, which is causing concern and putting pressure on resources. We're hoping it can be contained speedily.

The sky outside is black—these are the blackest clouds I have ever seen and I have stared fervently at every black cloud that has ever crossed my path. It casts an eerie hue that seems to demarcate the colors of Luanda, the white looks whiter, the Portuguese pink looks rosier. I will miss these beautiful skies.

Merry Christmas, Ethan.

Journal Entry: 28 December 2004

Christmas was a day I will never forget. Our celebrations started mid-morning at the first stop on our progressive party: there were six hosts and a crowd of twenty-three. By the penultimate course, numbers had dropped to fourteen. It was not your traditional Christmas fare, but we did well with what we had, and it was loads of fun and very distracting.

I had a couple of hours sleep after Christmas lunch before Simeon picked me up for dinner. I was looking forward to seeing what sort of gift he would select for me, knowing as he does, that I am inherently practical and have no interest in curios or adornments. I hoped he would not embarrass me with anything personal, like clothing.

He took me to a Portuguese restaurant on the Marginal. It is ritzy and expensive, and not a place any of us would ordinarily frequent, but it was Christmas and it was a nice gesture. The food was excellent, and the wine fabulous, like finding a nugget of gold in a coalmine, and it no doubt played a leading role in what followed.

First, there was the gift—a diamond-embedded cross on a gold chain. I was struck mute. I was stunned by the beauty of it, amazed that he would think to buy me something of Christian significance, and overcome that he would buy me something so personal. I was not surprised so much by the diamonds, after all, this is the Land of Diamonds—they practically grow on trees, but anywhere else, that would certainly have added to my shock. I have no idea how long we sat there with nothing said while I stared into my gift. Eventually, I opened the card, which read, "With all my love, Simeon."

That is pretty much how the evening ended. I don't know if I said thank you. I don't even remember the drive home or if he spoke. I guess he would have.

The next day I felt terrible, ungrateful, and confused. I may well have read too much into the words on the card, and the sentiment behind the gift. I really wanted to apologize, but it took me the entire day to work up the courage amidst frequent mind changes. Each time I said I should go to see Simeon, Jan agreed with me. Each time I said I shouldn't go, Jan agreed with me. He is no help at all during a personal crisis. In the end, Lucas drove me to Simeon's apartment, and waited patiently for me to leave his vehicle after more procrastinating.

There have been awkward moments between us before, but this was the peak—they don't get any more inept. I really felt sorry for Simeon—he looked hurt and not so happy to see me. When he sat down on the sofa to talk to me, he had obviously decided that he was going to say whatever was on his mind unconcerned for the consequences. However, he did not say a word—he kissed me, and I did not pull away.

The next morning Simeon made me a traditional Angolan breakfast of sweet rice (arroz doce). I tried to enjoy the incidental touches like when he handed me a coffee, and when he stroked my face. I have been without the sensation for so long. I craved and resented it. The last man to touch me, to love me, was Ethan and I felt I had betrayed him, but it is so nice to be loved by someone like Simeon Baptista. Simeon was happy and I didn't want to devastate everything with my ruminations. In many ways, he is much like Ethan.

Journal Entry: 2 January 2005

We spent New Year's Eve with Simeon's parents until midnight. I felt like a fraud being introduced to his family—there seemed to be an expectation regarding the nature of our relationship. After the family gathering, we headed into disco territory on the *Ilha de Luanda* to meet up with the rest of our crowd.

For the past week, Simeon and I have been a couple in all respects. From the outside looking in, an objective observer would definitely say that we were a couple, and we were treated as such—worse still, everyone seemed genuinely happy with the union and told us so. That made it so much harder.

At 4AM, we went down and sat on the beach. We kissed and it made me cry. I told him I wasn't ready for where we were going. I was glad it was dark and I could not see the way he looked at me, but I could feel his hurt. I asked him about the woman he loved—the one he said he wanted to marry, but that it was complicated. He looked at me, disbelieving, and said, "The woman is you. I love you, but you do not love me." The words pierced my heart. He was hoping for something back, but I said nothing. He stood up and walked away.

I looked out at the ocean wondering where Ethan might be. I guess some acorns don't grow when they fall from the tree.

Journal Entry: 20 January 2005

Matthew managed to get mum to a doctor and the news was not good—she has "probable Alzheimer's" which, 80% of the time, means it is in fact Alzheimer's. There is no single test to diagnose the disease conclusively, hence the use of "probable"—necessary also, I expect, to protect medical practitioners from lawsuits from a misdiagnosis.

Matthew is staying with her until the end of the month when he has to go to Washington to receive a journalism award, and to finish production of another documentary.

Then, he has promised, he will enter the realms of semi-retirement in Maine until admission to the asylum, bored into insanity. He plans to start work on his book to keep the ennui at bay. Life seems to have gone full circle for him—I picture him writing his book, sitting at the desk where he used to pretend to do his homework while drawing pictures of deathly beings.

I can't stop crying thinking about mum—a lifetime of torment and now this is how it will end for her. Why must some people endure so much and others so little? Matthew said there was no point me rushing home because there is nothing I can do. She is doing fine, he said. All the same, I'll be leaving here a month earlier than expected—only a matter of weeks now. I hope she'll be OK in the meantime. I will worry for every minute until I see her again.

Simeon has been unbelievable, not just with the news about mum, but since New Year's Day. He hasn't treated me differently despite how much I must have hurt him. I admire him so much. If we had met at some other point in time, before Ethan, then I really think we might have had a chance of a good life together. That is not to be.

People continue to come and go at our casa. Gisele left, and Ryan, Carmel, and Frances moved in. Ryan and Carmel are doctors from Canada, and Frances, from Ireland, is a nurse. We need more medical staff with the Marburg virus spreading up north. Jan is staying on a while longer until it has been contained. He is a good man, and a good friend. That will be my most treasured memory of my time here—the friendships, and Simeon.

Journal Entry: 6 February 2005

The Marburg outbreak is stretching everything and everyone to the limit. It is the worst outbreak in recorded history, and most of those who have died are children. It is an awful death—victims bleed from every organ and orifice in their body. Jan has just come back from Uige that has seen the worst of the outbreak. He is still quite shaken by it all—they come in, he says, covered in feces and vomit. There is no cure, other than death.

The virus is transmitted through contact with body fluid, blood or feces, so anyone who will have contact with the patients, or the vomit or feces, must wear a disposable suit with rubber boots, double masks, and double gloves. In some places, the only suits available are the ones we have, so medical assistance has been limited to what we can offer. Jan says it takes two hours to put the suits on and even longer to take them off because of the decontamination process. It is like a sauna inside so he is suffering dehydration, and everyone has been working sixteen or more hours every day. The diarrhea and vomiting is so frequent that a lot of time is spent cleaning the patients and the beds, with the suits on.

When they are nearing the end, the patients get very agitated and have to be restrained or they can rip the suits. Jan says they all worry, the doctors, not about death or dying, but of dying in this way.

Apart from establishing isolation units and maintaining hospital infection controls, we have been overseeing burial practices to ensure the virus accompanies the dead and not the living. It is hard on the families, but harder for the victims—as if it is not bad enough that they die such a death, they are denied a human touch when they need it most. It makes you want to reach out and hold their hand, and look into their eyes so they can see caring before they die. Imagine facing death alone, like Ethan, in the black, cold ocean, dragged down into his grave while life still pulsed within him. I wish my hand had been in his.

Journal Entry: 18 March 2005

My time here is almost at an end, and I have been blessed to have this opportunity, thanks to Sister Mary Catherine's brilliant suggestion. The people I've met—what can I say? They come here, giving their hearts and devotion to people they did not know, and risk their lives doing so. How can I one day inspire someone the way they have inspired me? When I find the answer to that question, I think I will have found the place where I can live, freed from the visions that haunt me, and the love that drains me.

The Angolan people are scarred more so than me, scarred with the red-dirt stain of poverty and lost limbs. The buildings are scarred with rust and bullet holes, but there is a sign of a new life emerging. The filthy streets are being cleaned, hospitals and schools are being built, and decayed buildings restored. The city now bustles with foreign banks and investors, and trade missions—everyone looking for a piece of this country with its rich oil reserves and bountiful diamond mines. Cranes testify that progress is in fact underway, but I see no change in the shantytowns where life is stagnant, where people just want a roof, walls with windows, running water, and food. The food supplies from the World Food Program will run out next year, and then what? Imagine if there was peace on Earth, and all the money spent on armies was spent on poverty—there would be no poverty, only peace. But that is not our destiny—we are all on the fast train to Armageddon, and it passes through Utopia without stopping.

This is a beautiful country with rainforests, waterfalls, and miles upon miles of pristine beaches. One day, it might also be a great country. I'd like to come back—perhaps I could practice law again, help the poor to own land or receive what is just, not justice—they are not the same thing.

Saying goodbye to Simeon will be difficult. I do believe I love him in my own way, but that is all there can be. I want to lay with him again, but I won't ask—it's not fair to treat him this way. After tomorrow, I will be gone. It is raining again, still.

Fifty-five

March 2005

AS the plane circled in anticipation of a descent, the dichotomy that was Angola and Maine became more evident: from pervasive red to contained green; from desecrated land to sanctuary; from death to life, worldliness to ignorance.

Carl shifted in her seat as she had done for most of the arduous journey. A bloated stomach pushed at her lungs refusing to subside even though she had not eaten for nineteen hours. The swelling was normal now—the flat board that had once ruled her mid region, displaced by a permanent protrusion without the promise of a confinement to end it all. Her empathy for the malnourished children of Angola was complete in every regard.

There was no sign of Helena when Carl stepped through the plastic floral arch into the Arrivals lounge at Maine's domestic airport. The letter announcing her return must still be in transit, she concluded, but anxiety welled anyway as she stretched out in the back of a Black & White taxi headed for her first home.

She tried to turn her mind away from what she had left and

what lay ahead by spotting any change along the route: a house painted a new shade, a new building, tree, garden, anything. She saw nothing as the scenery scuttled by, until the cab rolled to a stop in the leaf-filled curb out front of Orchard Road. The house was un-resplendent in its disrepair.

Carl waited for the taxi to pull away then struggled through the autumn foliage that covered the driveway. Her suitcase rocked from side to side on the cracked concrete, and shards of overgrown Paspalum slashed her ankles like barbwire. She left the suitcase on the bottom rung to the back stairs for later, when she might have more strength and enthusiasm. The back door—a mosaic of bare wood, chips of the once white undercoat, and olive paint—was wide open as usual. Carl called out from the threshold then continued despite the silence.

She passed through the kitchen stopping at the sink to gasp at the pile of dishes coated in gravy streaks, and caked-on remainders of a meal long ago passed. Ants feasted on the Formica bench top, the brown mass frantic to consume or move the unattended sandwich. The dining room table was a dune of newspapers with no sign of a surface or tablecloth.

"Who's there?" Helena called out.

"It's me, Mum. It's Carl."

"I'm in here, love, in the living room."

Carl walked through to their coat of many colors, the carpet that had once been Helena's great pride, and a tribute to her fiscal genius. The bright floral satellites were thread-barren after thirty years of footprints, and the carpet no longer overpowered the room as it had done in its heyday.

"How was work today? Where's Ethan?" Helena asked.

"He's…away…" Carl began. "I thought I'd stay with you for a while, if that's OK."

"Yes, of course, love. Come in, come in."

The magnitude of the crisis struck when Helena rose from the frayed armchair wearing a mismatched ensemble to accommodate every seasonal change. A loose, summery blouse accentuated the striped finger gloves with matching knee-high woolen socks, and a pair of stained shorts revealed the deepest wrinkling of dehydrated skin.

Tears wanted to fall, and Carl fought to keep them controlled. She glanced at her watch, expecting to see how much time remained before the end, or where to start with its beginning, then she hugged Helena tightly hoping it conveyed the requisite apology without the need for words.

Not knowing what to do amidst the sea of pressing issues, Carl settled for what was immediately manageable—the extermination of the ants in the kitchen. Helena watched on as Carl defeated the army, immobilizing the mass with Baygon, then with an egg lifter, carried the bread, jam, and dead colony to the rubbish bin.

"I couldn't find the peanut paste," Helena whispered and Carl thought of Matthew—he had said she was OK, no need to rush home, his touted journalistic observations flawed for clearly that was not the case. Carl finished with the kitchen, washed the dishes, and brought some semblance of order to the room that had once buzzed with extraordinary skill during the reign of Millie's Home-baked Treats.

Helena was next. Her hair, a once sensible, flawless bob straggled now, passing her ears for the first time with enough oil through the strands to run a car for an entire day. She could not be comfortable, Carl thought, for even at her largest, Helena had always been neat and clean with a lapse in hygiene never previously witnessed. Carl contemplated the right words to say without offending a fragile mind.

"Mum, you need a bath," she said.

"I can't remember," Helena whispered.

"You can't remember? What can't you remember? Come on, don't cry."

"The bathroom…what to do."

"You can't remember how to have a bath? It's OK," Carl said with a hug. "Come on, we'll work this out. Let's make a list of all the steps—you love lists, remem—"

Carl sifted through Helena's writing desk for paper. It was a monument to notes at all stages of completion. A bank statement was marked up with an attempted reconciliation, its numbers ridiculing a former master. Carl cursed Matthew again.

They sat down together at the dining room table. Carl cleared enough space for the sheet of paper so Helena could write the bathroom list—the words that would guide her written by her own hand while it still worked, and before everything became an involuntary scroll.

Carl washed Helena's hair, twice, prepared lunch, and talked until she could do no more. She returned for her suitcase at the bottom of the back stairs, and was able to stand just long enough to shower before she collapsed onto the old foam mattress that had supported her as a child. The time had come to resume a ritual established after Ethan died—crying until her head throbbed, but this time there was no medication to tame the pain and bring about the wonderland where anything was possible once more.

Carl woke late, not knowing where she was. She struggled to the bathroom then on to the kitchen that hummed: pans sizzled, toasters popped, and kettles whistled.

"Sit, love, I've made your favorite," Helena said as she placed a full plate of pikelets on the dining room table in front of Carl.

Carl stared at it, too sleepy to correct the error—pikelets were William's favorite. It was Coco Pops for Carl, cinnamon toast for Brian, and Matthew had favored vegemite, most likely because it was black like his artwork and his writing.

"Today is a good day," Helena said.

Carl smiled and felt some fear dissipate. She sliced the corner from a pikelet to celebrate. "Are you keeping these for any reason?" she asked, nodding at the pile of newspapers that covered the rest of the table. "You have more newspapers than the news agency."

"I...I'm not sure."

Carl reached for the broadsheets, all folded in the same way: into halves then quarters with the crossword at the forefront, partially completed. She checked a clue, seven across—super-predator, the largest and most powerful living cat. T-O-O-T-H filled the boxes. She tested another—a civil wrong. G-O-O-D was the answer. At least the words fit, Carl thought, but a seven-year-old would have done better.

"We should throw them out, Mum. You don't like clutter, remem—"

"Throw what out?"

"The papers? We should make room on the table so we can all sit here together, especially when Matthew comes."

Helena crumpled into a chair—the one Walter was in when he hit the floor after Matthew's assault. "I hate it when I can't remember," she cried, clasping her hands over her eyes. Carl noticed the cuts and burns to her hands, and shook her head.

"Don't worry, Mum. I'm here now. I'll remember for you."

"I don't want to be a burden."

"You could never be a burden." The words echoed, taking Carl back to when Grandma had said the same ones, so many years ago.

"Carla, I need to ask a favor of you."

"Sure, Mum, anything at all."

"I don't want to live like this."

"What do you mean?"

"I want you to help me…"

"Help you what?"

"End it."

"Oh, no, Mum, I can't do that. I'm sorry, anything else, but not that."

"I'm not insane, Carla. I know what's happening to me. My mind is disappearing and I can see it going."

"I know, Mum, but we'll be OK. We'll be OK."

Fifty-six

March 2005

CARL stumbled down the hallway to collapse onto the living room sofa, her stomach distended beyond the stretch capacity of her skin. She pushed at the swelling trying to disperse it, with no success.

"What's the matter?" Helena asked.

Carl lifted Ethan's pajama shirt to reveal the source of the protrusion.

"Are you pregnant, love?"

"No, no, Mum, nothing like that."

"What is it then?"

"Nothing to worry about. It's just an ongoing stomach problem."

"You do look pregnant."

Carl laughed, stopped suddenly and glared at the mass remembering nights with Simeon in Luanda then foolish thoughts surrendered to the facts: the bulge had not changed its nature or dimension in weeks.

"Can I get you some breakfast, love?"

"No thanks, Mum, no room in here for food. Coffee would

be good though."

Helena rushed to the kitchen, and Carl anticipated the soothing brew from her grandmother's old coffee pot.

"Need any help, Mum?" she called out after a while.

Helena returned. "Help with what, love?"

"You were going to make coffee?"

"Oh, sorry, love. I forgot."

"Don't worry, Mum, no urgency. Just follow the steps on the coffee-making list, one at a time." Carl listened for the sound of the pot filling with water and the clinking of china. "Did you find the coffee list? Let me know if you get stuck."

Helena appeared again in the living room with the coffee-making list. "I can't find 'stuck' on the list."

"Stuck? What's stuck?"

"You said to let you know about the stuck."

"Oh, yes, so I did. You know what? I'm feeling better. Let's make the coffee together."

"Are you pregnant, love?" Helena asked, as Carl pushed her frame up from the sofa, belly first.

"No, Mum. Just a swollen stomach, that's all."

Unease had pursued Carl since that first day back when she searched through Helena's desk for a sheet of paper to write the bathing list. While Helena dozed, Carl took a closer look.

She found an array of final notices scattered across the surface, with some inserted into the butt section of a checkbook waiting for a check to be written. The balance on the most recent statement appeared to be the cause, a once sagacious fiscal mind taunted by sums that would not add up. Carl sorted the bills and notices, and calculated the extent of the problem as best she could. A visit to the bank became the new imperative.

Helena did not want to go with Carl to the bank because of Mr. Chase, and took some convincing that Mr. Chase had passed on and away many years before and there were new, nice people there now.

Carl had not yet finalized the dressing list and the oversight revealed itself, Helena appearing ready for the outing dressed like a Lilliputian in Gulliver's clothing. Carl suppressed a laugh. "I've never liked that caftan," she said.

"What's a caftan?" Helena asked.

"The dress you're wearing. I remember Ethan asked you once if he could borrow it for the boat to use as a spinnaker. Do you remem—"

"Ethan has a boat?"

"He had a boat in Sydney, remem—. We went down to the marina one Christmas day and sat in the saloon area with dad and Andréa. That was a fun day for everybody." Carl smiled. "At least Ethan thought it was."

"I think I can remember that," she said. "Yeah, that was a nice day, and Matthew was there."

Carl sighed. "Let's find something more flattering for you to wear. To think you tried so hard to be this thin once and now here you are." Carl opened Helena's wardrobe and sighed once more—another decade had passed and nothing had changed within its walls. At least sixty patterns were fashionable again, but there was no Millie now to trim the breadth of fabric for the new frame. "This afternoon we'll sort through your clothes," said Carl. "We'll throw out the old stuff." That'll be most of it, she thought. "And organize the rest into seasons and occasions. Then we'll go shopping for some new dresses to make you sparkle like never before."

"I can't buy anything new until I've lost twenty pounds."

Carl nodded. "Yes, Mum. I remember." Some memories would never die, tucked away beyond the tentacles of disease.

It was a short drive on familiar ground to the main branch of the bank in the mall where Helena had held her account for decades.

"Good morning, Mrs. Baden," said the teller. "Did they catch the person who stole your purse?"

"What purse?" Helena asked.

The teller cocked her head to the side. "You came in last week to cancel your cards, remember, because your purse had been stolen."

"Oh, right," Carl interjected. "It hasn't been found yet. Thanks for asking."

"Your new cards are here, if you'd like to sign for them."

Helena poised a logo-embossed pen, and looked up at the teller who pointed at the spot.

"Just write your signature on the white strip," said Carl.

Helena stared to cry.

"Would you mind getting a glass of water, please?" Carl asked. "She's still a little upset…from losing her purse."

In the teller's absence, Carl showed Helena how to sign her name, the exercise pointless as no two signatures would ever be the same again. It cast a storm cloud over another imperative—the future management of her affairs, and her life. Carl and Matthew would have to assume control while she was still sound enough to meet the legal criteria. As soon as Matthew returned, they would attend the offices of Rey, Carol & Mendelson to sign powers of attorney. Carl hoped Matthew would hurry home for the mind they had known would soon be lost, and no one else could appreciate what that meant.

Fifty-seven

May 2005

MATTHEW stepped through the plastic floral archway that welcomed visitors to Maine. He walked with a bend, his legs still cocked at the knee from a long, economic flight. Carl cried at the sight, not at the form itself, but because he was there to share her burden.

"I need a decent coffee," he said bending to hug her. "You look awful."

"Nice to see you too, Matt…and so do you by the way."

"How's mum?"

"She has bad days and not-so-bad days."

"Does she still know you?"

"At this stage, but she's slipping away, fast—right before my eyes."

"It seems so sudden. I didn't expect this would happen for years, a decade or longer."

"Matt, when you wrote to me in January, you said she was OK. Was she really? Was she able to take care of herself back then?"

"Well, the house was a bit of a mess, and the yard, but I

arranged a housekeeper and a gardener, and everything else seemed fine."

"I wonder what happened to them. Clearly they haven't been around for a while."

"I don't know. Maybe she forgot to pay them and they just downed tools."

"Did you notice anything else back then? Was she, you know, clean?"

"Yeah, she seemed to be taking care of herself from what I could see although she was breaking new ground in the fashion stakes, but then who am I to judge?"

"So that was all there was? Her dress sense, and the house and yard were untidy?"

"She was a little forgetful. I found a carton of milk in the laundry, and she had trouble remembering stuff—everything became 'thingy'," he replied.

"The decline seems dramatic. Alzheimer's is supposed to progress at a rate of three to twenty years, and it's only been a year."

"But she might have had it for the past ten years and we just didn't notice."

"What a sad indictment on us if that's the truth."

Matthew grabbed his suitcase from the carousel, and they walked together toward the car.

"I have to warn you, Matt…it's harder than you think, seeing her like this. It's really important that you don't treat her differently even though she is."

"Of course, Carla. I'd never treat her differently."

"I didn't mean to suggest you would. I'm just trying to explain…it's hard not to get angry sometimes, and frustrated, like when she repeats the same thing over and over until you swear if she says it one more time you'll explode, then she does."

"I can be patient."

"And, one other thing…she forgets basic things…like going to the toilet. When she has an accident, she gets *really* upset and embarrassed. It's probably best if you leave those moments to me. Go to your room or somewhere else out of sight."

"If you think so, but I've seen a lot worse. It won't bother me."

"But it will bother her, and this is harder for her than it is for us."

"What about you, Carl? You really do look awful."

"I haven't been well for a while now, and seeing mum like this…I'm sure the stress isn't helping."

"Maybe we should think about a hospice."

"Definitely not. She should live out her days at Orchard Road. It's the least we can do." Carl paused. "It's good to have you back, Matt."

He placed an arm around her shoulder and they hugged. "So when's the baby due?"

"It's gas, Matthew, it'll pass."

"Make sure I'm not around when it does," he said with a laugh. "It won't be good for the ozone layer given the size of that thing."

"Did I say it was good to have you back? My mistake."

Carl made a doctor's appointment, leaving Matthew in charge at Orchard Road. She would be the easiest of patients having completed her diagnosis and solution: she needed something much stronger than a Rennie for her stomach, pills for the insomnia, and an elixir for the general malady. A squiggling across a script pad was all that was required.

The hour-long wait at the surgery passed by in no time thanks to an unexpected encounter with the former Olivia Naylor, now known by her more successful maiden name, Olivia Rey. Life had grayed her eyes too—their crystal shimmer wasted on a life choice. It seemed ironic, or fateful, that their respective journeys had brought them together in a doctor's surgery—a place of healing or of death. It seemed almost symbolic, Carl thought, in the strangest kind of way.

Carl followed the nurse, as ordered, down a long blue hallway to the marked entrance for Dr. Grant. She waited longer in his treatment room, thinking more of Olivia, and the two of them as children, with Tulip, not knowing then where life would take them. The recollection brought a smile, as in retrospect, it seemed like an easier time.

Dr. Grant disturbed the reflection, and began with a series of interfering questions. He was not the cooperative medico Carl had hoped for, ignoring her diagnosis and nominated drugs as if she had not spoken. Instead, he prodded, poked and pried, raised brows, pinched lips, and tapped at his table with an array of medical and stationery accoutrements. He ordered tests to prolong the production, purposefully, Carl believed, to remind her that a degree in medicine was required before proffering a diagnosis even for oneself.

Carl thought more of Olivia as she drove home to Orchard Road in Helena's sedan: a motorized contraption ten years passed the value of scrap metal. Up ahead, she saw Matthew running from one neighbor's door to the next. She pulled to the curb to wait, beeping the horn to catch his attention.

"What's up?" she asked, as he leaned into the open driver's window.

"Can't find Mum," he gasped.

"Good grief, Matthew. I leave you alone with her for two minutes and she disappears!"

"I'm sorry. She was there one minute, and gone the next."

"It's OK." Carl sighed. "It's not your fault she wanders. I'll drive around and see if I can find her. You keep on with the door-knock. She can't have gone far. Wait a second...is that—? I think that's her up there." Carl squinted. "What's she doing?"

"Picking leaves out of a tree by the look."

"What *is* she wearing? It's beige..."

"Nothing," Matthew replied with a smile.

"She looks like Eve in the Garden of Eden."

"But without the fig leaf."

"That's unfortunate," said Carl. "Get in, Constable Baden. Let's pick her up."

Fifty-eight

May 2005

CARL was ushered into the specialist's treatment room to wait in an expensive leather armchair. She wrestled for comfort, stretching her torso to release a confined, bloated stomach. Within minutes, she was dozing, insomnia wreaking havoc on her daylight hours. Technically, it was not insomnia at all, for Carl would be able to sleep if circumstances allowed it. Matthew had no problem sleeping through Helena's nocturnal scratchings—after decades in a war zone, a radio loud enough to wake the dead was, by comparison, intensely quiet. Sleep, for Carl, was more like an intermittent state of consciousness, but it had at least saved the dinner plates from the clothes dryer.

Dr. Mustaf interrupted a dream, startling Carl when he cleared his throat. He clasped his hands and rested his cherry lips on two rigid index fingers, and Carl struggled to keep up with the flow of information. At conclusion, she asked him to repeat the monologue, which he did with no sign of frustration or angst, and Carl wondered if he would be so patient after repeating the same story ten times or more, as she did with

Helena every day. She heard some of his words the second time around: ovarian cancer, surgery, as soon as possible. The timing was most inconvenient, but she promised to give the matter some urgent thought.

Helena was asleep on the lounge when Carl returned to Orchard Road, much to her relief. She followed the rapid tapping that emanated from the end bedroom, and stood at the doorway, unnoticed. She sat down on Matthew's bed and waited for an opportunity.

"I have news," she said.

Matthew continued to type, raising one finger to order silence. "Give me one second," he said. The rhythmic keyboard sped toward a crescendo with a period dotted dramatically to signify the end. He swiveled in his chair with similar theatrics to face Carl.

"So, what's the news?" he asked. "What did the doctor say?"

"I need surgery it seems."

"To remove the baby?"

She stared at him. "No…I have ovarian cancer."

Matthew smiled. "That's not funny."

"I'm not joking."

Matthew smiled again. "You are joking. You're too calm for someone who has just announced they have cancer."

"I wouldn't joke about something like this. I'm *calm* because I don't care. I'm not afraid to die."

"You're not going to die. When's the surgery?"

"I'm not having surgery."

"Now you're being ridiculous. If you need surgery, why wouldn't you have it? You're not making any sense, Carl. You must be in shock."

"Matthew, the reality is…I have nothing to live for. I've tried to find a reason these past few years since Ethan…but there's nothing, especially now with mum as she is. It's a relief actually, to know there is an end in sight."

"That's selfish, Carl."

"Why is it selfish? I'm not letting anyone down. Mum doesn't even know who I am half the time, and it's only going to get worse. It's not like I'll be dead tomorrow. I'll be here until she's gone."

"What about me, Carl?"

Carl laughed. "You don't need me, Matthew. You don't need anyone. You're almost thirty-five, and you haven't shared your life with anyone as far as I know. It doesn't get less needy than that."

"If you think that, then you don't know me. I need *you*. I've *always* needed you, since we were kids. You were always there for me. Nothing has changed."

"You've never said so…"

"What about Simeon?" Matthew asked after a time.

"Simeon? What about him? What's he got to do with this?"

"He loves you."

Carl laughed. "And you know this, how?"

"I'm a journalist—that's my job, to observe, witness the truth, and, I *know* because…he told me."

"He told you? Simeon said that to you?"

"Yes, he did."

"I didn't think men discussed that sort of thing."

"You haven't answered my question. What about Simeon? He's a good man."

"That's another world away, another lifetime, not this one." Carl stood to leave. "I'm tired. Can you keep an eye on mum while I have a lay down?"

"Sure, but think about what you just said to me—that I'm not a good enough reason for you to live."

"I'm sorry, Matthew. I didn't mean it that way. I will think about it. Make sure mum doesn't wander."

Fifty-nine

July 2005

HELENA'S descent was rapid. She could no longer walk unaided or sit without support. The mellowed smiles were gone, and her cragged head now flopped about like a rag doll.

Carl resisted perpetual, well-reasoned suggestions to place her in a hospice, to be cared for by professionals experienced in death as it comes when the brain fades into oblivion. Carl surprised herself with her dogmatic foolishness, and all because of a promise she made to Helena months earlier when she knew nothing of the carcinogenic cells that grew within her own body. This legitimately changed the terms of the promise, but Carl stuck rigidly to it.

The malignant tumors were not painful, making the pretense that everything was OK much easier. If it were not for the chronic fatigue and bloating, no one would even know her health was failing. Matthew persisted with demands that Carl seek treatment, "for his sake if nothing else". He seemed optimistic that he could change her mind, and Carl participated in the farce, "for his sake", meeting with Dr. Latseo, an oncologist, to learn more about the proposed surgery and her subsequent life span.

An invasive procedure was required, including a hysterectomy to be sure, but Carl still saw no point: her path was ending and she had been ready for it since Ethan died. If the solution had come in a pill, she would have obliged, but the more she learned of the treatment and all that it entailed, the less she wanted any part in it. Her only hope was to outlive Helena, and that seemed likely. Matthew did not really need her, and although his words had swayed her for a moment, and touched her heart, it made no sense to stay around for him, knowing as she did that he was a loner and a runner, and would be gone again at the first opportunity. Besides, she had barely seen him in the past decade although that did not affect how much she loved him.

The pneumonia came on suddenly, hospitalizing Carl at Maine Memorial Hospital. She worried during her conscious hours about Helena in Matthew's care—he did not talk to her as if she still lived somewhere within her gray flesh, and while he did not neglect her, ensuring her comfort and needs were met, he did so in a clinical, distant way, his way.

The pneumonia was a serious complication for Carl's weakened constitution and genuine fear arose that she might go before Helena, contrary to the plan. The fear forced her to take the cancer tests since she was already in the hospital, and had nothing better to do with her time except sleep.

Matthew, acting with wisdom and good sense, arranged Helena's placement in a hospice. Carl nodded powerless acceptance at the news, and cried over another unfulfilled promise. It sealed her fate—she was free to go, by pneumonia or cancer, whichever called first. She closed her swollen eyes, and fell into another drug-induced sleep where suppressed memories floated to the fore, and where people she loved lived again, but in strange places she did not recognize.

In her dream, Ethan had returned to her, but he had no face. She wanted to find it for him, but he could not remember where he had left it. All she could do was cry in frustration. The attacking rain woke her. She reached for the nurse-call,

Kevin appearing before the first press.

"What is it with you and rain?" he asked, pushing the curtains to expose the pale room to the winter dusk. He blackened the room before he left so Carl could stare into the bared pane to watch raindrops disintegrate upon impact with the glass.

Minutes later, Nurse Hilda bustled in. She turned the lights on, closed the curtains, and left Carl alone in the aseptic glow of over-luminous bulbs with no distraction from her thoughts. She stared at the bright floral pattern, which took her back to earlier times at Orchard Road where the carpet had similarly overpowered everything in its vicinity. Matthew would soon be its only occupant. It was best this way—to go as her grandmother had done, toward the white light without resistance.

When Carl woke next, daylight filtered through the bared window. She sensed a presence at the side of the room, blinked rapidly to clear the mirage and shook her head. The drugs had clearly taken control.

"Simeon? Is that you?" she whispered.

"It is, Carl," he said approaching her bed. "Matthew called me. I had to come."

"Matthew called you?"

"He did."

She smiled. "I don't know if you're real or not, but it is good to see you."

"I've missed you, Carl." He took her hands inside his and kissed her fingertips.

"What did Matthew tell you?" she asked.

"That you have refused treatment. Is it true?"

"I've done all the tests, for Matthew, but it is major surgery and I just can't see a point to it all."

"There is always a point to life, Carl. Did you not see that for yourself in Angola?"

She shrugged. "My mother doesn't know who I am anymore."

"I am truly sorry about that, Carl, but that's no reason to give up on you."

She sighed. "You said once that you loved me—"

"I said it more than once." He smiled.

"I just wanted to tell you…I'm glad that you do," she said, fighting for consciousness.

Two muscular frames dwarfed the pale wall, black and white, same height, arms folded, and ankles crossed. Matthew talked, Simeon listened then Kevin appeared to shoo them away.

"Gentlemen, you'll need to leave while I attend to my patient. You might want to try the *cuisine* they serve in the cafeteria."

"Can't be any worse than what we're used to," said Matthew with a laugh. "I'd even go so far as to say it would probably be superior to anything I've eaten in a while."

"Are you awake?" Kevin asked. "It's time for your shower, and I don't have all day." He disconnected the drip and helped Carl to sit. "He's as black as the ace of spades, that boyfriend of yours. You two are like the black and white minstrel show, you with your pasty white complexion. He's quite lovely, isn't he?"

"Yes, he is," Carl whispered.

"Is your brother straight?"

"I don't know for sure. I think so."

"No harm in asking. Now get up you lazy thing. Look at your greasy hair—that'll need a wash."

"I hope I'll get to fill in a feedback form when I check out," said Carl catching her breath. "I'll be giving you a zero."

"Well my dear, that depends on how you plan to check out. If you're going via reception then, yes, you'll get to complain about me, but if you're still planning to check out via the Pearly Gates, then you're going to miss your big chance. So what's it going to be?"

Carl smiled and shifted slowly to stand.

"You have that handsome man who's come all this way from another country just to see you. It doesn't make any sense for you to refuse treatment now, does it?"

"I'm still thinking about it."

"Happiness comes through doors you didn't realize you left open. Let it in, girlfriend."

"Maybe I could find out a little more about the surgery…since I'm here anyway."

"Good decision. Now sit on that stool under the shower while I fix your bed, and don't move from there."

Matthew was still ranting when he and Simeon returned from the hospital cafeteria. Carl smiled and remembered the little blue boy in the harness on the clothesline, and how he had scampered away to hide in the Rosella bushes. He scampered no more, but ran at speed into any danger zone. The exterior was steely, but within, there was still a weakness, something lost or broken he could not reveal or share with anyone.

"I love you guys," Carl whispered.

Simeon smiled. Matthew said nothing, but shifted restlessly in his soles. He did not have to say a word—he was there, in her room when she needed him most, with Simeon.

Kevin reappeared with another doctor whose eyes remained fixed on his clipboard. "*Carl* Marsh?" he asked, looking up at last.

"I'm Car—" Carl glanced at Simeon, to Matthew then back at Simeon. She loved him, them, more than she realized. There was time perhaps, for a new road, to go back to another time and start again. "I'm Carla Baden, doctor. Please call me Carla," she said.

Simeon smiled.

In a real sense, the hour is late, the clock of destiny is ticking out, and we must act now before it is too late.[1]

---

[1] Martin Luther King Jr., 24 March 1963

About the author

Leigh K. Cunningham is a lawyer with a career as a senior executive for a number of public companies in her home country of Australia. She has master's degrees in law and commerce, as well as an MBA (International Management). Leigh also has a law degree with honors.

RAIN was the winner in the literary fiction category at the 2011 National Indie Excellence Awards, and a silver medalist at the 2011 Independent Publisher Book Awards (IPPY) in the Regional Fiction: Australia and New Zealand category.

Leigh's first two children's books, THE GLASS TABLE and its sequel, SHARDS are recipients of silver medals from the Mom's Choice Awards.

Leigh has been married to Steve for 27 years (since 1983). They left their hometown of Rockhampton (Australia) in 1994, and lived in Melbourne and Sydney before moving to Singapore in 2004 where they now reside.

BEING ANTI-SOCIAL, for adult readers, is Leigh's next title due for release in 2012.

www.leighkcunningham.com

Made in the USA
Lexington, KY
17 January 2012